HIGHLAND MEMORIES

WILLA BLAIR

OLIVER
HEBER
BOOKS

If you've seen my social media (and you should!), you know I love animals. Especially kittens and cats. My two Wee Beasties, rescued calico cats, have been a source of joy during these tough times.
I appreciate the veterinary medical personnel who care for our animals, large and small, sick or injured. Many thanks to all of them.

ACKNOWLEDGMENTS

As always, my Beta readers are rock stars. My books would not be as good—or as long—without their thoughtful critique and ideas. I'd also like to mention two helpful critique partners, Nellie Krauss and Kit Hawthorne, both authors of fabulous novels, but also experienced ranchers. Any equine-related mistakes are entirely my own.

1

SCOTTISH HIGHLANDS, SPRING 1538

Lianna Lathan laughed as her mare, Brigh, raced across the sunlit glen below her clan's stronghold, the Aerie. She kept her fingers threaded loosely in Brigh's mane, trusting her mare to tell her if she needed a firmer grip with thighs or hands. Scents of horse and leather, springtime flowers, crushed grasses and the earth kicked up by Brigh's hooves filled Lianna's nose. Her heart pounded in time with Brigh's hammered strides, and her special sense let her revel in the mare's enjoyment of the run. For as long as Lianna could, she meant to relish the shared freedom Brigh gave her. They would race back toward the Aerie's high tor soon enough.

As the woods bordering the glen rose up before her, she slowed Brigh to catch her breath, and turned her along the edge of the trees. She kept her gaze on the woods, alert for danger. Pine and forest loam filled her nose, scents she associated with her father's displeasure.

Her agreement with her father, Toran, Laird Lathan, allowed her to ride through the glen as she liked, as long as she stayed in sight of the guards manning the Aerie's walls above her. She'd only disobeyed once, years before, not long after her first moon blood awakened her talent, making her feel as wild as the creatures that called to her. To earn her father's ire that day, she'd followed a chattering red squirrel into the trees. Over her mother's objections that her talent must be nurtured, her father had refused to allow her to ride in the glen for a month afterward. She knew better than to risk crossing him again.

But something moving in the trees ahead of her caught her eye, sending an unaccustomed shiver down her spine. She clicked her tongue and urged Brigh toward it with a light tap of her heels to her mount's sides. Brigh took a reluctant step forward, then paused as if asking, "Really? Ye ken what happened the last time." She seemed to have learned the laird's rules, too.

A riderless horse stepped into view between the trees. Saddled, head low, the stallion nickered and hobbled slowly toward her. Lianna didn't need her talent to know something was very wrong.

She twisted around in her saddle and waved at the Aerie's stone battlements to attract a guard's attention. Once she saw a guard wave in answer, she urged Brigh toward the strange horse. Several of the Aerie's guards would soon race down the tor to find her. Good. She might need their help.

"Come along, laddie," she crooned to the strange horse. Her special sense thrummed harder in her blood the closer she approached him.

Brigh whinnied and shook her head, making her tack ring. A warning?

The stallion stopped, legs braced wide apart, head low, as if he hadn't the strength to take another step.

"Bollocks. Something is very wrong with him," Lianna muttered and urged Brigh forward, under the trees. The sunlight dimmed to soft green, and shadows closed in around them. Lianna glanced in all directions, but nothing moved.

That was no mountain horse. A destrier, or another breed

of warhorse, big and black. If he wasn't in this condition, she'd have reason to fear him, but she sensed no threat.

For Brigh's sake, she stopped a few lengths from the strange horse and looked beyond him. "Where is yer rider?" There was no one, no rider, no sense of impending ambush, nothing. All the usual forest sounds continued, birds calling, squirrels chattering. A breeze wafted through the woods toward her, intensifying the tree and loam smells, but it brought along something else, as well. Horse sweat and something she couldn't identify —and didn't like.

She dismounted, went to the horse and knelt by his head, talking softly to keep him calm. "Are ye tired, laddie? Or is something else amiss? Why is yer saddle empty?" She hesitated to touch him, but she had to know. She placed a hand on his neck, then pulled it away, sickened. This animal was very ill. Silently, she warned Brigh not to come any closer. Lianna didn't know yet what ailed him, but if his rider was in the same condition, she must find him, and fast.

Before she could stand, the horse gathered himself and lifted his head, then moved a few steps away from her, deeper into the trees. There, he paused and looked back at her, entreaty in his dark, liquid gaze.

"Follow ye, then?" Along with his dire condition, she'd sensed his need to bring her with him. But where? She mounted Brigh and moved toward the horse. He turned his head away and led them into the trees. Before long, she saw where he was guiding her. A man lay on his back in a clearing just ahead. She rode around the ill horse into the clearing, dropped her reins and dismounted. With caution born of her father's concern, she studied the man and the ground around him as she crept closer.

Blood soaked his left sleeve and dripped from his scalp to stain the ground below his head. His face turned away from her, and tangled dark blond hair shielded it, but his chest rose, assuring her he lived. He didn't move as she bent and touched his neck with two fingertips. A strong heartbeat pulsed in his throat.

He couldn't have been lying there bleeding for long. The forest was full of predators and the scent of blood would've drawn them. And she was in no position to fight off a wolf pack. She glanced around, but nothing moved at ground level. Not yet.

She needed to help him up onto Brigh, and get him and his mount back to the Aerie. There, her mother could deal with him, and she could determine what was wrong with the stallion. The Aerie's guards had better find her soon.

She knelt and ran her fingers into his hair to find his wound. The obvious injury, a gashed knot on the side of his head, leaked blood. But she unlaced and pulled aside the bloody jerkin and the saffron shirt under it. Dark blond hair dusted his muscled chest and abdomen. She found no other injury to the warm skin of his shoulder under her palm.

The damage was confined to his head. Perhaps he hurt it when he fell from his mount. Concerned, she ran her fingers through his hair again. Long enough to brush his shoulders, it was thick and fine, a mix of light brown and wheat blond. She swept it back to expose the beard shadow on his cheek. She hadn't sensed any broken bones in his neck, so she gently turned his head.

She knew that face! David MacDhai!

She tumbled back onto her elbows, shocked. Her heart pounded as she recalled the last time she'd seen him, seven years ago, when his extended fostering at Lathan ended. He'd been tall but still slim by the time he left, towheaded and the handsomest lad she'd ever seen. She sat up and studied him. His shoulders had broadened and thickened with muscle. His arms had, too. His hands...she remembered those hands touching her. Teasing. Coaxing, and making her breathless with pleasure. Making her want him in a way she was too inno-cent to understand. Those hands, too, were broader, stronger, and rougher.

A lad no longer, he still had the power to fascinate her. She sucked in a breath and shook her head. Nay, not again. She'd learned her lesson.

They'd become close enough for her brothers to be suspi-cious of him. But it hadn't mattered. One day he'd simply disap-peared, leaving her brokenhearted. She'd dreamed of him ever since, but never thought to see him again. Certainly not like this!

> ✒

DAVID COULD HAVE SWORN he felt a woman's touch, but he kept going in and out of wakefulness. The last he recalled, he was in the middle of a forest, alone save for Athdar, his dying warhorse. His loyal mount. David could do nothing to save him. He hadn't reached the Aerie, the healer he sought, or the help he needed. He and Athdar were still in a forest. But where? Despair plunged him back into darkness.

He woke up thinking he had to have imagined her. The phantom woman. He forced his eyes open, blinded for several moments by the light flooding them. When he could focus, he saw nothing but green. Grass, and trees beyond that. He lay in a clearing, and his head hurt like hell. That brought a memory back. An accident. Athdar faltered, stumbled, and pitched David over his shoulder to the ground. He'd pulled himself up into the saddle, then continued on, Athdar struggling as his rider's scalp bled. David knew they weren't far from the Aerie, and if they could make it, there they would find help. For him and for Athdar.

Everything faded to black again. He came to as someone touched his chest, his belly. A thief! His heart pounded, driving spikes through his head. Before he could push the bandit away, the world faded again. When it came back, someone with gentle hands turned his head. Not a bandit. He hadn't been dreaming. Only a woman's hands could feel like that. Soft and sure, not rough and demanding.

Then gone.

He forced his eyes open again, winced as the light made his head throb, and blinked. When he could see, he found her. She'd backed away, eyes wide. Deep auburn hair, spread wild and windblown over her shoulders and into her face. And that face. Lovely, full lips, firm chin, milky skin blotched with berries. Had she fallen, too?

Nay, he knew her. Lianna Lathan! He'd arrived! But nay, he was not at the Aerie. Where was he? Of all the Lathans to find him, how had she? Luck, it seemed, was finally with him.

"Need the healer," he ground out. His dry throat refused to lend his voice any volume. Had she heard? "Need Aileanna," he said, trying again. "Foster mother. Ye remember me?"

"I do." She leaned forward and her gaze pinned him in place like a sword through his chest. "Not that I ever thought to see ye again."

She sounded angry. Why?

"Can ye sit up? I canna lift ye onto Brigh. Ye must help me."

He pushed up onto one arm. Hers around his back urged him upward. Her scent filled his nose, something light and flowery—Lianna, and horse. He turned his face into her neck and took a deep breath, wanting more.

"Come on," she chided, pushing his shoulder. "Ye canna lean on me and go back to sleep. I need ye to stand."

His head complained of the movement and his belly churned, but David ignored them. Lianna held him. Lianna filled his senses. His Lianna. She remembered him!

He remembered everything about her. He still regretted leaving her when he was sixteen and called back to his clan.

She'd been gangly, but pretty, with an air about her that drew him like bees to flowers. Budding into womanhood, she'd seemed older and wiser than her years. Not surprising, considering whose daughter she was.

With her aid, he pushed to his knees, then staggered to his feet, head pounding and gut churning with every movement. He leaned on her while he tried to gather his scattered wits, eyes closed and breathing hard. He was at sea, head spinning and belly protesting. She shifted, and without her, he would have fallen, but she steadied him. She had grown to be nearly as tall as he, perhaps a hand-width shorter, and strong, thank the saints, or he'd have pulled her down with him. Her horse approached at some signal he missed. He leaned against it as she lifted his arm to the pommel.

"Grasp it. Help me, damn it."

He couldn't get a grip. He opened his eyes, then squeezed them shut again as pain lanced from his eyeballs to the back of his head. His fingers slipped and his knees buckled, but Lianna didn't let him fall. She shoved him up against her horse.

He was injured. He needed Aileanna. How far from the Aerie were they?

Riders thundered up before he could ask. Lathan guards, by the way she shouted at them as rough hands pulled him away from her. She sounded angry as she took his hand and ordered her men, a warning urgent in her tone.

No matter. They'd help get him to her mother. Help tend Athdar.

Save his clan.

As he felt strong male hands lift his body, everything went dark again.

❧

BEFORE THE GUARDS left David to her care, Aileanna Lathan
made certain they carefully finished stripping the garments
from his upper body, the better to find any other injuries. But as
Lianna had suspected, all the blood came from his head
wound. "'Tis a good thing they didn't add to his troubles,"
Lianna groused to her mother as the men left. "When they
arrived, I was supporting him, trying to get him onto Brigh.
They thought he was attacking me. Blades came out. Can ye
imagine? He was all but unconscious, and they thought I was
being attacked. To save his life, I had to yell at them."

"How do ye think it looked to them as they rode toward ye?"

Lianna didn't answer. As usual, her mother was right.

Aileanna touched the wound on the side of David's head
and grimaced. She waved Lianna to a seat, and took a deep
breath. The tension in her forehead gave the only indication of
the pain she took from him as she used her formidable talent to
close the head wound she had earlier cleaned.

Lianna had learned at her mother's knee to assist her, and
knew not to draw her attention while she used her talent.
Lianna stayed silent and as still as her fascination with Aileanna's
patient let her.

David MacDhai. She could barely credit her eyes. She'd last
seen him as a sixteen-year-old lad, tall and full of easy humor.
He'd grown up. Oh, how he'd grown up! She wanted to trace
the curves of his chest and belly muscles. To feel the texture of
the golden-brown hair that dusted them and trailed below the
waistline of his trews to a bulge that could no longer be considered
in the least boyish. He'd earned a few scars along the way,
but except for his current condition, appeared strong and vital,
and so very male, Lianna had a hard time keeping her gaze on
her mother's work.

Finally, Aileanna opened her eyes, leaned back and sighed.

"He'll live. He needs a few days to rebuild his strength

before he can return to MacDhai." She said those words with her gaze still on the man she'd healed.

Lianna suspected she saw the young lad they once knew inside this strange man.

She turned to her daughter. "Why is he here, and in this condition?"

Lianna shook her head. "I dinna ken. He was mostly insensible when I found him. Once the guards stopped trying to kill him, I told them to bring him to ye right away, while I escorted his horse up the tor. The beast is ill. I dinna ken why yet, but I will."

"Then go out to the stable and do what ye do best, daughter, before whatever ails it spreads to any of ours. I'll have someone sit with Dhai until tomorrow. He'll wake by then, and we can get some answers. Oh, and stay out of yer Da's sight for a while yet. He's still *fashed* that ye took off into the forest alone."

"Ye ken why!" Lianna protested.

"I do, as does he, but ye ken he doesna calm down as easily as ye want him to do."

"Aye." Lianna stood. "I'm going. Send someone to check on me later."

"I'll come myself," Aileanna offered. "Ye may want some help."

Lianna kissed her mother's cheek, then pointed to the tray of food and drink waiting for her on the hearthside table. Her mother needed to refresh herself after such a prolonged use of her talent.

At the stable, someone had sense enough to move the Lathan steeds well away from David's horse. She found the stallion in the stall nearest the door, where he could be removed quickly if need be, with a shield of empty stalls around his.

The stable lad approached her as she studied the stallion from outside its stall. "He's a mean one. Ye need to have a care around him. He's been offered feed and water. He drank a wee, but I dinna think he ate anything."

"He's mean?"

"Aye. He tried to bite me when I grabbed the reins to lead him in there." He pointed into the stall. "If he werena so sick, I'd be minus one hand, maybe both. Do ye ken what's wrong with him?"

"'Tis too early to say, but 'tis bad. Go on now. Keep others away and let me work."

The lad eyed the dark horse with obvious misgiving. "I shouldna leave ye alone with him."

"He willna hurt me. See?" She reached into the stall and stroked the stallion's nose. He sniffed and backed away from her hand.

"I can scarce credit that. Yer da will have my hide if he harms ye."

"Nay, this lad hurts too much right now. Look at him. He's handsome and proud. He doesna like feeling this way any more than ye would."

The lad nodded. "Help him then, can ye?"

"I'll do my best."

The lad left her and she entered the stall. The horse flicked an ear as she approached, but didn't otherwise move. She laid a hand on his long, dark nose, centered herself and extended her talent. Immediately, she felt weak and tired, but not in any way that felt like the normal exhaustion any being would suffer after a long journey. The poor beast was fiercely thirsty, his heart raced, and tremors moved down his shoulder muscles as they shifted under her other hand. "What is this?" She'd never seen a horse in this condition.

Keeping one hand in contact, she moved down his side, touched along his ribs down to his belly, back up the other side and down again, several times. Something was wrong, but she couldn't yet tell what it was. With a sigh, she broke contact and stepped back.

"Ye've been at that for an hour," Aileanna told her.

Lianna jumped, startled. "I didna ken ye were there." Her mother sat on a bench just outside the stall, petting a cat in her lap. Another lay curled on the floor at her feet.

"I didna want to disturb ye—or let this lass interfere, either." She put down the cat and stood. "Did ye learn anything?"

"Only that I canna tell what I'm dealing with." She went on to describe what she'd noticed, which wasn't much. "The best I can think to do right now is keep him drinking and hope whatever it is will pass."

"Try some honey in the water ye give him. He might like it, and it will give him some strength. And make him drink dandelion tea, as well, to cleanse his blood. 'Tis worth a try." She stood and approached, then laid a hand on his forehead. "*Puir wee laddie.* What have ye gotten into?"

"Ye think 'tis something he ate?"

"I dinna ken. But we'll do what we can for him while we figure it out."

Two mornings later, David MacDhai studied the solemn faces arrayed around the table in the Lathan laird's solar. Toran, the laird; Aileanna, his wife; their son and heir Drummond; and daughter Lianna stared back at him, expectant.

David had fought to reach them. Now the urgency of his need weighed him down, his chest tight and his mouth dry. He fought to form words, and began with the horse they'd seen, the tale they knew. "I dinna ken what's wrong with Athdar," he told them. He kept his gaze on his foster mother, the healer, and away from her children. "'Tis why I came. My clan breeds and sells the finest horses in the Highlands." He turned to Toran. "Ye ken that. 'Tis how ye met my da. How I came to be here." He waved a hand, dismissing that part of his story. "Reivers are a constant challenge, but we ken how to deal with them. We depend on our horses for defense and as well as for income." He paused, took a breath, and turned back to Aileanna. "They're sickening, much the same as Athdar has, and I dinna ken how to stop it. We've tried everything our old healer and my stable master have recommended, but still, more horses sicken. 'Tis my responsibility to find out why. To find a cure. I need Aileanna's special help."

"Ye disappear for years, then show up, ask for our help, and expect our mother to travel all the way to MacDhai for ye?"

Drummond meant to intimidate him with his fierce glare, but David wasn't impressed. They'd never gotten along, less so after David bested him one too many times. Nay, better not to think of that now. He didn't need the distraction. Gaining the Lathan laird's agreement was too important.

"Nay, not for me," he answered and shifted his gaze to his foster father. "For my clan."

Toran held up a hand. "Start from the beginning, lad. *Yer* clan?"

David nodded. Without Toran's agreement to send the help David needed, this journey would be for naught. "Aye. I'm laird now." A ripple of movement drew his gaze around the table as he told them, "Da died almost a year ago. I'd been living in France." His gaze strayed to Lianna. How would she react to this part of his history? "I dinna ken what he told ye at the time," he said, returning his attention to Toran, "but ye ken I was suddenly called home from fostering. He kept me home for two years, training, learning more than I ever thought possible to ken about horses, before he sent me to the Continent. MacDhai is nothing without its horses. He sent me to find good breeding stock to strengthen our stable. Spain first, then France. But...things happened. I stayed there longer than expected." This was not the time to tell them the reason. "I returned as soon as word reached me that he'd passed." He paused a beat, his gaze raking over his audience, but only so that he could see the frown on Lianna's face. The set of her shoulders, mirroring her brother's.

Drummond's antipathy concerned him, but David counted on his foster father to understand his need, and for Lianna to forgive years of no contact between them.

"I've been gone so long," he said, "I'm a stranger to my own people."

"And to us," Drummond muttered.

"Aye, and I'm sorry for that," David answered. He pulled his gaze from Lianna to her father. Toran was canny. Besides being his heir, Drummond served as Toran's right-hand man. No doubt Toran allowed him to poke and prod and see what he could force from David that he would never otherwise admit. Toran knew his sons had all but started a feud with David before he left Lathan. Did the laird know why there was bad blood between them? Or had the furor died down once David was out of their reach?

Toran nodded, but didn't amplify his son's comment. Instead, he turned to Aileanna. "Do ye ken what might cause the horses to fall ill?"

She shook her head. "There are many things, but I'm nay the one to ask. Lianna has devoted her talent to animals. I'll help her as I'm able, but only while the beast is here."

Drummond snickered.

David pretended not to hear him. No doubt Drummond meant that term "beast" applied to him, not to his horse. Aileanna sent her son a quelling frown, then turned to Lianna. "'Tis on yer shoulders, lass."

Lianna crossed her arms, glanced from her mother to her father, then pressed her lips together. "I'll do what I can to make Athdar well enough to travel. I fear whatever he suffers from willna be so easily discovered—or vanquished." She turned to David. "This could take some time. How eager are ye to return?"

"I'm eager to return, but most eager to return with an answer."

"Ye say yer clan doesna ken ye," Toran said. "Does someone ye trust hold the clan in yer stead?"

Of course, Toran would be concerned for his position as laird.

David trusted the cousin he'd left in charge. Kerr held the clan while news of the old laird's death reached David in France and relinquished it back to him without objection when he returned. Kerr had done so despite the objections, David later learned, of two of the council, who had remained silent since he took over. "Ye ken why I couldna send another MacDhai to ye. Not for this. Not when the healer's talent," he said and nodded to Aileanna, "may be the only thing that can help us. I would not share her abilities with anyone, not without yer leave." He looked back to Toran. "To answer yer question, aye, I trust him well enough. But the sooner I return, the better."

He'd left something behind more precious to him than the clan itself. He hoped that had not been a mistake.

LIANNA DIDN'T WANT to feel sorry for David, but some small part of her did. He had struggled to get here. His horse had nearly died. And he faced the long trip back to MacDhai, possibly without the answers he needed—and possibly without Athdar.

He might not have accepted it yet, but everything he said he cared about depended on her. She couldn't let herself get lost in memories of the lad she'd known and the feelings she'd had for him. She'd fought them down years ago. Here sat a man. A laird. She must focus on the needs of his clan, his horses, and nothing more. "I must do a great deal more with Athdar before I can say with any certainty, but if, as ye say, others in yer stable have the same symptoms, well, 'tis naught I've seen before. It could be that his sickness is not natural."

"What?" David stood, his chair clattering to the floor behind him. "Someone is..."

"Poisoning yer horses? Possibly. I'm learning what I can from Athdar while I try to make him better, but..."

"Ye must come back to MacDhai with me," David declared.

"Is that needful?" Toran turned his attention from David to Lianna.

Hating the desperation in David's voice, she locked her gaze with her father. "I dinna ken—*yet*," she added after a pause, because of David's choked sound of protest. "But if I go to MacDhai, perchance I can help."

"The hell ye will," Drummond responded as he surged to his feet. "Ye willna go anywhere with him."

"Sit down." Toran's abrupt command cut through the tension suddenly clogging the room.

David righted his chair. He and Drummond took their seats and eyed each other as though expecting dirks to come out.

"Whatever was between ye was over..." Toran paused and fixed Drummond with a frown, "long ago." He continued in a calmer tone. "Yer sister is of an age to make her own decisions."

"Not where that bastard is concerned," Drummond ground out.

"Enough." Toran slapped a hand on the tabletop.

The expressions that crossed David's face made Lianna ashamed of her brother. She didn't see anger in David's countenance as much as dismay, sadness, even fear. For his horses? His clan? Did he think Drummond would convince their father to forbid her to help him? He knew Toran better than that.

But he'd been away for seven years. Perhaps he was no longer certain of anything, or anyone.

"Who else can help, Drummond?" Lianna asked, squaring on her stubborn, overprotective, much-loved older brother. "Can ye? Will ye let MacDhai lose its horses, its livelihood, over something years past?" She couldn't believe she was sitting here arguing in favor of going to MacDhai.

"They're of nay concern to us."

"There's a treaty between our clans," she reminded him before her father could. "And David is now the MacDhai." She stood and glared at her brother. "Ye may not care about the treaty, though ye should." She glanced at her father. He remained silent as she berated his oldest son. "'Tisna my first concern, either, but I'm not the heir. I do care about the horses, especially if someone is poisoning them." She held up a hand as Drummond sputtered and David paled. "I dinna ken that for certain," she said to David. "Not yet. I need more time with Athdar. He may yet tell me what is wrong. If not," she said and turned back to take in her parents and her brother with her determined frown, "I *will* go to MacDhai with its laird."

DAVID COULD HAVE CHEERED over the warning Lianna had just give her brother. But Drummond's determination to deny the help David needed made his gut hollow out. Still, she hadn't refused to come to MacDhai with him. And if she came, he'd have time, precious time, with her.

But only if she couldn't solve the puzzle with Athdar's help. Or perhaps even if she did.

"The Scottish horses got sick first," he said, as brother and sister frowned at each other. He cut his gaze to Toran and the healer, sitting side by side. Through all their years together, they remained steadfast in support of each other. He could see it in them, even now. With Aileanna on his side, Toran would approve of Lianna's determination to help him, not her brother's objections. "Only a little," he continued, his gaze still on them. "But one of the stable lads noticed something was wrong. Then a few got worse. We tried everything we could think of.

Stabling them instead of letting them roam in the glen. Different food, water mixed with ale. Naught helped. The bigger horses I brought back from Spain and France sickened next. Andalusians from Spain. Percherons from France. Hardy stock, mostly mares I counted on to breed with ours and strengthen our stable. Even they were not spared."

"Have ye lost any? Have any died?" Aileanna's eyes were full of sympathy, and David appreciated that she understood how devastating this had been. And still was.

"None yet, at least not by the time I left. Things could be worse by now."

"If Lianna is right about poison, whom would ye suspect?"

Toran's question landed like a kick to David's belly. His trusted circle was small. Too small. "There are several possibilities. First, I would look to neighboring clans. The MacPhersons, or someone who works for them. Our clans have been at odds for generations. Mackintosh, too, perhaps, but less likely, save for an incident that took place while I was still fostered here. One or two others within the clan who would have been rivals for the position I hold. Or some person, some reason that I dinna suspect, perhaps naught to do with me."

"Ye said ye spent time in France. Could someone from there have cause and the means to do this?"

David didn't want to think anyone there could be involved. "From such a distance? Unlikely. I had to leave with little preparation when I received word about Da, but I left no enemies behind, not that I'm aware."

"How long has Athdar been sick?" Lianna's frown told him she had considered a variety of causes, and judging by her expression, none of them were good.

"He was fine when I left, but started sickening late the first day out. I thought about turning back, but believed we could make it here. And there was no guarantee that the next horse I chose wouldna suffer the same. We rode hard and long. I may have pushed him too hard."

"Aye," Lianna agreed. "By the time ye reached us, ye both were exhausted, which may have made Athdar sicken faster. But ye couldna have kenned that would happen."

"If ye canna help him...if I've brought some sickness to the Aerie..." David choked to a stop, dismay souring his belly. "I should not have come."

"Nonsense," Aileanna spoke up, her voice filling the tense silence. "Where else could ye go for help? Nay, ye were right to come to us. Lianna will go with ye if she deems she must." Aileanna turned to her husband, who nodded. "But before that decision is made, we have work to do here. David, ye will come with me. I want another look at yer head. Lianna, get to the stable."

"And Drummond," Toran finished for her, "will remain with me. We have much to discuss."

Aileanna, David, and Lianna stood and quit the solar. Outside the door, Lianna opened her mouth as if to speak.

"I'll meet ye in my herbal," Aileanna told him before her daughter could say a word. "Ye do recall where it is?"

He glanced from Aileanna to her daughter, reading the hesitation in Lianna's eyes. "Aye. I'll be there in a moment. Thank ye."

Aileanna nodded and went on her way.

David turned to Lianna. "Thank ye for agreeing to help me. I regret that in doing so, ye may have to spend some time away from yer husband and family."

Surprise flickered in her eyes. "I am not married." She paused, color rising to her cheeks.

Not married? David's chest filled with heat, and his heart beat faster. He fought down his reaction. This hallway was no place to discuss that. "Why did ye wish to speak to me?"

"I only want to apologize for Drummond. He can be over-bearing. He's protective of me."

"As he should be."

"Aye, well, that doesna give him leave to be insufferably rude." Glancing at the laird's solar door, she crossed her arms. "He'll be laird someday. He should act like it, especially when dealing with another clan's laird. I expect that's what Da is telling him right now."

David fought the urge to touch her arm and shook his head instead. "Ye needna apologize. He and I never got along."

"Because of me." She uncrossed her arms and clasped her hands at her waist.

"Not entirely," David admitted. "Jamie was more of a friend to me, Drummond a rival. But as Laird Lathan said, ye are of an age to make yer own decisions. So is his heir."

David studied Lianna for a moment. She withstood his inspection calmly, as if waiting for him to say something else. And with no hint in her expression or demeanor of the attraction they used to share. She'd outgrown it. And him, it seemed. She treated him not as a friend, but as a visiting ally and laird, as she'd reminded her brother. "Very well," he said, relenting, for the moment, from his focus on her. "Thank ye."

"Think naught of it," she told him, and went on her way.

David watched her go down the hall, liking her confident stride and the sway of her hips. Her concern for her brother and her clan. And his horses.

Not married.

Despite the distance she seemed determined to keep between them, hope swelled and filled his chest, robbing him of breath.

3

D avid sat on a stool in the herbal as the healer inspected his injury.

"Ye took quite a tumble," she muttered as she parted his hair. "Ye havena had another headache, have ye? Or felt queasy?"

"Nay." He felt good, especially after hearing Lianna's news.

She patted his shoulder. "Yer heart is beating a wee fast, but ye are healing well, Dhai."

How long had it been since someone had called him by that name? He'd been David to everyone in Spain and France, and David or Laird to his clan after his return, rather than his childhood Gaelic name. "I would expect nay less under yer care," he told her and smiled, then sobered. "Athdar is always steady. In battle, I never have to think about keeping him under me. He surprised me when he stumbled and threw me. When I woke, I feared Athdar would be down and I would have to..."

"Dinna think like that." She stepped back, hands on hips. "Ye are here, getting the care ye need. So is he. We'll figure this out, laddie."

He nodded, lips pursed as he gazed at his bent knees. "So much depends on it."

"*Dinna fash*, Dhai."

"Good advice, but I canna take it."

"Go on with ye and find yer bed. Ye need more rest. By tomorrow, ye will be well recovered. Today, I want ye to stay quiet. I'll have someone collect ye before the evening meal." She shooed him off the stool and out of her herbal.

David wanted to do as the healer suggested, but he could think of only one place to go. The one place he wanted to be in this whole keep. At the stable, with Athdar. And Lianna.

He couldn't get over the change in her. From coltish to womanly, and stronger than she'd been seven years ago, or she'd never have been able to help him up from the ground. Her younger self had only hinted at the beauty she would become. She was the same Lianna he remembered, tormenting her brothers at every opportunity, but she was more. She had filled out delectably, now more polished, more desirable than ever. She had auburn hair like her triplet brothers, Drummond and Jamie. The younger twins, Tavish and Lianna's sister, Eilidh, did, too. Lianna's warm cream skin was freckled lightly by the sun. With her love of animals, he had no doubt she spent a good deal of her time out-of-doors. He'd seen her only a few minutes at a time, yet already he was as smitten as he'd been as a lad.

Drummond and one of the twins, his younger brother Tavish, met him in the hallway that led from the herbal and kitchen to the great hall. David glanced around, alert. They were alone.

David raised his hands, palms out. "I'm not looking for trouble, lads," he told them.

"Why else are ye here?" Drummond punctuated his demand by pushing David's shoulder, backing him against the wall. "Ye were always trouble."

Tavish stood by, as silent and watchful as David remembered him to be. He didn't know what talent Tavish had inherited, or if he had one at all. As a young lad, he'd always been distant, a deep thinker who said little. Yet David had noticed when Tavish did deign to speak, his family listened.

"Ye heard why I'm here," David told Drummond and clenched his fists while he fought the urge to smash one of them into his jaw. Must they still do this, after all these years? They'd never gotten along, but Drummond treated him worse once he realized how his sister felt about him.

"I ken what ye told the laird. 'Tis quite a tale. A mysterious illness only the Lathan healer can solve. Ach, nay, 'tis only the horses affected," he taunted, "so Lianna must go with ye."

"I came for Aileanna. If Lianna goes, 'tis her choice."

Drummond got right up in David's face. "Ye ken it isna. Ye counted on her being the same lass ye beguiled all those years ago. The lass with an affinity for animals, not people. Trailed about the keep by dogs and cats and any other creature that happened to be near. She cared for ye, though I'll never understand why, and ye left her without a word. Ye showed her how little ye cared for her. I'll not let ye hurt her again."

"I did write to her. She never answered."

"I dinna believe ye. Ye left and never looked back. Ye lied to her then and ye are lying now. Ye have nay honor, MacDhai, and if it were not for that damned treaty, I'd gut ye where ye stand."

"Ye could try." David shoved Drummond off of him. He didn't want to fight a man trying to protect his sister, no matter how wrong he was about the circumstances of their parting.

"Ye canna take him," Tavish taunted. "And ye canna take us both."

"I willna try to take either of ye," David told them. "I have more respect for yer da than to bring a fight into his own hall."

"Respect?" Drummond laughed. "Is that what ye call it?"

"Aye. For yer da and yer mother. And yer sisters."

Drummond's fists clenched.

David ignored them. "Yer family treated me fairly when I fostered here. As for the two of ye…"

❧

"THE TWO OF ye had better go," Lianna warned, her voice ringing ahead of her in the enclosed hallway. She hurried forward, thanking the saints she'd come along when she did. "Before I tell Da what ye are doing," she warned when she reached the three men. "Drummond, Da told ye to stop yer nonsense. I'm fine, and even if I werena, I can fight my own battles."

David stood still, apparently content to watch her berate her brothers.

"'Tis my responsibility to protect ye. I'll not let him harm ye again."

"Ye are not the laird yet." Lianna huffed out a sigh, adding some energy to it for effect. She'd had years of Drummond's protectiveness. "And David never harmed me," she added. Not physically, anyway, unless she counted her broken heart. "Brother, I appreciate yer good intentions. But this is not the way to carry them out. And I'm telling ye, I will do what I deem is needed. Ye," she said and poked him in the chest with her index finger, "willna have any say in what I choose to do." She planted her hands on her hips. "Now stop yer strutting—ye, too, Tavish—and leave the MacDhai in peace. Ma will be furious if ye make her heal him again."

David frowned at that.

But really, what did he expect? He was recovering from a serious injury, and Lianna was certain she'd arrived in time to prevent another.

She was grateful her brothers worried about her, but

MacDhai's problem was hers to deal with. Caring for animals was her calling, her talent. She didn't want to go to MacDhai. But if hers was the talent the horses needed, she'd go, though she wished she could go with anyone but David MacDhai. She would not lose her heart over him. Not again.

"There will be no peace until he's gone from here," Tavish observed.

David studied the expression on his face before sliding his gaze to her.

She realized he'd never seen Tavish in one of his spells—or when he pretended to be in one. He seemed to look inward, to touch something beyond the real world, and it could be unsettling to watch him.

"The only threat to the peace in the Aerie is ye and yer brother," Lianna said with a frown at Drummond, then punched Tavish's arm to bring his focus back to them. "Dinna try to fool me with that far-seeing guise of yers. I've kenned ye too long to fall for it."

Tavish frowned, but didn't say anything. Drummond studied him with a frown of his own, shoved him down the hall, and followed on his heels.

David watched them for a moment, as if making sure they weren't coming back, then turned to her. "I'm sorry to be the cause of trouble between ye and yer brothers."

"'Tis nothing new."

"And I am grateful ye are willing to help."

"Ye said that already." She glanced after her brothers, then turned back to David. "The laird has agreed. Depending on what I learn from Athdar, if I must, I will go and help put an end to whatever—or whoever—is behind the sickness." And she'd have guards with her, so she'd never have to be alone with this man as she was now.

She took a deep breath, then realized her mistake. Standing so near him, she smelled his musk, a scent deeper and more complex than he'd had as a lad. Now he was grown, unwelcome attraction sizzled in her blood. She didn't know how, but she would have to rid herself of the need growing stronger within her each time she was near him. She would have to avoid him when they were not working with his horses.

"Nonetheless," he said, "I'm grateful for yer offer of help, and for yer timely arrival. I dinna ken how far Drummond intended to take his threats. I didna want to fight them."

Even his voice made her blood sing. She took a step away from him, then another, as though preparing to follow her brothers. "He kens better than to shed blood. Da would lock him up. Tavish and ye, too, until ye all cooled off. Better Da doesna hear what just happened here."

"He willna hear it from me." He leaned back against the wall and his gaze dropped.

"Ye'd best go lie down," Lianna told him. "Ye are not yet recovered."

"I'm well enough."

"Is that what my mother told ye?" She could see the denial in his eyes. "Go on. 'Tis a good thing I came along before my brothers made things worse for ye."

Lianna left David to find his chamber. She headed for the stable to work off her frustration with her brothers and with David MacDhai. The blue eyes were the same, deep-set and arresting. But the jaw was sharper, his face broader and weathered, and combined with his commanding height and muscled frame, her body's response to him was more than she could wish away.

The faint laugh lines at the corners of his eyes told her he'd had much to laugh about in the past. There had been some time in the past seven years when he'd been happy. Before his father died, and he'd taken on the responsibilities of the laird. Before this disaster struck.

The lad he'd been had stolen her young heart. David had taught her a great deal, but he'd refused to take her innocence. He had more honor than her brothers gave him credit for. If only they knew the truth—but nay, it wouldn't have mattered to them.

So why, when he seemed to care so much for her, had he disappeared from her life? She could still recall the day he left as if it just happened. He hadn't said goodbye. From the Aerie's open gates, she'd watched him ride away. He never looked back. She'd stood there, fists and jaw clenched against crying out his name, so that only her tears spoke for her. But he did not see them.

He'd told her father he'd been home for a few years before his father sent him to the Continent. Yet she'd never heard from him. Her letters to him had never been answered. It didn't seem like the David she'd known, to forget her so completely. But he had, and now, she vowed she would not let him hurt her again.

She reached Athdar's stall and forced herself to stop thinking about his master. The horse needed her skill, her talent, and her total concentration. "There ye are, laddie," she cooed to him. He no longer stood with the splayed, exhausted posture that was all he'd been able to manage when she found him. His movements were more sure as he crossed the stall and looked over the half-door, then butted her shoulder with his nose. "Aye, ye ken who's been making ye feel better." She rubbed his nose and fed him a small apple she'd gotten from Cook. "Are ye still scaring away all the stable lads?"

He gave her a side-eyed stare, as if he'd understood, and her question did not merit an answer.

"Of course ye are. Well," she said as she opened the stall door, "let me in, and we'll see if ye are fit to deal with today."

He shuffled back, communicating calm, and allowed her to

join him. She checked the feed trough. He'd eaten well of the special feed of oats, dandelion greens, and apple bits she'd mixed for him, and he drank most of the honey water mixed with dandelion tea in his bucket. "I'll fetch ye some hay in a minute," she told him, then studied the ground around him. She didn't see any droppings yet. They would tell her something about his health, but she could wait for them. She reached up and ran a hand along his neck to his withers, then placed both hands on his back, leaned her forehead between them and *reached*. His heart rate was down and her palms were dry, so the strange sweating had ceased. So had the tremors in his muscles. She straightened and patted him. "Ye are doing better today, Athdar. Let's get ye more to drink. I think that helps ye as much as anything else I do."

She refilled the bucket with plain water and put it in front of him. Obedient, he dropped his nose into it. She watched, pleased, as the water level fell. When he finished, she moved it out of the way and saddled him. "'Tis time for ye to go for a walk, laddie," she told him as she tightened the cinches. He turned his head, watching her as she checked the tack. His stance shifted, then he stilled and allowed her to mount.

He didn't react to her weight on his back. Encouraged, she flicked the reins and walked him out of the stall, then out of the stable. He moved with ease, as though he'd never been ill and weak. Since he obeyed her commands to turn and halt, she signaled to the gate guard. At his wave, she rode Athdar out of the Aerie's walls, down the tor and into the glen. There she gave him his head, letting him wander at will, pause to relieve himself of all he'd been drinking, then wander some more. The water he passed was a lighter red than when he first arrived, encouraging her that her treatment was working. The dark color she'd seen in it then had worried her, but she hadn't sensed any bleeding to cause it.

"Are ye ready for more, Athdar?"

As soon as her heels touched his sides, he moved, at a canter at first, then she let him run. Under the watchful eyes of the Aerie's guards up on its walls, they galloped down the glen and back again. "Ye did well, laddie," she told him, and patted his neck as she slowed him to a walk to cool him. She didn't want to tire him, but to better judge his recovery while he stretched his legs.

She let Athdar sample the glen's grass, thankful that he was so much better. David's gratitude for saving his horse would please her, but she had to keep reminding herself that he wasn't the lad who'd been her friend, who showed her he thought her beautiful. The one she'd thought herself in love with. He'd changed in seven years. They both had.

She looked up the tor to the Aerie's open gates, where the people lived that she truly loved, though sometimes she wanted to throttle at least one of them. Drummond needed to stop taking every burden on himself. He'd treated the new MacDhai laird unfairly and unwisely. But in a way, Drummond was right. This new David didn't know everything about her any more. She'd learned a lot in seven years of not hearing from him. One of those things, she thought as she rode Athdar back up the tor to the Aerie's gates, was to guard her heart.

When she reached the gate, David stood in the opening, disbelief in his wide-eyed expression, a sharp crease between his brows hinting at—what? Anger? Nay, surely not. The emotions on his face stole her breath. He stepped forward to stroke Athdar's muzzle, then met her gaze. "How? He willna let anyone ride him but me."

"He let *me*," Lianna said, failing to understand why David was not as pleased by her demonstration of Athdar's progress as she'd expected.

Aye, anger glinted in his gaze. "He could have tossed ye off and hurt ye. Killed ye, even."

"Nay, he couldna." Her simple denial seemed to set him back.

He paused for a breath, and Lianna could have sworn she saw the sheen of tears in his eyes. Certainly not.

Then he colored and his jaw tensed. "What did ye think ye were doing? He was near to death just days ago."

"Have ye forgotten what my talent is? 'Tis the reason ye are here." She almost told him she wasn't the one who'd ridden Athdar nearly to death, but she held her tongue. "In case ye failed to notice," she replied instead, glaring down at him, "I have saved yer bloody horse." She patted Athdar's neck and slid off him, then stepped forward and handed David the reins.

4

The next morning dawned gray, with a cool mist that threatened to turn to drizzle or rain, but Lianna didn't care. She looked around the bailey as she tightened Brigh's girth. Bhaltair, her father's chief guard, and five of his men checked their mounts, their weapons, and other gear, or moved into and out of the stable. She patted Brigh's neck. "Not long now, my lass. We'll be on our way soon."

Jenny, her closest companion, save for her younger sister, Eilidh, came out of the keep and found her among all the men and horses. "Have ye all ye will need?"

"I hope so. What about ye?" Since Lianna didn't know anyone at MacDhai, Jenny would serve as her female companion on this journey.

"The same."

"Yer mount is ready," Lianna told her and lifted her chin toward the stable entrance. One of the lads led out Jenny's favorite, another mare, smaller than Brigh, but swift. "Are ye?"

"As much as I can be. I've never traveled so far."

"Nor I. Da keeps his lasses close. I sometimes wish we could foster away as the lads do."

"Ach, what would yer mother think if she heard ye say that? She depends on both of her daughters."

"I'd be more worried about what Da would say."

Jenny laughed as she left her.

Lianna looked around as Jenny walked to her mare. Her father was sending David, Jenny, and her with an escort worthy of their status. She hoped they reassured Jenny.

She found David in the chaos, standing next to Athdar, talking to her father. Getting last-minute instructions, no doubt. David had voiced concerns about Athdar being ready to travel. But after yesterday's run in the glen, the stallion was restless in his stall. Lianna judged him well enough for the trip, and Aileanna seconded her opinion, reassuring David. Besides, Lianna would be there if he fell ill again.

Drummond and Tavish were nowhere to be seen. Likely Da had warned them to stay inside the keep. They weren't coming on this trip, and he wouldn't want any tension with them to mar David's leave-taking. Or hers.

Her mother approached and took her hand. "I almost wish I was going with ye. I havena had an adventure since before ye were born."

Lianna's eyes widened in surprise. "I clearly recall ye declaring ye'd had enough adventure back then to last ye a lifetime."

Aileanna cupped her daughter's cheek and gave her a wistful smile. "Aye, ye are right. This is yer adventure. Yer time. But if ye need anything, send one of the guards. We'll send all the help ye need and more. Ye ken that, aye?"

"Of course, I do, Mother. I'll miss ye and Da. And Eilidh. And maybe the lads," she added with a twist to her lips.

Aileanna laughed, cocked an elbow and planted her hands on her hips. "Drummond only wants ye to be safe and happy."

Lianna grimaced. "I wish he was a wee bit less intense about it. Tavish, too, in his own weird way."

"Well, they willna be there to hover over ye at MacDhai. But yer da is sending some of his best men."

"I ken it." Lianna's gaze roved over her traveling companions again, stopping at the big, blond man who captained them. "Bhaltair alone could fight off a score of men." David was big, but Bhaltair was even bigger.

"I hope he doesna need to," Aileanna remarked with a frown.

Lianna snorted. "That makes two of us."

"That makes two of ye to do what?" Toran's deep voice came from behind Lianna.

Aileanna looked over her eldest daughter's shoulder and smiled as her husband approached. "We were just discussing the men ye are sending with yer daughter and Dhai. A worthy escort, my love."

"Of course. Speaking of the MacDhai, I believe he's ready. Are ye, daughter?"

Lianna's heart clenched. She hated saying goodbye, but it wasn't forever. She'd return as soon as David's problem was solved. "I am, Da. I'll miss ye."

He pulled her into his big arms and crushed her to his chest. "I'll miss ye, too, my wee love. Take care of yerself, and dinna do anything foolish." He released her with a kiss to the top of her head, then pushed her toward her mother.

Lianna hugged Aileanna, but not before she noted the sheen of tears in her mother's eyes.

"Be well, daughter. May ye find the cause of Dhai's problems." Her mother kissed her cheek. "And yer happiness, too. Dhai is a good man."

Lianna drew back in surprise. "Mother! What are ye trying to say? He's a laird! He must be married. Or betrothed?"

"Ready?" David's voice rang out before Aileanna could answer. His gaze swept over the riders in the bailey, then paused on Lianna.

"Go on with ye," Aileanna told her, and stepped back, eyes glistening.

Lianna's eyes burned and welled up. Her mother acted as though she would go off to MacDhai and never return. She grabbed Brigh's reins and mounted. "I'll be home before ye ken I've gone," she promised, and turned Brigh to form up beside Athdar.

David nodded to her, then glanced around at Jenny and their escort. They were all mounted and ready to go. He patted Athdar's neck, raised an arm and gestured forward, then led them out of the Aerie's gates, down the tor, and across the glen.

There, before they entered the woods, Bhaltair took point with David. The other guards arrayed themselves alongside Lianna and Jenny, and at the rear, behind the pack horses carrying their supplies, including a goodly apothecary selected from Aileanna's store of herbs and preparations. Lianna still wasn't certain what had helped Athdar, or what else she might need for any purpose, so she carried as much as she could.

She knew the escort was there to protect them, but she preferred riding on her own. Brigh pranced, frustrated at following Bhaltair's mount. Athdar kept pace to his side, David's gaze on their surroundings, much as the rest of their escort was doing.

Lianna gave in and patted Brigh's neck. "Settle down, lass. We've a long way to go. No sense wearing yerself out trying to lead."

❧

DURING THE FIRST part of their journey, David's mind was on their surroundings as he scanned the trees for hidden dangers on four feet and on two. A rider alone might be overlooked, but a group as large as theirs could not pass unnoticed through forest, much less through open fields or past outlying cottages.

At least in the open, they could see trouble coming. Every time they entered woods, David's hackles went up and he fought the urge to edge Athdar closer to Brigh. Lianna rode in the center of the group, passing the time chatting with Jenny, but David noticed that she watched their surroundings as carefully as her guards. She'd trained with her brothers, after all, and could help defend herself and Jenny. As much as he wished she didn't need it, he approved of her vigilance.

The men changed positions several times during the morning when Bhaltair signaled one of the Lathan guards to replace the man at point. David saw the sense in that. Constant watchfulness was tiring and whoever rode point had to assess the trail ahead as well as look for trouble approaching. David offered to take point alone, but Bhaltair shook his head. "Nay, we'll need ye there as we near MacDhai. What are we likely to be up against as we get closer?"

"Reivers after our stock are the biggest problem. Small bands of lost men, or raiders from a nearby clan. MacPhersons."

"Small bands we can handle."

David hoped Bhaltair's confidence was well placed.

"And once we're there?"

David shrugged. "Until we ken who is harming the horses and why, 'tis hard to say. There are some who do not approve of me as laird. And too few that I can trust without reservation."

"Are ye in danger from within yer clan?"

"What laird isna?"

"Toran, for one."

"Aye, so far as I used to ken," David agreed. "I'm glad to hear ye say 'tis still true."

"Does Lianna ken how things stand at MacDhai?"

"Not much, nay. She heard what I told Toran, but I dinna want her worried about me. She'll have enough weighing on her with the horses." He glanced around and met her gaze.

Could she hear them? He didn't think so. But he'd caught her watching him. Warmth filled his chest, then dissipated as he continued speaking to Bhaltair. "I dinna want to put her in jeopardy. If she involves herself in clan disputes, she will be."

"Ye ken the lass. Ye willna keep her from anything she sets her mind to."

"Ye must. We must."

Bhaltair snorted.

At the midday stop in a clearing by a burn, Lianna and Jenny sought privacy behind some undergrowth downstream while the men tended the horses. David was tempted to go with them as guard, but Bhaltair must have seen his frown as his gaze followed the women, and he shook his head. David stayed with the men but kept his gaze on the women until they disappeared in the trees. Then he followed them to the edge of the copse and waited, determined to be nearby if trouble found them.

The women returned quickly, and after a simple meal of bread, cheese, and dried venison, everyone mounted up and continued on. Bhaltair's placement of the guards and the point man put David next to Lianna.

"Ye had us leave so early, ye must talk to me to help me stay alert," she said, pulling Brigh closer to Athdar. She smothered a yawn. The afternoon had turned warm and the woods were full of birdsong.

"Ye were talking to Jenny all morning."

"And now I'm talking to ye." She looked around. "This reminds me of a long trip we made with Da to Fletcher."

David glanced around to assure himself their guards were paying attention to their surroundings. "I remember that journey." He wanted her to continue talking to him. Perhaps their shared memories would bridge some of the distance currently between them. "Ye wouldna stay within the circle of guards yer da set because ye complained the ride made ye sleepy and ye wanted to explore, so he tied a lead from yer mount to yer mother's."

"And I spent the rest of the trip sulking. He embarrassed me, and Mother let him get away with it."

"She worried for yer safety, too."

"They only made me more determined to get away."

"I recall ye disappeared that evening long enough to rile yer da. I'll never forget the look on his face before he sent out searchers. He tallied every man in the camp to make sure one hadna sneaked away with ye. I was old enough to be pleased to be counted among the suspects."

"Pleased?" Disbelief rang clear in her tone.

"Aye. Male pride is a foolish thing. And, to be honest, I was terrified. Yer da can bring a man to his knees with one grim look."

"I ken that look. It doesna work on me."

"Or on yer mother. But it did on me. I'd thought to leave the camp for privacy before settling down to sleep. At that look, I was glad to be right where he could see me, and not off in the trees." He paused a moment, remembering what came next. "Ye ken yer expression was just like his when ye returned."

Lianna frowned. "Two of the guards found me. I hadn't gone far. I thought I heard wildcat kittens and followed the sound."

"Ye couldha been hurt if an adult cat found ye with them. Or even killed. Yer da was furious."

"I'm lucky he didna tie me to my mother for the rest of the trip, rather than her horse."

David snorted, imagining Aileanna being tethered to the rebellious lass. "I'd say yer mother was the lucky one."

Lianna's soft laugh, the first he'd heard since they reunited, danced along David's nerve endings. He welcomed the sound. She seemed determined to keep some distance between them. As though she didn't recall their past affection the same way he did. Or he'd hurt her. Leaving the Aerie had been hard on him, too, but his father's missive left him no alternative but to return to MacDhai. As he rode down the tor, he'd known she'd be watching, and she'd see his tears. So he'd kept his posture straight, his gaze on the path ahead, and never looked back.

Though he'd thought she'd find out from her father, David had written to her to explain why he left so suddenly and how sorry he was about the way he left.

She'd spurned his letters. And him.

Now, she seemed comfortable with him only when discussing the horses. She'd put their past firmly behind her. Could he?

Bhaltair's next guard rotation moved David away from her. She stayed near Jenny or her Lathan guards when they camped that night. Was she avoiding him? The next night, she did the same. He studied her across the campfire. The flames threw a flickering glow on her face, and dancing light and shadow on her hair, reminding him of the rebellious lass who'd sat fuming after guards brought her back to her father's camp. Now, her long, graceful fingers were wrapped around a cup she lifted to press against full lips and sip. God's blood, she made him jealous at every turn. First of Athdar, then Jenny, and now he was jealous of her cup. The thought of touching those lips, of kissing them, made him hard. Thinking of the time they had missed—time they might have had together—made his chest ache. He was eager for another chance with her—if she ever allowed it. But could he put himself through that again? Wanting her? Not having her? He clenched a fist, then cursed himself for a fool.

They would reach MacDhai tomorrow. How would she feel about what awaited them there? He would not wish away what he had in France. Any thought of Mirielle always brought a smile to his lips. Would Lianna accept his family?

She was the lass who'd first stolen his heart. He'd done his best to forget her, to leave her in his past. He'd tried to lock away his feelings for her in his memories. They had been distant and fading more each year—each day—they spent apart. Seeing her now, like this, he knew how completely he'd failed.

Lianna was strong, decisive, sometimes impulsive, but always caring. He had no doubt she would do everything she could to help his horses. But his problems in the clan might be the cause of the horses' illness. As much as David wanted her to stay, those problems might be enough to convince her—or her guards—to return to the Aerie. She'd heard him tell her father he was a stranger to his own people. After nearly a year as laird, he still felt more like an outsider than the man in charge. Would Lianna be disappointed in him? He imagined her expression and his belly clenched. He found he wanted her respect as well as her help.

To distract himself, he twisted around and studied the horses. They would be the first to react to any nearby predators, but for now, they were calm. At the edge of their camp, Athdar was tied off to one side, Lianna's Brigh next to him, then the rest of the Lathan mounts. Lianna had spent some time each evening with Athdar while he and the other men made camp. David didn't know what she did as she leaned close to his mount, but if Athdar was willing to permit her nearness, who was he to question it? His warhorse had made it clear he would not suffer the attentions of Lianna's guards or their mounts. Only her and, grudgingly, it seemed, Brigh. He took comfort that if something happened to him, Athdar would feel at home with them.

He twisted back to the campfire in time to see Bhaltair walk over and settle beside Lianna, cup in hand. He took a drink then said something that made her laugh.

David's melancholy fled, and he tensed, his chest burning like the flames between them. Her father trusted Bhaltair.

David knew how dangerous it could be to marry her away from the Aerie. That danger was likely the reason she was still unwed. Could Bhaltair be considered a match for her? Watching her talk and laugh with the big man, David's irritation grew, churning his gut. He had no right to be jealous. He'd been out of her life for seven years. He couldn't appear out of her past one day, and the next sennight expect to claim her as his.

But he hadn't seen any sign that Lianna returned Bhaltair's interest—if David was seeing the kind of interest that he imagined. She treated him as any man of long acquaintance. Any man beholden to her father. She was friendly. But David wondered if there was more in her conversation, her smiles, and her laughter, for Bhaltair.

He tossed the rest of his drink, stood, and stalked away from the campfire, unwilling to watch any longer. Perhaps she'd be happier with a man like the big guard captain. Someone she'd seen every day of her life. Someone with whom she could stay at the Aerie, protected and in familiar surroundings. Someone she'd fallen in love with? David cringed as he moved into the trees. He would watch and wait. He wanted her in his life, but no matter how it hurt him, he would not destroy hers if she wanted someone else.

THE NEXT DAY, Lianna was sure they'd been riding for weeks instead of days. She wasn't accustomed to traveling so far. Despite the steady seat Brigh gave her, her entire lower half hurt. Whenever they stopped to rest the horses and she dismounted, muscles that had tensed to hold her in the saddle were forced to move and stretch. Until the cramping eased and she could walk, she'd hang on to Brigh and use some words under her breath that her father would not approve. She patted

Brigh's neck as they rode along, resolved that she and her horse needed to spend a lot more time in the glen from now on.

David rode ahead of her, at the front of their escort, as he had done much of the past three days. This morning, he promised they were close to MacDhai. His expression, when he said it, had confused her, a brief, wistful smile that fell into a frown. Was he dreading the return to his clan? Did he fear news of more sick—or worse, dead—horses? Or had something else changed his mood?

She studied his broad back, the flex of muscle in his arms and shoulders as he rode, the way his waist tightened as he twisted to speak to one of their escorts. She could watch him for hours. She had. Studying David made her forget the soreness in her thighs, and made her long for soreness of a very different kind.

They'd almost been lovers, once, after her body had changed from lass to woman, after she'd shed her first moon blood. If not for David's sense of honor, he would have been her first, perhaps her only. She pressed her lips together. That was in their past.

Most lasses her age were already wedded, with a babe in arms and another clinging to their skirts. Not her. Because of her talent, she couldn't wed just anyone. Her father wanted her to go somewhere she'd be safe and happy. Well-matched. So far, they failed to agree on any man, or any clan, he suggested. She'd convinced herself that she would always care more for animals than any man. She might never wed. Then she found David MacDhai lying on the ground, bleeding, and her heart suddenly felt whole again.

She thought back to how careful he'd been with her, how caring. A man like David wouldn't have a string of conquests in his past. He'd find one special lass and care for her. Love her. Marry her. Aye, that sounded more like the David she knew. By now, he must be married.

If so, he could break her heart again. Though they'd spoken little during this journey, last night, across the campfire, he'd watched her more closely than he had any other evening. What had he been thinking? He'd said nothing out loud, but his eyes...could she believe the desire she saw in them? She reminded herself she would not fall for him again.

She should hope he was married. She'd find out soon enough. Today, in fact. She fought the shiver that threatened to hollow her insides and fill her with cold dismay. If he had a wife, she would do what she came for, find out what ailed the MacDhai horses, and if possible, heal them. Then she'd return home, no worse off than she'd been the last seven years. Better, in fact. She would be certain David was forever out of her reach. And if she told herself that lie often enough, she might start to believe it.

Another hour passed before David raised an arm, stopping them. He turned to Bhaltair and exchanged a few words, then rode ahead, leaving her and her escort behind. She moved Brigh to the front in time to see David and Athdar halfway down a slope, headed toward an extended tower house castle, surrounded by a wall and the emerald green grass of its glen, a small village off to one side. Mountains towered behind it.

"We wait here," Bhaltair told her. "For the MacDhai to return."

"Why did he go alone?" Lianna thought she knew the answer to the question, but felt compelled to ask.

"To ensure ye will be safe," Bhaltair answered.

She nodded, having feared as much. David didn't trust his own people. Because he felt they didn't trust him? Or because he suspected at least one of them of harming the horses?

"What if he doesna come back?"

"We are to turn around and return to the Aerie."

Lianna's heart sank. Surely not. There were sick animals

that needed her. And worse was possible. "If David doesna return, he will need our help."

"Or he'll already be dead, lass." At Lianna's gasp, he continued. "If I were here with only my men, I might at least demand to see him—or his body. But I canna risk ye and Jenny. Ye ken that. Yer da expects me to return ye safely to the Aerie."

"If David doesna return to us, I canna go back without kenning what happened to him. And helping him, if I'm able."

"Lass..."

"He must be safe. If the horses are as important to this clan as David said, and I have come to help heal them, they will let me in. And since he has brought help for his clan, they should be glad of his return." Lianna kept her gaze on the distant keep, willing David to reappear.

Brigh pawed at the ground, seemingly eager to reach their destination, or determined to follow Athdar.

Lianna had noticed them getting along much better as the miles fell away behind them. Perhaps Athdar associated Brigh with feeling better, with Lianna helping David. She knew Brigh's moods well enough to know her mare would accept Athdar when it came time for her to mate. If they were still here. And if David permitted it. She hadn't thought to ask him, but perhaps she would suggest it.

Suddenly, David appeared, riding hard toward them. Dear God, what was wrong? Was Bhaltair right? Had he been threatened?

"Come ahead," he shouted as he neared them. "I need Lianna at the stable."

Lianna kicked Brigh into motion and galloped out to meet him, relief easing her chest that David was unharmed, giving her space to breathe. "What's amiss?"

"One of the Percherons is down, damn it. It doesna look good."

Her relief was short-lived, giving way to bees buzzing in her chest as a chill spread down her arms to her fingers. How bad was it? She fought the cold sensation as she raced to the MacDhai keep. Inside its walls, they stopped and slid from their mounts. The rest of the Lathans came in right behind them.

"Keep Brigh and the other Lathan mounts separate from ours," David warned the lad who came to take the reins from her. "Put them in the back stable." The lad nodded, wide-eyed, took their reins and led Athdar and Brigh toward the stables.

"Papa!" Suddenly a wee blonde lass ran from the door of the keep straight at David. "*Papa, tu m'as manqué*," she cried again as he knelt to wrap her in his arms and scoop her up.

Lianna's heart sank, but she couldn't tear her gaze away.

"Mirielle, *ma belle, ça va*? I missed ye, too." David's expression softened as he cuddled the wee lass.

He had a daughter. What Lianna had feared must be true. He also had a wife.

5

David hugged the lass to him, murmuring into her ear. To Lianna, she appeared to be no more than three or four years old. She was lovely, and quite happy to see her father.

A blonde woman came out of the keep, calling, "Mirielle!" and clearly looking for David's daughter. Hers, too? She looked a little older than David, but still, she might be his wife.

David stood with his daughter in his arms. "Clémence, I have her."

"Mirielle! Ah, David, you are 'ome."

The woman spoke with a heavy French accent, but she didn't come to greet David as Lianna thought a wife would do after a lengthy separation.

Lianna stood by, pain lancing through her chest, while the wee lass clung to her father's neck, happy tears coursing down her sweet, chubby cheeks. She wished she could cry as openly as Mirielle, but held herself in check. David had a family, and it didn't include her. Now she knew it never would.

She should be relieved. She would be once she got away from here. She shifted her stance, ready to follow Brigh into the stable.

David murmured to his daughter again. He attempted to unwrap her from his neck, but she clung even harder. "Clémence, if ye will, take her for now. I'll be in once I see to the horses. Ah, Lianna, this is Clémence, Mirielle's nurse. Clémence, this is Lianna Lathan, come to help find out what is sickening the horses. And Jenny. They," he nodded to the big Lathan men surrounding them, "are her escort and guards. Please tell Cook we have guests, and ask the steward to find chambers for everyone."

"*D'accord*," the woman replied while she helped David transfer Mirielle into her arms. The child cried out and reached for her father, but he stepped back.

"I'll be in soon, Mirielle. *Wheesht* now, and go with yer nurse. I willna be long away from ye again."

That soothed her, and she allowed the nurse to turn and take her back into the keep.

"I'm sorry about that," David said, his attention shifting to the Lathans before his gaze cut to Lianna. His expression communicated regret, concern, embarrassment, even fear, as he met her gaze. Still, he said nothing more about his child—or her mother. Instead, he asked, "I ken ye must be tired, and ye just arrived. Are ye able to see to the Percheron?"

"*Dinna fash*," she told him, head high and shoulders back. She kept as firm a grip on her emotions as she could manage around the shards of the dreams she'd revived when she found David in the woods. Damn her memories! She had fooled herself into thinking she'd let him go. She wished she could forget the feelings she'd once had for him. The pain of shattering them again hurt worse than the first time. "'Tis why I'm here." She moved toward the stable, not waiting for David to show her the way. She'd seen where Brigh had been taken. And she couldn't look at him now.

Once she entered the stable, David caught up to her and led

her to the stall where the ill Percheron lay. "The stable master said she's been down since late this morning."

"It hasna been long, then, but 'tis not a good sign." She took a breath, letting the familiar scents of horses, hay, and leather calm her. She needed that calm, that distance from her tattered emotions, to be able to read the mare. Her own racing heart and hollowed belly would block her perception of the mare's condition.

"What do ye need, Lianna?"

"Give me a moment and I'll tell ye." She knelt by the mare and placed one hand on her forelock, another on her long, sweat-soaked neck. The mare's pain, thirst, and weakness flooded Lianna's senses. The horse lifted her head, eyes wide and fearful, and immediately, the muscles under Lianna's hand shook. "Lay ye down, lass," Lianna crooned, and smoothed a hand over the mare's neck until she again rested her head in the straw covering the stall's floor.

Lianna dropped her hands into her lap for a moment, then pushed to her feet, turned and faced David. The apprehension on his face was enough to make her want to lie, to let him believe all was going to be well, but she couldn't do that to him. Or to herself. "'Tisna good," she murmured, and his expression crumpled, a hand coming up to cover his face. She took one step toward him, but forced herself to stop. Best she tell him rather than trying to comfort him. He had a wife for that. "I'll do what I can for her, but she's in much worse shape than Athdar was when I found him. I dinna ken if I can save her."

"I...damn it! I didna bring her and the rest of them all the way from the Continent to let something—or someone—kill them here. I need these horses. My clan needs them."

"I hear ye, David, I do. And I'll do all I can. Where are the others?"

Wordless, he led her to five more stalls. In them, horses were on their feet, but listless, though they took halting steps toward her, and in two cases, shafts of sunlight highlighted sweat-dampened coats and tremors in their muscles. "'Tis the same, aye?"

"It appears so. Show me where their water comes from."

"'Tis the same well the people drink from. None are sick with anything like this. It canna be the water."

"If the well is tainted, it might not manifest the same way in people. But I think ye are right."

"Then what could it be?"

"Food, perhaps. Or pasture. Something in the glen. I canna say." She rubbed her forehead with the back of her hand, exhausted before she even began to do what she must do for these animals.

"Ye are tired. Come, ye need to eat and sleep before we look any further."

Defeated, she nodded. She'd be stronger and think more clearly after some rest. "Ye should have the lads bring them water. Keep them drinking while I'm gone, especially the Percheron. Get water into her any way they can. Where is Brigh?"

"Behind ye," David said and gestured. The stable had another section of stalls, visible through a double doorway.

Lianna turned to find Brigh's head over her stall door, leaning out. "There ye are, my beauty. I'll be back soon." She dared not touch Brigh after touching the sick Percheron, not until she knew more about what they were up against. Instead, she headed for the stable door, not sure where to go from there, but certain David would see to her.

And perhaps introduce her to his wife.

DAVID'S EMOTIONS clashed as he walked Lianna back to the keep. Fear for his prize breeding stock, desire for the woman he hoped could save them, and urgency to see Mirielle all roiled around in his chest. His daughter would be frantic by now, knowing he was home. He hadn't yet set foot inside his own hall. It was time.

And perhaps, too, time to tell Lianna how Mirielle came to be. Soon. First he must get her settled somewhere she could regain her strength. The trip had been long and hard. She needed time to prepare before dealing with the ill horses. Time he would use to talk to Kerr and find out what had happened here during his absence.

The steward met them in the great hall, waiting for them. "Yer men and Lady Jenny have been seen to, milady, and with the MacDhai's permission," he added, turning to David, "I've reserved a guest chamber near yers for the lady."

David nodded. "Ye should go refresh yerself," David told her, "I'll have food and drink sent up to ye." He could smell something mouth-watering and knew Cook was preparing the evening meal, but she would have something ready at all times. "And a bath, perhaps?"

"Of course, milady," the steward said at David's suggestion. "If ye will follow me, I'll take ye to yer chamber."

"Go on, Lianna. Take some time for yerself."

She looked back toward the doorway to the bailey—and the stable beyond it. "I willna be long, David. I have much to do."

"Ye've had a tiring trip." He could see her determination in her gaze, but also the dark circles under her eyes. "Rest while ye can. Ye saw the horses. They can wait a few hours more."

"Not the first mare. I need to go back to her. And find out more about the rest."

David knew he'd get nowhere arguing with her. Aileanna had once described to him her compulsion to heal. Likely Lianna labored under the same compulsion now. "I'll speak to Kerr. He'll ken more. If there's anything urgent, I'll fetch ye."

She shook her head. "I should be at the stables. 'Tis why ye brought me here."

"Dinna be stubborn, lass. Ye ken ye must rest or ye willna be able to—"

"I'll go change," she said, interrupting him. "Have someone send up a basin of hot water. Not a tub. I'll want a bath after I'm done, not now. And aye, food and drink."

"I ken it. Go on. The steward will see to what ye need." He tried to say with his eyes what he could not say in front of the steward. He knew the toll dealing with the horses would take on her.

"Ye'll find me in the stables with the mare in an hour."

David nodded, knowing she was right. Stubborn and argumentative, aye, but also right.

He meant to look in on Mirielle first, but saw Kerr in the laird's solar as he passed the open door.

"Ye are back! The steward told me he was making room for strangers. Did ye find the healer ye went to fetch?" He rose and met David inside the door.

"Aye, she's here." No sense explaining about Aileanna when Lianna had made the trip. "What happened while I was away?"

"Another Percheron and two of the Andalusians are ill, and more of the Scottish horses. We havena found the cause. I hope yer healer can."

"I, too. What have ye tried?"

"The same things we did before ye left. Naught has worked."

"Has anything else happened? Anyone gone missing or behaving oddly?"

"Nay, not that I've seen, and none reported to me." He ran a hand through his hair. "This illness is a damn shame."

David clenched a fist. "'Twill be a damn tragedy if we dinna find the cause and cure it. No one will buy MacDhai horses if they hear they might spread a strange malady."

"'Tis good ye were able to bring back the healer ye sought. Ours has proven to be of little use."

David nodded and glanced at his desk. Kerr had organized the documents on it into neater stacks than he ever managed. David hoped he'd been able to make sense of them. For months, they'd frustrated David's efforts, so he'd turned his attention to planning a better future for the clan—until this crisis began. But he had done something no one else in the clan could do. In Lianna, he'd brought the best hope for his clan that he could provide, whether they knew it or not. Now that he was back, it was time for him to take up his other responsibilities. "I'm going to spend a few minutes with Mirielle. If ye think of anything else, ye ken where to find me—the nursery or the stable. Ye can tell me about all that," he said, and gestured at the desk, "later."

Kerr nodded.

David went upstairs to the nursery and opened the door to his daughter's chamber as quietly as he could. She might be sleeping. But nay, she shrieked as soon as she saw him and ran into his arms. "Papa!"

He hugged her to him and inhaled the sweet scent of her skin and hair. "Have ye been a good lass while I've been gone?"

"Aye, Papa. I have been *tres bonne*."

He glanced up at Clémence, who laid aside the book she'd been reading to his daughter and nodded. "She missed you, of course," she told him.

"Very well, *ma petite fille*, ye have earned a treat. What say ye to supper with yer papa in the great hall tonight?"

"*Oui*, papa! I will be *une très bonne fille*."

"A very good wee lass, aye, I'm certain ye will."

He spent a few more minutes with her in his lap until she drifted off to sleep. "I'm sorry," he told Clémence. "I fear she willna sleep well tonight."

"Do not worry, *monsieur*. She has been too excited to sit still since she first saw you, and supper will be enough to tire her again."

"Very well." He stood and put Mirielle in her bed, then moved to the door. "Bring her to supper, if ye will."

"Of course, *monsieur*."

As he made his way to the stables to meet Lianna, he felt better, knowing his daughter was safe. He trusted Kerr, but he'd missed her. He hadn't realized how much until he spent these last few minutes holding her in his arms.

After passing one of Lianna's Lathan guards, Ailbeart, posted outside the stable door, David found her in the Percheron mare's stall. She lay across the mare's midsection, not moving. David froze, uncertain. He couldn't tell if she was breathing, but from his experience with her mother, he knew better than to interrupt her if she was deep into healing. Yet if the horse died while she linked to it, dear God, how would he explain to her parents that he'd let her die, too? He had to know she was alive.

He dropped to his knees beside her. Fighting to remain calm as dread emptied a space in his belly, then filled it with acid, he touched her shoulder. "Lianna, 'tis David."

She didn't respond, so he squeezed her shoulder and spoke again, panic spiking his heartbeat and sending shards of ice along his veins. "Lianna? Come back to me. I need to ken ye are well."

Finally, her ribs expanded with a breath.

He choked in a breath of his own.

Her hands clenched as she pushed herself upright, but she left them in contact with her patient. "Why?" She didn't open her eyes, but her tone made her irritation clear.

"Ye were not breathing, lass! Ye scared the life out of me." He dropped his face into his hand for a moment, then frowned, though he knew she would not see his displeasure. "I'll stay and watch over ye." He wanted to touch the mare, but dared not, as long as Lianna was in contact with her. "Does she still live?"

"Aye, barely."

Her breathlessness told David he'd arrived just in time. He started to insist Lianna move away from the Percheron. Saving its life was not worth the risk of losing hers, but she spoke first.

"Find some clean water and mix it with honey," she ordered before he could pull her away. "Like we did with Athdar. I canna get her to stand. If ye can get some of it into her, it will help her. Give her strength. Until she's on her feet, I dinna ken if she will live."

David blanched. "Only if ye will let go of her and rest while I do," he bargained. When she pushed away from the mare, he left to do her bidding.

He spent the next several hours with Ailbeart, the Lathan guard, mixing honey water for the mare, and forcing Lianna to stop for rest, food, and drink when it was clear she had nothing more to give. Ailbeart had gone back to Cook for more honey when the mare suddenly groaned, lifted her head and rolled to her belly. As she pushed up on her forelegs, Lianna kept hands on her.

"Come on, lass, ye can do it," Lianna murmured over and over, like a litany.

Was it meant to reassure the horse, or herself? David couldn't say. "Can I help?" He didn't know if Lianna heard him until she nodded. He moved to the opposite side of the mare and forced his arms under her haunches. He couldn't lift her, but he hoped the little he could do would be enough to encourage her to get up.

She scrambled like a newborn foal. Lianna kept talking to her, kept her hands on her, lending whatever her talent allowed. By the third time the mare lost her footing, David didn't think they would succeed. Then she pushed onto her front legs and jerked herself upright.

Lianna slid her hands up the mare's shoulder and wrapped her arms around her neck. David stayed by her hindquarters, exulting, terrified and determined. If she fell again, he couldn't stop her, but he'd damn well do anything he could to help her get up again. He didn't like the tremors he could see rippling through the mare's hindquarters, but he trusted that Lianna would deal with them.

Lianna took the mare's head in her hands, leaned her forehead to the mare's and spoke so softly, David couldn't hear what she said. But the mare nickered back to her, and that seemed to reassure Lianna.

"Do we have more water for her?"

"Aye." David brought two buckets and put them down in front of the mare.

"Drink lass," Lianna encouraged her. The mare dropped her head, and for a moment, David feared she would go down again, but she stayed on her feet as she nosed the buckets and drank.

"We can leave her for now," Lianna said, finally lifting her hands from the mare and stepping back, "but leave her more water, and naught to eat until tomorrow. I need to find fresh dandelions for her and the sick horses. Until I do, perhaps the cook has some that will do for a tea."

"Ailbeart and I made several more buckets of honey water for her."

"Good," she said, but her gaze remained on the mare. "Share a scant handful of salt between them, I think, and put them in her stall. Tell the lads to leave her alone unless she goes down again." Her gaze stayed on the mare. "If she does, get me, no matter the hour."

"They'll get me first. I'll come for ye."

Lianna cut him a glance. "As long as ye do."

David looked toward the stable door. The gloaming was upon them. And he'd promised Mirielle she could have supper with him tonight. He glanced down at himself. His clothes were filthy from the stall and sticky from honey. "I need to change, then it will be time for supper. Let's go."

Lianna studied him for a moment. "Is yer wife pleased to see ye returned to her?"

David swallowed, knowing he should have told Lianna about France before they arrived here. Seeing Mirielle must have been a shock. But why pick now, after all they'd just been through, to ask about her mother? "I dinna have a wife."

"Ye have a daughter."

"Aye, but her mother died. Days after she delivered Mirielle. A fever took her."

Lianna closed her eyes and shook her head. "I'm sorry."

For a moment, David believed she was. There was a hint of sympathy, of embarrassment, in her gaze when she looked at him. Then her jaw tightened.

"So, ye have been busy these last seven years. No wonder I never heard from ye."

Aghast, David watched as she patted the mare one last time, turned and left the stall. What did she mean, she never heard from him? He wrote to her. She never responded. He knew she had to be exhausted, but her comment stung. He walked back to the hall behind her, unable to think of anything to say that wouldn't escalate into an argument. He didn't dare start anything that might make her gather her guards and leave. Instead, he hurried to his chamber to change, and collect his daughter.

As he'd expected, Mirielle was excited to be allowed to eat with the clan rather than being confined to her chamber with her nurse. She put her tiny hand in his and chattered all the way down to the great hall. David placed her beside him at the table and looked up in time to see Lianna enter and look around as if trying to find her guards. He stood and beckoned her over.

She mounted the steps and approached the table, and he pulled out the chair on his other side. "Sit with me, if ye will," he told her. "Ye havena met my daughter, Mirielle. Lass, this lady is Lianna Lathan. She's here to help our horses."

"I saw you arrive," the girl said, eyes wide as Lianna smiled down at her.

David was grateful for that smile. After her comment as they left the stable, he appreciated the effort she made to charm his daughter.

"I saw ye, too, lass. Ye are a bonny one."

Mirielle hesitated, so David stepped in. "Say *thank ye*," he told her.

"Thank ye," Mirielle piped up. "Are you going to have your supper with us?"

"I suppose I am," Lianna agreed and took the seat David offered.

It didn't take long for the day's excitement to catch up with his daughter. A full stomach did her in, and before she could fall into her trencher, sound asleep, he gathered her onto his lap. Once she slept, he signaled for Clémence to take her back to the nursery.

"She's lovely," Lianna remarked when Mirielle had been taken away. "I am sorry about her mother. And about what I said before. In the stable."

"Ye are exhausted, Lianna."

"'Tis nay excuse. I'm sorry."

"I, too, but that was more than three years ago. In France, before Da died and I had to return. Mirielle is doing well here, I suppose. Her nurse, my wife's cousin Clémence, was her wet nurse. She lost a babe, but has helped raise Mirielle as her mother would have wanted, speaking French. She's learning to be a Highland lass from me." That earned him a snort of laughter. "From living here, too, thank ye. Dinna be surprised if she mixes languages and nonsense ensues."

"Most three-year-olds can be counted on to speak nonsense."

David chuckled. "I suppose so." He glanced around the hall. "There are yer men, just coming in. And there, by the hearth, is Kerr, my cousin who held MacDhai for me while I journeyed to Lathan." When Lianna hid a yawn behind her hand, he added, "I ken ye are tired. If ye have replenished yerself, I'll ask one of yer men to escort ye back to yer chamber."

"I am ready. I can get Bhaltair…"

"Nay, I dinna want ye to cross the hall alone, now that it is filling up. Ye are still a stranger. I'll not have ye accosted." He signaled for a serving lass and asked her to collect the man Lianna pointed out to her. As he made his way across the hall toward them, Lianna stood. "I'll see ye in the morning."

"And not before. That is my hope."

"The mare should continue to improve during the night. Tomorrow, I'll do more with her, and see the other sick horses, too."

"Rest well," David said, nodded to Bhaltair, and watched Lianna walk away from him until she passed out of sight up the stairs to the sleeping chambers.

Kerr approached and settled into the chair Lianna left. "Ye make a lovely family, the healer, yer daughter, and ye."

David pursed his lips and fought down the hope that flared in his chest, bright and hot. "Appearances can be deceiving."

6

B reakfast was never Lianna's favorite meal, but she knew better than to attempt what she had to do today without being well fed. Her reserves of strength and stamina would be tested by the mare alone, and she didn't know what else awaited her with the other MacDhai horses.

She'd almost finished when a young hound limped into the hall ahead of a gangly lad, and made its way toward her.

The lad gave an impatient whistle and gestured for the dog to come to him. With a final hopeful look at her, the dog returned to its master, and they settled at a nearby table. Lianna expected it often hung about the great hall hoping for some morsel to be dropped. She turned back to her meal.

There was no mistaking the sound when the dog let out a loud yelp. As Lianna turned toward it, it whined and hunkered down, inching away from the lad. The lad held up a piece of meat and the young hound paused, eyeing it hungrily, then scooted toward the lad. Instead of tossing the meat to the dog, as soon as it got close enough, the lad kicked it.

Lianna winced, certain she'd heard ribs crack. The dog

yelped again and backed away even faster. Lianna stood and marched over to the lad.

"What do ye think ye are doing?"

He met her demand with insolent silence, glanced at her dismissively and turned his attention back to the dog. When he held up the scrap of meat, Lianna ripped it from his grip and tossed it to the hungry hound. "If ye ever kick that dog again, or any other, I'll…"

"Ye'll what?" The lad rose. "Ye dinna belong here. I dinna have to listen to ye."

He was nearly her height. Thin, but possibly muscular enough to challenge her in a fight. He probably thought so. But he didn't know she had three brothers, so perhaps she would surprise him. She knew how to fight and where to hurt a man. Before she could widen her stance, another voice intruded.

"Ye do have to listen to me," David announced, coming at the lad from the side. "And obey." His scowl made it clear he would not tolerate any argument.

The lad blanched and seemed to shrink, but only for a moment. His color came back and he straightened defiantly. "I didna do anything."

"Save tormenting that young hound, offering, then with-holding food, and kicking it hard enough to break ribs when it ventured too close," Lianna said, glaring at the lad. "'Tis barely more than a puppy. That doesna make ye tough, or a man. It makes ye crass and cowardly and cruel."

"And assigned to remove waste from the keep. For a month," David said.

"From the kitchen? Or the stable?" The lad's eyes grew wide, as if he couldn't believe he'd be given such a lowly task.

"All of it. Chamber pots, too. Ye'll bury it all. That should keep ye too busy to torment helpless animals."

"Helpless? That cur tried to bite me."

"With good reason." David narrowed his eyes. "And if I hear

any more complaints about ye, ye'll be doing that job all summer."

"'Tisna fair!"

"But 'tis fair to harm a lowly animal? What's next? A wean? A lass?" David's fists clenched at his sides. "Get out of my sight. Ye have work to do."

Once the lad stomped away, Lianna approached the dog, who lay on his side, still whimpering, his suspicious gaze on her as she knelt in front of him. She held out a hand to let him sniff her and decide she was no threat. He allowed her to touch his side. His whimper and her talent told her the lad—or someone else—had hit this dog more than once.

"How is he?" David asked softly.

"Cracked ribs. That lad should be punished for treating an animal this way. And 'tis not the first time. This hound has older, healed and half-healed injuries. I think he's been tortured since he was a wee puppy, and kept hungry enough for that lad to entice him with food, even when he knows he'll be harmed."

"I ken that lad. The laird hanged his da four years ago for leading a ring of thieves stealing from neighboring crofters. His mother lives in the village now, taking in mending and such to support them. Likely that pup came in with him, which means 'tis been subjected to that treatment all its life. I fear ye may have more than horses to care for while ye are here."

"I agree. Is there someplace quiet where I can help this wee lad?" She reached out to stroke the dog's head, saddened when he ducked away from her before he realized she wouldn't hurt him and allowed her touch.

"Aye, we've an herbal that is little used. Our healer is old and canna do much anymore. I'll take ye there, then I believe 'tis time I paid a visit to that lad's mother. He may be angry at what happened to his da, or to his mother and him, but that doesna give him the right to harm helpless creatures."

Guilt filled Lianna over her earlier comment about the lad. "I hate to think it, but chances are he's been treated much the same by a parent or someone close to him."

"I fear so. Come, let's take care of this wee dog, then I'll go find out."

David led her and the limping hound to the keep's herbal, down a hallway from the kitchen. Dust covered the scraps of dried leaves, old pots and jars that remained on scarred tables. A large, heavy-looking cabinet, doors locked with a padlock, stood against what Lianna assumed was an outside wall. She would not find anything she needed in this neglected space.

"Where is the healer?" Lianna looked around the chamber, dismayed.

"The old woman sickened during the winter and never recovered her strength. She lives, but doesna do much in here anymore. Her apprentice didna survive. A lung sickness took six of our clan."

"I'm so sorry. Perhaps I can set this to rights so that a new healer can make use of it after I've gone."

"If I can find one, aye." David looked around, despair pinching his face. "Da left so many things to chance, and to wither away. I dinna ken how to deal with it all, but I will. Somehow."

Lianna put a sympathetic hand on his arm. "I'm certain ye will. Now, help me lift our friend onto that table. Then ye can go."

David carefully lifted the dog by wrapping his arms around his four legs and placed him on the work surface Lianna indicated. "I'm surprised he let me do that." He scratched behind the dog's ears. "Maybe because he trusts ye, he trusted me. I wonder what his name is."

"I didna hear the lad speak to him at all. Perhaps he doesna have one."

"I'll find out," he said, gave the dog a final pat and turned to go.

Lianna watched David until he disappeared out the door. "He's a good laird," she told the dog. "He's trying to be even an even better one. Now, can ye lie down for me?"

He settled on his haunches before he eased himself down and stretched out. She put both hands on the dog's ribs and let her healing talent tingle out of her fingertips into his side. She sensed his fright as the warm sensation wrapped around his injuries, and spoke soothingly to calm him. As the pain in his side eased, so did his anxiety. Her own ribs started to ache, but she knew her discomfort was mild compared to what he had suffered.

His older injuries took more time to study. Several had healed out of alignment. When she understood what she would need to do, she put the dog in a healing sleep and undertook the painful process of breaking and realigning several small bones in his front paws, and a larger one in his front leg. His hips looked as though they belonged to an old dog, not a young one. She did everything she could, then lifted her aching hands, stepped back, and rubbed her hip with her forearm. "Sleep, laddie. I'll go for some food and water for both of us. I promise ye are going to feel better when ye wake."

Then the tears came. She ached with fatigue and the residue of the hound's injuries, but mostly she was heartsick that someone would treat an animal this way. From puppyhood to now, this dog had been made to suffer for its food, the worst kind of cruelty. It was a miracle he would tolerate any human at all.

That ended today.

"I'll take ye back to Lathan with me, if I must," she vowed, rubbing her arm, "and any of yer kin who've been treated badly, too."

She dried her eyes and made her way to the kitchen, begged

enough food for herself and two more hearty men besides. Cook put it in a large bowl and gave her a pitcher of water and another of cider on a tray Lianna carried back down the hall to the herbal.

She let the dog sleep while she ate her fill, and drank the cider. Then she cut the remaining meat and vegetables into small pieces, added a good measure of water to the bowl, and placed it by his head. After she touched him to wake him up, his nose twitched. He was back with her.

"Smell that, do ye? 'Tis right there, just waiting for ye. All ye can eat and drink, laddie."

He lifted his head and looked at her, his expression clearly dubious.

After the way he'd been treated, she shouldn't be surprised, but it broke her heart yet again. She pointed to the bowl. "All for ye." Understanding his reluctance, she stepped back and took a seat on a nearby stool. "I'll not stop ye. Go on. Eat."

He gave her one more look that said, "I canna take it if ye, too, torture me," then pushed up to his paws, shook himself, and dipped his nose into the bowl. His gaze never left her as he began to eat.

Tears rolled down Lianna's cheeks yet again. "Good lad," she said, encouraging him. He needed food to finish healing. "I'll not let ye starve ever again," she promised. "Ye are safe with me."

WHEN HE GOT BACK to the keep, David went first to the herbal, but no one was there. Relieved that Lianna had finished with the young hound, he went to the next most likely place she'd be and found her in the stable with the Percheron mare and the wee dog she'd treated.

"He looks much better," David said when he saw that she

wasn't in her healing trance. "His name is Albie." As he said that name, the dog cowered. "But I think he needs a new one."

"I saw that," Lianna said. Anger heightened the color in her cheeks. "How badly did they treat him to make him fear even his name?" She crossed her arms. "So what do ye propose?"

"For his name?" David leaned on the stall's side wall and thought.

"He's a strong laddie," Lianna told him. "He'll do well from now on."

"How about Conall, then? It means strong wolf."

"Perfect! Do ye like that name, laddie? Ye can be Conall, and never hear the one ye hate, ever again."

Conall jumped to his feet and barked.

"So ye *do* like that!" Lianna met David's gaze. "He doesna have to go back to them, does he? I willna allow it."

"Nay, he'll stay here."

"With me, aye. And I'll take him back to Lathan to keep him away from that awful lad. What did ye find out about his family?"

David frowned, not wanting to share what he'd found, but knowing he'd have to tell her. She'd ask until he did. "I'll tell ye, but first, how is the mare?"

"Resting. I put her into a healing sleep after I got her to drink more honey water. She's stronger and her symptoms have lessened. I still dinna ken what caused them, but if we keep to the same care, and I make some dandelion tea for her, she should recover. I'm hopeful that she'll do as well as Athdar did."

"Have ye seen any of the others?"

"Nay. I'm sorry, I was about to start. Conall kept me busy, didn't ye lad?" She ruffled the fur at his neck, and he licked her hand.

"He kens ye helped him," David observed.

"I think so. He had been beaten many times. He was in pain,

but had to be kept constantly hungry to allow that horrid lad anywhere near him."

David pursed his lips. "I fear that horrid lad harms any animal he can reach. His mother claimed it started after his da died, and she could do naught about it."

"Ye almost make me feel sympathy for them," Lianna admitted. "But there's no excuse..."

"I agree. I've ordered the lad fostered away."

Lianna sucked in a breath.

"*Dinna fash.* I'll warn the laird who takes him to keep an eye on him."

"Good. The lad will be gone long enough to have a chance at a new way of life."

"As I was?"

Lianna pursed her lips, looked away, and nodded.

David wasn't sure what she meant by avoiding his gaze. Before his life took an unexpected turn, he'd come to the Aerie learn to be a warrior, and to learn from her father to be a laird. He was tempted to ask her what was wrong, but after all this time, he wasn't sure he needed to know. "I have letters to write to place the son in fostering. I'll see ye at supper?"

"Of course." She kept her gaze averted as he left.

ONCE DAVID LEFT, Lianna stood and straightened her skirt. She needed to forget him. She was here to deal with horses, so that is what she would do.

She left the mare's stall, Conall at her heels, closed the door behind them, then walked from stall to stall.

She touched each horse in the stable. Some were perfectly healthy, others showed weak signs of the affliction. None were as ill as the mare had been. Brigh greeted her and Lianna spent some time introducing Conall to Brigh. After some initial distrust, they seemed to accept each other. But as Lianna turned to go, Conall on her heels, Brigh neighed. Lianna turned back to her. "I ken it, lass. Ye canna go everywhere Conall can. But I need to ride the glens around here, so we'll go places wee Conall canna. Does that suit ye?"

Brigh chuffed and bobbed her head. "Nay, lass. We're not going now. I'll come back to ye when 'tis time."

"She seems to understand ye." A man came up behind Lianna, stopping a few paces away to study Brigh with a practiced eye. "She's a smart one."

"Aye, she is." Lianna took a breath to slow her racing heart and crossed her arms. Who was he and how long had he been watching? "I raised her. Trained her. Spent more time with her than anyone. I'm Lianna Lathan."

"I ken who ye are. I'm the stable master, called Tadgh."

The stable master was a big man, though not as big as Bhaltair. Perhaps David's age or a little older, he had kind eyes set wide in a broad face, light hair, and strong hands. "I'm pleased to meet ye. What can ye tell me about the horses, the illness..."

"Little enough," he said, cutting her off. "I tried putting horses out to pasture, bringing them into the stable. The laird suggested changing their food, withholding food. We tried everything either of us could think of. Some horses seemed to get better on their own, others worse. I dinna ken why."

He leaned heavily muscled forearms on the top of the stall door, gaze on Brigh. "This lass hasna come down with it. Nor any other Lathan horse. Not yet, at least. If ye care for her, ye will take her from here as quickly as ye can." He gave Lianna a rueful smile. "Unless ye find the culprit—and the cure—of course."

"I hope to do just that." A chill ran down Lianna's back. Had he just threatened Brigh? Or did he mean what he said to be helpful, to protect Brigh and the other Lathan mounts? She didn't know him, so didn't know how to interpret his words or his tone. But his expression told her he meant well, so she didn't call for the guard she knew was just outside the stable.

"Ye didna mention changing the source of their water."

"I didna think it necessary, since the animals and the people drink from the same well."

"Yet, could it be poisoned somehow? Something that affects horses more than people? Or the keep's hounds and cats?"

"What do ye have in mind?"

"Honestly, I dinna ken. There's a burn nearby. We crossed it on the way here. Do ye ever take water from it?"

"Not since the well was dug. But 'tis worth a try. There's a loch, too, though not as close by. I'll send some lads to the burn each morn with buckets. They might not spill it all on the way back."

"Have ye a wagon?"

"That would make better sense, would it not?"

He rolled his eyes, and Lianna liked that he could make fun of himself.

"Aye, we do. I'll send the lads come sunup. We'll see if water from a different source makes a difference."

"Thank ye. I dinna ken what else to try that ye havena already done." She turned back to Brigh then thought better of it and asked, "Have ye more horses somewhere else? Already out to pasture or in another stable somewhere?"

"Some are out to pasture, some with the men patrolling the borders of MacDhai land, others belong to folk in the village yonder," he said and pointed. "None are ill in the village, not that I ken."

Lianna nodded. "I'll check on the others as I am able." That was interesting. So something, or someone, in the keep was behind this.

7

Lianna's conversation with Tadgh was still on her mind the next morning. She had been too busy to interact with many of the MacDhai residents. Perhaps it was time to remedy that omission. She might find out more that way. She'd start with the old healer. Nay, the cook, after she broke her fast. Cooks and cooks' helpers often knew more about the goings-on in a keep than anyone else, and she and the healer were most likely to have access to poisonous plants.

After she met with those two, she'd talk to David about what Tadgh told her, to see if he recalled anything else they'd tried before he left for the Aerie. The more information she had, the better she could treat the illness without wasting time using methods already proven not to work.

In the great hall, she ate her porridge and watched the people around her. Who could be behind the trouble at MacDhai? Everything seemed normal on the surface, save that everyone studiously ignored her. Serving girls moved among the tables, putting down food or taking away the remains. A man, who from his size must be the blacksmith, rose from a table near the hearth and crossed near her without acknowledging her presence. The man he'd been with lingered for a few more minutes, finishing his meal, then he, too, left without comment.

She was beginning to feel invisible when one of her Lathan guards, Damhan, came in from outside and sat beside her, his large, brown-haired presence immediately comforting.

"Good morrow," he said, "I hope ye dinna mind some company." He widened his green eyes and lifted an eyebrow in question.

She gave him a grateful smile. "I'm glad of it. Other than the serving lasses, no one here seems to be willing to notice me. Or speak to me."

"So much for Highland hospitality," he said in agreement, then leaned aside to allow the serving lass to put food in front of him. "If I were the laird, I'd watch my back," he added after the servant moved away from them. He dug in to his food.

Lianna's hands went cold. "What makes ye say that?" If there was an urgent threat, David must be told.

"I've never seen a clan behave this way with guests," he told her.

She had to wait for him to take another bite and swallow before he continued.

"'Tis not simply that the MacDhai has been away for years. This has been going on since the old laird was in charge, or I miss my guess. I've heard of problems with Clan MacPherson, and there's another clan's name I've heard. Mackintosh. I dinna ken the story, but there must be one. Perhaps 'tis only because of the threat to the horses, but many people seem on edge."

"If there is a story, surely David is aware. He mentioned trouble with both of them to my da."

"Aye? Either way, I think one of us should be close to ye at all times. I'll talk to Bhaltair."

"Talk all ye will, but I willna agree to be escorted within the keep unless ye can keep up with me—and out of my way. I've too much to do here. 'Tis enough that ye are nearby. I havena been threatened. I must be free to move about."

"They canna threaten ye if they're not speaking to ye."

Disquieted by the warnings Damhan gave her, Lianna took her leave and headed for the kitchen.

Cook was in her element, sleeves rolled up, elbow-deep mixing dough and shouting at her helpers as she kept an eye on the goings-on in her kitchen. She paused when she noticed Lianna enter.

The heat from the hearth and all the active bodies was oppressive, but Lianna couldn't let it bother her. She was here to get information she thought David could not. "Good day," she offered as she approached the table Cook leaned over.

"What brings ye here, milady?"

"I come to seek yer aid, if ye will show me what herbs and flavorings ye keep on hand. I seek something to help the clan's horses. Fresh dandelion greens, and more."

"Ach, the ones getting ill, I ken it." Cook straightened and gestured at shelves on the wall opposite the hearth. "What I have is there."

Bottles and tied bunches of herbs, some fresh, some dried, lined the lower shelf. Lianna moved to inspect them. "Do ye prepare these yerself?"

"For the most part, aye, from the walled garden. Others the healer, or rather, lately, the younger lasses forage for in the glen and the woods." Cook gestured at the shelf. "Do ye see what ye seek?"

Lianna studied the stock, picked up a jar and sniffed the contents, then shook her head. "Thank ye, but nay, none of these. What ye have here I would expect any good cook to keep on hand, but they are not what I think might help. I need fresh dandelions. And a place to make large amounts of dandelion tea." The herbs she brought with her wouldn't last long, but based on what she'd learned at the Aerie with Athdar, water fortified with honey and salt, and dandelion tea, seemed to work. If Cook could brew more of that, it would ease Lianna's burden.

"I can help ye with that. I'll have the lasses gather as much as they can find."

Lianna spent a pleasant few minutes while she waited for Cook to finish with her bread dough, taking in the scents of flour and yeast, and the stew bubbling in the kitchen's great hearth. It reminded her of the Aerie's kitchen, and the time she, her brother Jamie, and David had been kicking a ball around the bailey. Well, Jamie and David had been. She'd been watching because the lads wouldn't let her play in her skirts. She'd told them she wouldn't trip, but David had insisted he didn't want to see her get hurt. Jamie had snorted at that. Brothers! They were caught out by a sudden rainstorm that drenched them to the skin before they could run inside. They headed for the warmest place in the keep—the kitchen. The Lathan cook sat them at a worktable nearest the heat of the great hearth and plied them with warm cider and sweet bread, talking and laughing with them while they dried and she and her staff prepared the next meal.

How could she recall memories like that without pining for David? She supposed the comfort of a busy kitchen and a friendly cook were just the sort of things she'd missed since she arrived here.

Once the MacDhai cook finished kneading her dough and dropped a cloth over it, she seemed prepared to talk. "That needs to rest a wee, and so do I." She sat opposite Lianna. "The laird spent years with ye," Cook observed, "but has said little about his time there."

"There's little to tell, really," Lianna told her. "We're a clan much like MacDhai." A lie, but she couldn't tell Cook what made the Lathans special. No wonder David had never said much about his time at the Aerie.

"And I'm a fox." Cook gave her an assessing stare, putting Lianna on guard. "The lad came back with a distant look in his eye. That's before his da sent him abroad. He returned from there a man, but a sad one."

"I ken it." Well, what could she say? "He got along with my brother Jamie, but not with the other two. He was always very good with horses. Now that I'm here, I understand why, but his skill challenged my oldest brother, who liked to think he was the best Lathan rider."

"Tell me more."

"They nearly came to blows," Lianna told her, grimacing at the memory, then grinning, "because David beat Drummond in a race by six lengths. The most anyone had ever bested him. Drummond didna take it well."

"Nay?"

"Well, perhaps David rubbed salt in the wound by offering to teach Drummond to ride."

Cook's eyes widened, then she threw back her head and laughed. "That sounds like the David I remember."

Lianna laughed with her, but only for a moment. The feud between them began that day. And apparently, in Drummond's mind, at least, it never ended.

Lianna suddenly felt the need to change the subject. "What can ye tell me about MacDhai that its cook would ken, but no one else?"

"I presume ye dinna care to ken who likes which dish, or whose belly grumbles over what."

"Ach, nay. Thank ye for sparing me that. Did ye grow up here? Was yer mother the cook before ye?"

"Nay, she wasna. My da was a crofter. We lived outside the village. I always liked watching the fields grow thick with grains and vegetables and fruits. My ma was a good cook, and we were prosperous enough that she let me try different combinations of ingredients on my own." She looked away. "Then David's grandfather took fifty men and fought with the king at Flodden. We lost my da that day, and the clan lost many more husbands and fathers. Ma and I couldna farm on our own, so we came to the keep and worked for the old cook. Eventually, I took over."

"Yer mother?"

"Gone, the fever that took several of the clan a few years ago."

"I heard. I'm sorry." Lianna folded her hands together on the tabletop.

"David's father did what he could for the clan, but he needed a seneschal to keep track of everything. David would have done that, I suppose, but the old laird sent him away. Something about a girl, I heard. I dinna ken more than that."

Really? Lianna leaned forward. "I wish ye did. I'd like to hear that story."

"Ach, every lass for miles around had her eye on that lad. He couldna help but find one or two to his liking." She laughed again. "But he treated them well, so I canna imagine what he did to be banished for those years until the old laird died."

"He was looking for good breeding stock—horses," Lianna quickly amended, and she saw the glint in Cook's eye.

Cook laughed again. "And he found both, aye. Wee Mirielle is an angel. And now, to have to fight to save the horses..." She looked down and shook her head, then up again. "MacDhai depends on its horses, ye ken. We breed the best."

Cook's tale only added to the mystery of David's past, but his present was what brought Lianna here. "Do ye have any idea who is behind the trouble?"

"I wish I did. I'd use that cleaver on them, I would." She nodded toward the large, heavy blade on the next table.

Lianna got no sense from her of discontent aimed at David. She was not behind poisoning the horses. After a few more minutes that garnered a large pot Cook promised she would dedicate to dandelion tea, Lianna left her to her work.

Next, she sought the healer in her herbal. The last time Lianna had been there, with Conall, it had been empty. But now, the old woman was in there, so Lianna paused in the doorway, waiting to be noticed as the healer muttered over several small piles of herbs. She took a pinch from a few, and added them to a steaming pot. The steam's odor was unpleasant and Lianna wondered how the old woman tolerated standing so near it. Perhaps her sense of smell had faded with age.

Finally, the old healer looked up and saw her. "Ye. What do ye want?"

"What are ye making?" Lianna thought she might disarm the woman by starting with the obvious question.

"Rat poison," she said and cackled. "Stinks, aye?"

Lianna approached and was tempted to back away. It was eye-watering up close. "It does."

"'Tis my own recipe," she boasted. "'Twill cool down to a paste the rats love. But not for long." She cackled again, then gave Lianna a penetrating stare. "Now yer curiosity is satisfied, why are ye here?"

"I want to talk to ye about what might be making the horses sick. Ye've lived here all yer life, I'm told. So ye must ken the plants and trees in the area. I dinna think there are many plants in the Highlands harmful to horses. So what could it be?"

"Why are ye asking me? Ye are a healer." She stirred the contents of the pot again, then turned to scowl at Lianna. "Ah, of course. Ye come here to accuse me, aye? To find out what potion only I might be able to make?" She pointed toward the door. "This is my place, and has been longer than ye have been alive. Who do ye think ye are, coming in here and asking me questions like this? I'll complain to the MacDhai, I will!"

"I dinna mean to upset ye," Lianna said, trying to calm her. But the old woman refused to be mollified.

"Go on. Get out. Ye are not welcome here. Not in my herbal and not at MacDhai."

Lianna put her hands on her hips. "How can ye say that? Yer laird brought me. Ye ken why I'm here."

"Aye, I do. He's had his eye on ye ever since ye arrived. Has he seduced ye yet? He's a popular one with the lasses."

"What? Nay!" Lianna could feel her face heating. Is this why people avoided her? What they thought? That David brought her to be his leman? "Ye couldna be more wrong."

"Ye dinna fool me, lass. I ken the looks he gives ye. There's no mistaking it in a man. Best ye go back where ye came from before he forces ye to do something ye'll regret."

Like talking to this nasty old woman? Lianna threw up her hands and left the herbal. She'd come back to inspect the healer's stores sometime when she wasn't there.

Away from the healer's toxic presence, Lianna realized the old woman had deftly changed the subject to one certain to upset and divert her.

Something was very wrong at MacDhai.

As she entered the great hall, she saw that most of the tables had emptied and serving lasses moved among them, carrying away used cups and wooden trenchers, then scrubbing the tabletops. Bhaltair sat with Damhan. Damhan looked up and saw her, smiled and stood. Bhaltair glanced up at him, then looked around and saw her. He stood, too, then gestured for her to sit.

She refused. "I ken what ye are going to say, and I told Damhan how I felt about it already. I'm sure he told ye."

"He did." Bhaltair frowned at her. "I am no longer certain merely having us with ye in the keep is the protection yer da had in mind. The MacDhai has more problems than we ken.

We can stay with ye, and yet leave ye free to go about yer duties."

"And how would ye do that?"

"By having one of us here in the great hall with ye, another in the stable, all of us out riding with ye, and..."

"And sleeping in my chamber, too?"

"Nay, though we will if we must. For now, one of us will sleep on the floor outside yer door..."

"And have the whole keep talking about me?" As if they weren't already? Nay, the healer must have lied. "Ye go too far, Bhaltair. I am not in danger here." Not yet, anyway. She thought back to the old healer's assertion that she wasn't welcome at MacDhai. Given the way people avoided her, there was probably some truth to what she claimed. But that didn't necessarily constitute a threat. And some, like Cook and Tadgh, were friendly enough, once she made a point to speak with them.

"Ye dinna ken that." He crossed his arms over his massive chest, frowning.

"Because ye think the clan distrusts David, so they must also distrust me." With a growl of frustration, Lianna sank to the bench and they resumed their seats. "Keep yer eyes open and listen," she told them. "I dinna think I have been a target, but if poisoning the horses doesn't accomplish the attacker's goal, then because I am helping to thwart them, ye are right to be watchful. Jenny could be a target, too. So could I, to get to David. Or, who better to use to get to him than his daughter? David can protect himself. I can, too." She held up a hand as Bhaltair opened his mouth to object. "I ken what ye are going to say. Da sent ye here to look after me. That doesna mean ye have to sleep outside my door." She shook her head. "Protect Jenny and the lass."

"Our job is to protect ye," Bhaltair argued, clearly frustrated with her refusal to take a threat against her seriously. "And

Jenny." He sat back and glanced at Damhan. "We should take ye home."

Lianna shook her head. "I'm not finished here. The problem isn't solved. And I'm telling ye I'm not a target—not yet, anyway. Protect the wee lass. Unobtrusively. She spends most of her time in the nursery, where she should be safe, with her nurse, Clémence. But keep an eye on her, too. She might be part of this."

"Whatever *this* is," Damhan grumbled.

"Just keep yer eyes and ears open. Ye may notice something. David may not ken whom to trust, but I do. I trust all of ye."

They grumbled some more, but eventually agreed. Then Bhaltair threw down a gauntlet she could not ignore. "At first sign of any threat directed at ye or Jenny, we'll pull ye out and take ye home."

Lianna refused, but she knew he was right. Her father would be beyond furious if anything happened to her, and these men would suffer for it. "I dinna ken if it means anything, but keep an eye on the old healer, too. I've talked to Cook and to her. Either could have compounded a poison, but I dinna think Cook would do something like that. Or have the opportunity. She has too many helpers around her. As for the old healer? She's cross and unfriendly, but to be fair, that doesna mean she's behind the trouble here, either." Lianna was too embarrassed to mention what the old healer had said to her about David.

"But she could be," Damhan added.

"Aye. She bears watching." But if she was involved, she had to have help, and that would be even worse.

&.

LIANNA ENTERED the solar and sank into a chair across from David's desk with a sigh. He hadn't expected to see her. His body tightened with surprise and longing. Yet, as he listened to her morning's activities, her frustration was evident. He wanted to go to her, take her in his arms, and soothe both their worries. But he knew she wouldn't welcome his touch, not at the moment.

Her lack of progress finding a source of poison, and her encounter with the old healer frustrated him, too. Her idea that either she or the cook might be able to compound a poison made sense, and he agreed the cook didn't seem the one to do it.

"The old healer is nothing like my mother," she said with a shudder. "It rankles to even mention the two of them in the same sentence. I wish I had more to tell ye."

David could swear there *was* more she wasn't telling him.

"She's a nasty old woman. Ye'd do well to replace her. Soon," she added with uncharacteristic rancor.

David snorted. That must have been quite a conversation. "She's been the clan's healer for my and at least part of my father's lifetime. She canna last much longer, so aye, I ken that."

"I'm sorry. I'm still annoyed from speaking with her."

"Ye mentioned wanting to see more of the glen," David said, changing the subject to something he thought would please her.

Lianna appeared to appreciate the diversion. Her eyes lit up and she said, "Aye, I want to ride the ground around MacDhai." Then her expression grew solemn. "And see if anything is growing that could sicken yer horses. Gather dandelions, too. After the midday meal, perhaps."

"I'll go with ye," David said and stood. He'd been sorting through one pile of documents Kerr had recommended he give more study. Instead, spending time on horseback with Lianna gave him something to look forward to.

"I've already told the Lathan guards, and they'll come with

me. I ken ye are busy enough without devoting yer afternoon to me."

David rounded the desk, forcing his smile to remain neutral, and not filled with the desire her comment elicited. What he would give to devote his afternoon to her. But not as she expected. "There's naught I'd rather do," he said, and took her arm, urging her out of the solar. "Besides, ye dinna ken where the horses are usually pastured. I can help narrow the search."

Lianna gave him a long look as they crossed the great hall.

David led her to a table near the hearth. For privacy, he placed them across the room from Bhaltair, her determined shadow. The man could still see her and keep watch, but he wouldn't hear every word they said.

"What are ye avoiding?"

She was too astute, by far. "Piles of my father's papers covered with numbers that dinna make sense."

"Then ye should keep working until they do."

He signaled for the serving lass to bring their midday meal. "I've put them off for months. They're history, and I'm more interested in securing our future."

"Records are kept for a reason—crop cycles, prices, trends."

"They willna make any more sense after we ride than they do now, so I may as well do something I enjoy for a few hours. Even better if it helps the horses. They are the clan's future." Riding, though enjoyable, paled in comparison to spending time with Lianna. But he couldn't bring himself to say the words. He needed to keep their interactions cordial, keep her focused on staying busy and perhaps, in time, he could rekindle the attraction they'd shared as teens. His revelation about Lucienne was too recent and too raw for him to push Lianna very fast.

"Do ye mind if Conall comes with us? The lads have him

out in the stable, or he'd have followed me about the keep this morning."

"Ye have a new shadow, do ye?"

"Aye. Ye ken I collect beasts, large and wee." She put an elbow on the tabletop and leaned her chin on her fist. "The wee dog has been so mistreated all his life, I mean to see he's never harmed again. I'll admit to being reluctant to leave him behind when I leave the keep."

"Even to ride the glens?"

"Aye."

Their food arrived, putting a stop to conversation for a few minutes. As they finished their meal, David saw Bhaltair nod to Lianna and head out into the bailey. She stood. "I'll go change. I'll meet ye in a few minutes."

By the time Lianna reached the stable, the Lathan guards were leading out their own mounts. David had quickly saddled Athdar and mounted up, waiting with her men. Seeing her, Conall danced around the horses, trying to get to her.

"Conall!" Lianna's cry and snapped fingers brought him to heel and out of danger from the much larger horses' hooves. She bent to ruffle the fur on his head. "Ye wee daftie. I dinna want to have to fix ye again."

"Brigh is waiting for ye," Bhaltair, told her.

Lianna nodded and headed for Brigh's stall. Soon, Lianna led her out into the sunlight. Bhaltair lifted her to Brigh's back.

A spasm of jealousy rushed hot and urgent through David's chest and burned into his belly when Bhaltair's gaze raked him, but the man turned away to his own mount. Had that look been proprietary? David didn't know the man well enough to be sure.

"Ready?" Lianna's question snapped his attention back to her.

"Conall?"

"Here," she answered.

David finally noticed the pup draped across her thighs. Someone must have handed him up to her while his attention focused on Bhaltair.

"Let's go." He clenched his teeth and led the way out of the gate. They passed the village and rode through a stand of trees before heading out into the glen. There, David circled Athdar back to her. "This area is the closest pasture, but there are several beyond it, where we move the horses throughout the warm season to higher ground."

"Very well. This could take some time. I feel guilty for taking ye away from yer incomprehensible numbers."

He snorted. "Ye needna. They'll be there when we return."

"Follow me, then," Lianna told him and entered the pasture at a walk.

Athdar whinnied, and David suspected he was annoyed at not being allowed to run. Open ground stretched before them. "Athdar needs some exercise. I'll give him his head and circle back to ye."

Lianna nodded, her gaze on the ground, so David turned Athdar away, kicked him into motion and let him go. He'd let him run long enough to work out the stiffness of being confined in his stall for the last couple of days.

He glanced back once to ensure Lianna's men remained vigilant. They did, but Bhaltair watched Athdar's progress. David's hackles rose. What was the man's interest in Lianna?

§&

DAVID RETURNED and Athdar seemed calmer, but Lianna grew more frustrated as they rode. She saw nothing that would account for Athdar's or the Percheron mare's symptoms, nothing that would poison a full-grown horse. The thin scattering of early season yellow buttercups and single wild foxglove plant she spotted didn't help. They were dangerous, but none grew in sufficient quantity to explain the amount or variation in illness she'd observed. The pastured horses, cropping spring grass, seemed not to notice them. Rather, they gravitated toward her. Eventually, she collected a following of MacDhai horses. David seemed amused, and the Lathan guards, used to her affinity for animals, and theirs for her, merely shrugged it off.

An hour into the search, she got off Brigh and put Conall down to walk with her. The hound ran around, enjoying his pain-free liberty and the warm day, much as she would be if she weren't so focused on her quest. Still, it felt good to stretch her legs, and walking let her collect dandelions when she happened across them.

She was so insistent on continuing that with David's agreement, Bhaltair even sent one of the men back to the keep for water, cider, and food for them and the horses. They'd shared their light meal in a shaded wood, then David led them to the farthest pasture.

She rode around it first, randomly, in no particular pattern, but none of the mid-spring grasses, wildflowers, or seedlings dropping from trees here and there seemed out of place. Butterflies flitted among the wildflowers and bird song rang in the glen despite the presence of people, horses, and one young hound.

Her guards ranged out from her in a loose circle, but David stayed at her side, pointing out this tree or that hill or the bothy where herdsmen and guards could shelter in a sudden storm. Clearly he loved this land, even if he hadn't yet gained his footing as leader of his clan. Watching him, seeing his pride reflected in his voice, she knew he would. Curing the horses and finding the culprit would help.

They dismounted and David asked, "What are ye hoping to find?"

He'd asked the same question before, and she'd simply

shrugged. But she owed him an answer for his persistence in staying with her.

"Enough of one or two toxic plants to make Athdar and the mare as sick as they were, and the others, too. It would take a great deal more than I've seen. And what I've seen, especially this far out, seems untouched, not bitten off or trampled as a horse might do."

"The horses havena come this far yet. Ye've had yer nose pointed at the ground, so ye might not have noticed, but we've climbed to higher ground. Summer pasture."

"So whatever has harmed them blooms in spring. But even closer to the keep, there was little sign..."

"Then perhaps the cause is not a wild herb, as ye thought. Or else 'tis something already picked and gone."

"Or 'tis more than one thing, which might explain the different symptoms." She shrugged. "We've done all we can here today. I need to get back and see how the mare and the others are doing." She glanced around, then frowned. "Where's Conall?" She didn't see him, and David's expression as he looked around them told her he didn't either. The hound wasn't in the tall grass, nor did she see him with any of their guards.

"There's a stand of trees over there," David said and pointed. "He might have seen something worth chasing into it."

Lianna nodded and strode toward it, calling, "Conall!" every few steps. When the dog failed to appear, she broke into a run. "Conall! Where are ye, lad?" She didn't stop to see if the guards followed.

In the trees, David grabbed her arm. "Slow down before ye trip over something," he warned, then added his voice to hers, calling the dog.

Deeper into the trees, she finally heard something. A whine, then a soft bark.

"He's hurt," she said and hurried toward the sound.

They found Conall at the base of a large, sturdy-branched

Dule tree, one leg bent at an unnatural angle. He woofed when he saw them coming, then glared back up into the tree, where a red squirrel stared down at him.

"Dinna tell me ye tried to climb after that squirrel," Lianna scolded as she knelt beside him and placed her hands above and below the break. "Daft dog! Ye broke the one leg that yer former master hadn't damaged."

"How can that be?"

"He was fed so poorly, his bones are weak, but they'll improve with good food and time," Lianna told him as she examined the dog.

"Can I help?" David knelt on Conall's other side.

"Aye. Hold him still, and watch his head. He may try to bite, even though I'm going to make him sleep."

David put a hand above the dog's muzzle, another on his torso. "Go ahead."

Lianna *reached* to make Conall drowse, muted his pain, then grasped both sides of the break, pulled and reseated the bone into its proper position. Conall let out a faint yelp, but David held him still while she knitted the break back together.

"Sorry, laddie," she said when she finished and woke him fully. She nodded to David to release him, then patted Conall's head. "I ken that hurt a wee." She rubbed her own leg. "What did ye think to do if ye caught the squirrel? Carry it back down the tree?" She looked to David. "If ye will find a straight bit of wood, I'll wrap that leg, so he canna move it. We'll need to carry him back to the horses. And ye," she added, frowning at Conall, "will have to stay quiet for a few days. Do ye ken? And dinna ever think about climbing any more trees."

She bent down and placed a light kiss on his head. Before she could move away, he reached up and licked her cheek. "Ach, laddie, ye're a sly one, ye are," she told him and chuckled.

David moved off to find what she'd requested. Bhaltair,

whom she hadn't noticed standing a few feet away while she tended Conall, approached, his expression thunderous.

"What do ye think ye are doing, running into the woods away from us?"

She pulled the scarf from around her neck and folded it into a long strip, ready to use when David returned. "Did ye hear us calling for this daft dog? He's hurt," she told Bhaltair. "David's gone after a stick I can use to brace his leg." She glanced up to find the squirrel had come down the tree, closer to her. Leery of Conall and, she supposed, Bhaltair, who stood with arms crossed over his chest, frowning, it stayed out of reach.

She turned her gaze to their surroundings. Only then did she notice the ground where they sat. Hundreds of wing-shaped seeds lay scattered under the squirrel's tree. Something about them prickled the back of her neck, but she couldn't think why. She scraped up a double-handful and passed them to Bhaltair to tuck away and save for her. As David approached, he nodded to Bhaltair, and distracted her with wrapping Conall's leg.

"How is he?"

"He'll do. Best we get ye home," she said to Conall as David helped her up. Then he lifted the dog, Lianna supporting Conall's leg until David stood on his own two feet, holding Conall against his broad chest. Lianna allowed herself a moment to be jealous of her pet, then put the thought out of her mind. Being wrapped in David's arms, her head on his shoulder, like Conall's, was a dream she denied herself. At least if she were in his place, her tongue wouldn't be hanging out like Conall's.

"He's heavier than he looks," David remarked as they set off toward their horses, Bhaltair leading the way. He'd left his mount just outside the trees, but walked with them instead of mounting up.

Lianna favored her leg as she walked, wishing the pain away. Stubbornly, it remained to plague her. "He's all bone and muscle," she answered. "The way they starved him, there's nay any fat on him, poor wee laddie."

"Aye, that makes sense," David agreed.

Quickly fed up with walking on her sore leg, as soon as they were out of the trees, Lianna whistled. Brigh trotted toward them and nickered a greeting as she reached them. Lianna mounted and David handed up Conall. He and Bhaltair walked on either side of Brigh, Bhaltair leading his mount by its reins until they reached Athdar.

"That's enough excitement for one afternoon," Lianna told her dog as they rode back toward the MacDhai keep with the other guards. David, riding beside her, seemed to be deep in thought. "What *fashes* ye?"

"When I had my hands on him, and ye were doing whatever it is ye do..."

"Ye felt something?"

"Aye. Warmth, calm, a tingle. I dinna ken how to describe it."

"I do. I didna realize ye would feel anything. Are ye well?"

David laughed. "Better than well. Humbled. I thought I kenned what ye can do. But I never really did until now. When yer mother helped me, she put me to sleep. I never felt a thing. I feel cheated."

"I can remedy that. Where would ye like me to hit ye? Or would ye prefer to be stabbed?"

"Neither, thank ye," he said and chuckled.

"Ye shouldna feel cheated. Fixing an injury can hurt. Does hurt," she added, rubbing her leg. "She spared ye that."

"I'll remember to thank her the next time I see her."

8

David rode at Lianna's side, but for a change, his gaze was on his hands rather than on her or the surrounding area. For once, he was willing to trust her Lathan guards to spot any trouble before it reached them.

His mind was on what he'd felt while she treated Conall's leg. What had he missed when he first got to the Aerie while Aileanna healed his head? He remembered going in and out of awareness, having a fierce headache and a roiling belly, then nothing. He wished he'd been aware of what Aileanna had done to him. He'd give a lot to know if mother and daughter shared the same...he didn't even know what to call it. Sensation? Touch? Or was it individual to each, just as each of them were an individual person in every other way.

Still, what a gift they shared! And what a burden. He'd noticed Lianna limping before she whistled for Brigh, yet she'd never complained. How much pain did Aileanna bear for the people she helped? How much had she borne for him?

Toran was right to protect Lianna as he had. This was not a lass to barter to another clan for any reason other than to keep her safe and happy. It was a responsibility David would gladly assume. He understood much better now what she could do, what it cost her, and how others might fear her ability. But he wanted to believe that once the people of MacDhai got to know her, they would love her, and accept her talent. And that he could be the one to keep her safe and happy.

The more he thought about her ability, the more something niggled at the back of his mind. Something from long ago. He'd been hurt in training. Knocked out by a wooden sword. When he woke up, his upper arm had been strapped to his side. He remembered keeping it wrapped for a few days, and being fine after that. Aileanna told him that besides being hit in the head with a baton during sword practice, when he fell, he dislocated his shoulder. He hadn't noticed her favoring her arm or her head, but perhaps her talent behaved differently. Or she'd recovered by the time he woke up.

Aileanna's talent was an accepted part of life in the Lathan clan. His memories of her talent had propelled him back to the Aerie for help. He'd heard many tales. He'd even seen her treat the sick and injured a few times, but she always disappeared afterward to eat and rest. Now he understood why.

He shook his head, and the movement attracted Lianna's attention.

"What?"

She rode with the reins in one hand, the other stroking Conall's rough coat, keeping him calm.

Envy of the hound roared through him. What he'd give to have her touch him that way.

"Do ye recall years ago, yer mother treating me for an accident on the practice ground. A head wound..."

"And dislocated shoulder. Aye, I do." She nodded, thoughtfully, her gaze dropping back to Conall for a moment, then returning to him, her hand still on the dog's back. "I worried about ye for all the days ye had yer arm bound to yer side."

"Ye never told me that."

"Of course I didna. Ye hadna been with us for very long. I didna ken ye, and ye were an older lad."

"Only two years."

"Still, ye wouldna have cared whether a wee lass worried for ye."

"Mayhap, but it was ye. And that changed everything."

"What changed?"

"I found out ye are special, too. I'd lived at the Aerie a long time before I saw ye heal a sparrow's broken wing. Ye didna ken I was there. At the time, I thought I imagined seeing the broken wing before ye knelt by the bird on the ground. I couldna see what ye did, but after a few minutes, ye picked it up, tossed it in the air and it flew away."

"It could have been stunned, not injured."

"Aye, that's possible, but kenning what I do now, I'm certain ye healed it. I remember wishing I could draw or paint. I wanted to capture the image of ye kneeling with yer arm upraised, yer hand open, and the bird just out of reach, flying free. The joyous expression on yer face as ye watched it go..." He paused and shrugged. "'Tis fortunate I have a good memory. Usually," he added. Aileanna must have treated him and made him forget, somehow.

"I dinna recall doing that. Or rather, I've done something similar many times, so I dinna recall that particular time. If I had been aware of ye watching, I wouldha been more careful."

"Why? Ye were with yer clan, fully safe and cared for by people who understood yer gift. Ye had nay reason to hide."

"Ye were there. That shouldha been reason enough."

"Because I was a stranger."

"Aye."

"But we became friends. More than friends. And ye learned to trust me."

Lianna glanced aside at their escort. The Lathans rode far enough ahead and behind them that they probably couldn't hear, or at least understand, most of their conversation. She met his gaze, her lips compressed until she spoke. "Aye, perhaps I did, but then ye left without saying goodbye." With that, she looked away and resumed petting Conall.

David winced. Aye, he left. Her opinion of him from that time on was utterly clear. But they'd been close before he was called home, and if he could convince her he hadn't forgotten her, they would be again. He just needed time.

And answers.

Everything depended on her. She held his future in her slim, beautiful hands. The hands currently ruffling Conall's fur. The hands he longed to feel touching him as lovingly as she touched the dog. He forced his gaze away.

§.

KERR JOINED David in his solar soon after they returned. "Still not making any progress on that?" He grinned and gestured toward the open ledger and loose pages on the desk between them.

David turned his frown from the ledger he should be working on to Kerr. "Nay." Instead, he'd been musing about whether Lianna would ever welcome his advances and accept him as her husband, but he wasn't going to share that with Kerr. "I havena. Nor has Lianna found the source of the poison. Our ride today was interrupted by daft Conall chasing a squirrel. He's all right, but he learned dogs are not meant to climb trees. Lianna has been over the glen and seen nothing to suggest the horses are being sickened by anything they find there."

"A natural illness?"

David shrugged. "'Tis possible, but I hope it isna true. I dinna ken how to fight something like that. A conspiracy of men, as terrible as that may be, seems simpler."

Kerr dropped into a chair. "I must have gone out to the stable to talk to Tadgh after ye came in. Ye say Lianna hasna found the answer, yet he swears the horses are better. Something she's doing is helping them. Tadgh mentioned a lot of water and dandelion tea."

David turned his whisky glass in his hand, thinking about her ability. As much as he would like to tell Kerr what she could do, he had to protect her from any who might learn of it and before they got to know her, come to fear her. No one in MacDhai knew what she and her mother could do. It was not his place to tell them. Not yet.

She had saved Athdar. The Percheron mare was improving, as were other horses who'd shown signs of the same illness, but whose conditions were not as dire. Without Lianna, they all might have died eventually. The thought of the effect on MacDhai if that happened made him toss back the whisky in his glass, nearly choking as it burned down his throat to his belly. Without her...

"If the solution is that simple," Kerr continued when David didn't respond, "when are ye going to send her home? Some in the clan dinna like her men watching them."

David pinned Kerr with a frown. "Not until we ken who is behind this and why. Her men are helping me...us...do that. Perhaps the ones who dinna like it are the ones we should look at more closely." Once she solved the mystery of the horses' illness, would she choose to go back to Lathan, leaving him as he'd once left her? He didn't want to be without her. Not just for the sake of the horses. For his sake, too. And his daughter's. Mirielle needed a mother. Aye, she had a nurse, but that wasn't the same thing, as well he knew. His mother had died when he was only six.

How would Lianna react to his advances? Could they begin anew?

"Some of the council are among them."

Kerr's statement startled David out of his thoughts as he continued to add even more.

"The old healer," Kerr said. "Even Molly, who claims they leer at her when she goes to the well for water for her bairn."

"Which Molly?"

"The one whose husband was injured in the last skirmish with reivers. If what I hear is true, I dinna think he's much use to her now," he added with a twist of his lips. "She seeks out male attention like a tavern doxy. No doubt the Lathan guards have seen her."

"I'll warn Bhaltair to keep his men clear of her."

He'd always known some in the clan did not agree with his father's decision about him, or about changing the clan's breeding practices for the horses. They did not support him, despite how he tried to make life better for his people.

Then someone started poisoning the horses. It made an insidious sort of sense. Making them ill, even killing one or two, would threaten the clan's livelihood, and his ability as laird to use the horses to protect MacDhai from their enemies. All to discredit him. To prove him incompetent to be laird. To give the council reason to banish him back to France, and replace him with...who? Kerr? Or someone else? He believed Kerr was loyal. He depended on Kerr. So, who else would concoct such a plot, then wait as long as they had for it to take effect?

He needed to know who his enemies were. David hated to give Kerr the impression he suspected him of being behind the clan's problems, but if he didn't get answers that reassured him, Kerr would indeed be a suspect. He was here. David would start with him, learn what he could, and go from there.

He leaned his elbows on the desk, doing his best not to look threatening. "I dinna wish to ask ye these questions, but I must. We've been all but brothers our entire lives, and ye have held MacDhai for me."

"And that makes me most likely to want to replace ye. Is

that where ye are headed? I wondered how long it would take ye to ask me."

David pursed his lips and nodded. "I dinna want to believe ye capable of such, but ye ken why I have to ask."

"I do. I swore fealty to ye when ye returned to become laird. I meant every word. Ye can trust me. Having served as chief in yer absence, I can tell ye honestly, I dinna want the job. The headaches. The horses. Ye have a bond with them like no other —until Lianna Lathan arrived. I dinna envy ye carrying the weight of trying to save them."

Everything Kerr said, the way he said it, the way he sat, the relaxed and open gestures of his hands, told David he was sincere. "Yet if anything ever happens to me, ye ken I trust ye to care for the clan as I would. To raise any son I might have to be a good laird."

"Aye. I'm honored, and grateful for yer trust. Ye have mine, as well."

David nodded. "I'm honored, too." He leaned back, relieved, his muscles loosening as he moved. He spread his hands. "So who else might have designs on this position? One man, or a conspiracy of several in the clan? The ill horses would certainly seem to play right into a plan to discredit me, whether they're truly part of a conspiracy, or not."

Kerr nodded. "I have had the same thought. One man could gather something to poison them, or purchase something in the village. Or several could play different parts, including making certain the horses eat or drink whatever it is. But ye ken it may be none of the clan. It may be naught but a passing illness, or something new in the glen."

David poured another dram for himself, and one for Kerr. "Who on the council is complaining? Perhaps they have more reason that most to fear eyes on them."

"Old Rab, for one. I can vouch for him. He has nay interest in being laird." Kerr took a sip and studied his glass for a moment, then lifted his gaze to David. "But I would keep an eye on Alastair. He's still young enough to be ambitious. He voted against ye, not that yer da cared a whit about what anyone on his council wanted. I can think of a few others, once they've had too much ale, and lasses' attention in the hall after supper loosens their lips. Talk to Griffith and old James, too. They're yer strongest supporters on the council, and they're crafty enough to ken, any time trouble is brewing, who might be stirring the pot." After another sip, he added, "Two more names come to mind. Dugall is a blowhard, but perhaps he has grand plans. And there's Iagan."

David snorted. "Dugall is a loner. How would he pull together enough support to do any of this?"

Kerr nodded. "He wouldna be able to build a group of any size. But one or two might do."

"'Tis the problem. It might only take one or two. If ye'll talk to Dugall, ye may get more from him than I could. As for Iagan, I dinna think he'd have the bollocks to challenge me. Besides, we were once friends."

"I'll talk to Dugall. But dinna make light of Iagan." Kerr shook his head. "There's more to him now than there was when he was a lad."

"A few stone?"

"Aye, and there's more muscle under his belly than anyone looking at him would ken."

David nodded. "I'll keep that in mind."

"So, Iagan and some of his masons. Dugall, the same. I dinna take them seriously, but they're not above a drunken brawl now and again. If they start something with the Lathans—"

"Chances are, the Lathans will finish it."

Kerr nodded. "That's good then."

"Why do ye say that?"

"As long as no one dies, they'll leave eventually, and in the meantime, they become a common enemy, uniting the clan against them."

"And against me. I brought them here."

"Not if yer lass really does save the horses."

But as Lianna healed the horses, she disrupted the plans of whoever meant to remove him as chief. She would be a target, too. He needed to speak to Bhaltair. To warn him that he and his men needed to keep even closer watch on their mistress.

"Ye brought her," Kerr added. "The guards just came along to do what guards do." He tossed off his drink and stood. "I'll see ye at supper."

David nodded dismissal and turned to watch the coals in the hearth. *Yer lass*, Kerr said. He wanted that more than Kerr knew. The warm glow reminded David of the passion he once shared with Lianna. Much like these coals, heated, but low. Now they were grown, he was sure they would burst into flame —if only she'd let him near her. He wanted to rekindle their passion. But how?

Was Mirielle part of the solution? If Lianna spent time with his daughter, would a bond form between them that would help him convince her to stay? Or would his daughter be hurt when Lianna chose to leave?

He had to try. He'd let Mirielle spend time with her and hope she'd prove open to being a mother to his daughter, as well as his wife and mother to any other children they might have in the future. He took another drink of the whisky, more measured this time, then set the glass aside.

BEFORE DINNER THAT EVENING, Lianna asked Jenny to do something special with her hair. She usually wore it down, sometimes in a braid. Jenny twisted it up and fussed over it while Lianna relaxed and let her thoughts drift to David.

They'd been young and she'd been foolish to think she knew him back then. He seemed interested in her now. Yet she didn't know this new David well enough to know if he would abandon her again, or if she had seen a glimmer in his gaze of the feelings he'd once had for her. She couldn't help think that despite his marriage, despite having given his heart to another woman and having a child with her, perhaps he could love her again. Nay, he still made her foolish. She couldn't allow that.

By the time Jenny held up a small looking glass for Lianna to see what she'd done, Lianna had begun to regret asking for her help. Changing her appearance this way might be too obvious, not only to David, but to the others in the great hall. She didn't want to appear to pursue him. She considered asking Jenny to take it all down, but the pleased anticipation on her face as she waited for Lianna's reaction stopped her. "'Tis beautiful. Thank ye," Lianna said as she turned her head from side to side, the better to see what Jenny had done.

When she entered the great hall, David wasn't in his usual seat at the high table. She took her place where he'd seated her the evening before, beside his, and waited. Servants brought out trenchers and began putting food on the tables. She waved them away. She'd wait for their laird.

Her men sat against the far wall, taking up most of one table. They'd aligned so that men seated on either side could see and reach her quickly if the need arose. That, she was certain, was Bhaltair's doing.

He was the most senior among the men, though he was probably close to David's age, she realized, which might explain some of the looks the two men aimed at each other. Jealousy? Or simply Bhaltair knowing something of their history and warning David to watch his step? The notion amused her, but worried her as well. The Lathans were guests here. She didn't need a romantic rivalry to develop between her head guard and David. She didn't think of Bhaltair that way, and never had.

After the third servant offered her a trencher, she waved the lass away and stood. David was late. Or not coming. Either way, she'd sit here no longer. It seemed as though every eye in the hall followed her from the high table down two steps and across the chamber toward the table where her men sat.

As she crossed, she heard comments, first barely above a whisper, then a few braver and louder. "She doesna deserve to sit with the laird." "What's she doing at the high table?" "Who'd let her travel without a male relative? Look at her. She must be a loose woman, not a wise one." The comments stung, but Lianna held her head up and never let her pace or her posture falter. She reached the table where her men stood, waiting for her, gazes scanning the room for trouble, and sank onto the bench with the wall at her back. If there was going to be trouble, she wanted to see it coming.

Her men sat down around her and passed her choice morsels on their trenchers before they resumed eating. A serving girl brought more food and a cup for her. Soon, another brought a full pitcher of ale.

"Have ye any cider?" Lianna might need the strength that came from the cider's sweetness, and didn't want to dull her senses with ale.

"I'll bring some," the lass agreed.

Lianna ate in silence, finished her meal, and leaned back, in no hurry to leave the hall. She would not allow anyone to think they'd chased her out with their comments.

David had still not appeared. She spared a moment to hope he was well. Then glanced around the room. A few heads were turned her way, but most seemed to have forgotten she was there. She wondered how her sitting with her guards, six very large, very strong Lathan men, appeared to the MacDhais. Then she snorted and stood to leave, her men standing with her to escort her upstairs. She didn't care.

9

The next morning, Lianna was still unhappy that David had not appeared at supper, leaving her to be subjected to the comments she'd heard as she crossed the great hall to sit with the other Lathans. To be fair, he was not responsible for escorting her everywhere, or for everything his people did or said. She didn't have to like the way she was treated last evening, but she hadn't been harmed. She hadn't really been threatened. She couldn't blame David, though she wanted to. Where had he been? Was he so unaccustomed to guests that he'd forgotten his duty as host?

As she walked through the bailey toward the stables, she fought to set aside thoughts of him, her gaze on her destination. A squeaky bark stopped her. She turned toward the sound in time to see a young puppy leave a lass at the top of hay piled against the outer wall and scamper down, its gaze fixed on her. It stumbled, then tumbled down, landing hard. Lianna winced. That had to hurt. She hurried toward it, and picked it up. She sensed nothing broken, a happy change after her experience with Conall. She'd done more for his injuries than she'd want any animal to need. She settled onto the hay and petted the squirming puppy as the lass climbed down to her.

"Dinna hurt it!"

She was crying. Lianna could sympathize with her concern for the pup. "He's fine, lass. What's his name?" She handed the puppy to her.

The lass clutched it to her chest and it licked her chin. Tears forgotten, she giggled, she lifted it, and it licked her face. The lass buried her face in his side, then looked at Lianna.

"Beau. His name is Beau."

"He's a handsome lad," Lianna told her as a cat padded up to her and jumped in her lap. "Hello, wee cat." Lianna smoothed her fur and she curled up. Then Lianna turned back to the lass. "What's yer name?"

"I'm Jane."

"I'm Lianna."

"I ken who ye are. Ye came to help the horses."

"I did." Lianna smiled as another cat, younger this time, and already pregnant, arrived, followed soon after by a deerhound and a smaller dog of mixed parentage.

"Why are they coming to ye?"

Her new friend Jane looked more curious than concerned, so Lianna reached over and petted Beau, then did the same to the deerhound and the smaller dog. She made room for the pregnant cat beside her. "Because animals like me. And I like them."

"I like them, too, but they dinna come to me like they do to ye."

"Perhaps if ye stay very still and think welcoming thoughts, they'll begin to," Lianna told her. "All creatures are drawn to peace and joy."

A child following another dog arrived then, and soon, Lianna found herself surrounded by children and animals. She told them stories, keeping a close eye on the adults who passed by in case anyone looked ready to object or cause trouble. But no one did. After a while, a few women joined the group and told a few tales of their own.

Lianna smiled and scratched the cat in her lap behind its ears. Perhaps the way to the clan's acceptance was through its animals, the children who loved them, and the parents who loved them.

DAVID STOOD at his chamber's window and observed the comings and goings in the bailey with a critical eye. Kerr had already been in to tell him about the comments directed at Lianna during supper last evening, and to chastise him for leaving her alone at the high table waiting for him. David's initial reaction had been to protest that he hadn't told her to meet him, but thinking back, he couldn't be sure. Then, picturing Lianna sitting alone at the high table and being subjected to such scathing criticism when she left it, heat flashed through his body. He clenched his jaw. What happened to her was his fault.

Unaware they were being watched, men and women moved around below him, intent on everyday errands, as though no one had insulted Lianna to her face. His guest. The woman taking pain and exhaustion in her stride as she fought to save his clan. For him.

Which of them had called Lianna loose? If he ever found out, he'd make them regret it. And which had told her she didn't belong at the high table? Only he had the right to make that decision. And after she sat next to him the evening prior, in questioning her place there, they questioned his authority. Openly. Publicly.

Right now, he was too angry to be able to decide which was worse, but both made his blood run cold, then hot, then cold again. Furious, and yes, fearful for her sake. Angry for his own, and at himself.

David wanted to know what Bhaltair heard. He stepped back from the window, about to go look for him, when he noticed Lianna crossing the bailey. As usual, her beauty, her confident stride, and her kindness ensnared him. She was on the way to check on his horses, to help any that were ill, and to take on their pain. He clenched his fists. He would not allow her to be mistreated by anyone.

When she ran to a wee puppy lying on the ground below a stack of hay, he leaned toward the window, the better to see her. A lass climbed down and joined her after she picked it up, then a cat, a few more dogs and cats, and more children. He could tell she'd started telling stories, and the group grew with every new tale until some older lasses and mothers joined in.

David watched from his window, transfixed.

As far as he knew, Lianna had not met the first lass and could not know who she was, but her kindness to the child spoke volumes to David, especially after what she'd endured at the hands of some in the clan last evening. She protected the puppy and she charmed the children. She would be a good mother someday.

He turned from the window and left his chamber in search of Bhaltair. He found him in the great hall with Ailbeart and another Lathan guard, Damhan. "Who's watching Lianna?" He didn't mean for his question to sound peremptory, but the Lathans stood at the sound of his voice.

"Cole is watching her," Bhaltair answered, "and Hamish is in the stable with our mounts. Brodie was up all night. He's sleeping."

"Thank ye. Please, sit. I want to talk about what happened at supper."

Bhaltair nodded, frowning. "What do ye want to ken?"

"Kerr told me what he heard. I want yer take on what was said, and how Lianna reacted."

Bhaltair confirmed what Kerr told David, and added a few nuances Kerr had either left out or been unaware of. "Lianna held up her head, stayed, ate with us, and acted as if the comments directed at her meant nothing," Bhaltair informed him. "She ignored them."

His tone betrayed tension, but not, David judged, the tension of someone ready to do violence.

"People here dinna ken her," Damhan added, "or they wouldna speak as they did."

"I agree." David turned his attention back to Bhaltair. "Did ye sense a threat?"

"Nay. And Lianna showed them she's not one to back down."

"Aye, she is that," David said, and stood. "I'm sorry it happened. I'll apologize to her. And I'm glad 'twas no worse. I'll see that it doesna happen again."

He came away impressed with the Bhaltair's intelligence and grasp of the implications of what he'd observed the evening before. What David did not sense was a romantic interest in Lianna. Bhaltair spoke as one angered for the person he protected, not someone he cared about in any other way. He saw her as his responsibility, not his intended bride. Had Bhaltair been in love with Lianna and heard those comments last evening, likely clan MacDhai would be short a few members. He was glad neither Bhaltair nor any of his men had been provoked to violence on Lianna's behalf.

Together, they would protect her. But only David would win her.

David could picture her crossing the room as if what she heard had not wounded her. But he knew it had. So did Bhaltair. David thought back to looking down on Lianna in the bailey with her collection of animals and bairns, and was even more impressed with her kindness and caring toward a member of the same clan that rebuked her.

He headed to the stable, knowing he'd find her there. He owed her an apology for the actions of his people.

§.

LIANNA HAD INSPECTED everything in several of the stalls, raked the hay, examined the tack, the water in the horses' buckets, and the oats in the feedbags when she noticed David leaning against the wall, watching her.

She frowned. "How long have ye been there?"

"Not long. What are ye doing?"

She'd been shaking her head, muttering to herself, and getting nowhere. "Searching. There's got to be an answer. If it's not in the glen, it has to be here." She spread her arms and gestured at the stalls around them.

He straightened and walked toward her.

She fisted her hands, frowning. "There has to be a reason." She ran a hand through her hair, half unraveling her braid. "And I must find it."

He took her in his arms.

She stiffened. "David..." His scent and heat arrowed straight to her heart.

"I owe ye an apology," he murmured. "I heard what happened at supper last night. I'm sorry I wasna there."

"Nothing happened." She shook her head against his muscled shoulder.

He hugged her closer. "Ye dinna need to protect them."

His voice rumbled against her ear. She wanted to melt against him, to rest her head on his shoulder and let him comfort her, but if she did, she'd be lost. Again.

"Some of the people of this clan—my clan—were rude and cruel," he insisted. "I heard what was said from several sources, and I willna stand for it." He tipped her chin up and met her gaze. "I dinna mean to excuse what they said, but they dinna ken what ye are doing for them. If they did, they would behave differently. I will see to it that ye will not suffer the like again."

She drew her brows together. "Nay! If ye say anything, they will fear me." She tried to pull back, but he held her fast. "They'll blame ye for bringing me here."

David shook his head, determination in his gaze. "They will honor ye. Once they understand. Just as yer father's allies accepted what yer mother could do."

"It willna matter if I canna do what I came to do." She pushed against his chest, and this time, he let her go.

"We'll figure it out. With yer talent, 'tis only a matter of time."

"I havena yet," she objected, but he shook his head to silence her.

"Look about ye." He nodded down the central hallway. "The horses are better."

She turned away and rested her forearms on the stall's wall. Anything to keep from falling into David's embrace. "'Tis not as if I've done much for them."

"Ye ken when they've been poisoned before they get sick. Ye keep them alive. And I saw what ye did with the puppy in the bailey."

She glanced around. "Ye did? How?"

He stepped closer and rested a hand on her shoulder. "From my chamber window. I happened to look out at the right time. Ye were kind to the lass—and the puppy."

His heat and approval warmed her and melted the hard edges of her resolve. "She didna mean for it to be hurt."

"I ken it." He released her and stepped away. "Ye drew quite a crowd of animals and people. After last night, 'twas the best thing ye could have done."

Surprised, she turned and met his gaze, quizzical.

"'Tis not like I did it on purpose. The animals just came to me, and with the lass already there, others followed, then their mothers. We talked and told stories. 'Twasna anything I planned."

"Perhaps not, but perhaps the way to acceptance is through the puppies and kittens. Small creatures my people care about. Today was a good start. Let them see how their pets are drawn to ye. When they see the animals trust ye, surely they will ken they can, too."

"I had the same thought, but I havena done anything for them. Only Conall."

"I saw them gather around ye. They stayed and more joined ye. They will talk to others. Give it time."

She tensed with frustration. "Do we have time? If the poisonings continue, how much time do ye think yer horses have before one or more of them succumbs?"

David's face fell.

Surely he hadn't forgotten the stakes that brought her here.

"We canna ken. We can only do as we have done, help the horses who are ill and continue to search for the person or group doing this."

"And if ye canna find them? Then what?"

David ran a hand through his hair, pushing it back from his forehead. "I must. If I mean to remain the MacDhai, this is a test I canna fail."

"I want to help ye, David. I do. I dinna ken how else to do it."

"Ye've already done so much for me," he told her and cupped her face, his gaze locked with hers. He took a breath, then told her, "I never forgot ye. I never could." He bent to take her lips.

She turned her face away. "I canna, David. Not again."

He reared back, disappointment in his gaze. "Ye ken I have feelings for ye, Lianna. Can ye forget the past? Forgive me?"

"There's naught to forgive." Her feelings for him were her own fault. How she nursed them after he left was none of his doing. She didn't trust herself around him. Not when he was this close.

"Ye have the same full heart ye had as a lass, only now ye are grown. I want to make new memories with ye. When ye are ready."

She understood what he didn't say. He wanted a future with her. But would she ever be ready for him? She'd tried to keep her memories of him, her feelings for him, in the past, but they hadn't stayed there. She'd come here still believing she needed to protect herself from him. What if she was wrong?

10

The next morning, Lianna woke from dreams of David's kisses. In them, he held her with no thought for anything but her. His kisses went on and on, making her feel loved and wanted in ways she only experienced with him as a lass too young to understand heartache. Her body responded with sensations she didn't know how to name. She sat up in bed, her heart still pounding and her core clenched and crying out for something she feared only her dream-David would ever give her.

Even in her dreams, he hadn't said *forever*.

Perhaps even her dreams were wrong. Perhaps the real David would never touch her so intimately. But someone might, someday, even if that someone was not him. But oh, what if he *was* the one?

David had said he never forgot her. He wanted to make new memories with her. Why would he say such a thing? Because he wanted her as his wife? The thought stole her breath as longing flooded her, and her heart beat a wild rhythm inside her chest.

Did she want that, too? Since he left her behind at the

Aerie, she hadn't seriously considered the possibility of marriage and children. And since she'd found him in the woods below the Aerie, she'd turned him away every time he tried to get close to her. She raked her fingers through her hair, then clenched them and tugged. She had to stop this.

Someone knocked softly on her door, and Lianna realized she'd slept later than she'd planned. Jenny entered and without a word of greeting, went right to her trunk for fresh clothes.

"Good morrow," Lianna told her.

"Ach, Lianna, I'm sorry to wake ye. And good morrow to ye," the lass said as she stood and shook out the last clean dress Lianna brought with her. "I'll see the rest of yer things are washed this morning, so they're ready for ye to use tomorrow."

"Thank ye, Jenny. I'm sorry ye have had to become my maid."

"*Dinna fash.* What ye are doing is too important to be bothered with such as this." She gestured toward the dress.

"Still, I appreciate yer help. 'Tis good to have a friend here."

Lianna watched her as she gathered up the dirty clothes Lianna had traveled in and worn the last two days, including the one drenched and sticky with honey. She seemed distracted.

"Is there a problem, Jenny? Ye are more quiet than usual." Normally, she was cheerful and annoyingly talkative in the morning.

Jenny turned to face her, clutching the soiled dress as though she couldn't bear to part with it. "'Tis naught."

"I ken ye better than that. What's amiss?"

Finally, Jenny sighed and dropped her shoulders. "I feel unwelcome," she said, reluctance in her expression and posture. "Except for Tadgh, I suppose. He talks to me."

"Aye, I've spoken to him. He seems a good man."

Jenny looked away with a sad smile, her lips compressed, as if recalling some time spent with the stable master or wishing for more. Then she sobered. "'Tis almost as if the people here think I'm a spy, though who I'm supposed to be spying for, I dinna ken." She shrugged. "Or something else is going on. They stop speaking to each other when they see me coming. They avoid me. 'Tis silly, I ken it."

"'Tisna. I've been treated the same by most of the people here. Has anyone threatened ye?"

"Nay, not truly. Avoided me, more like. Except for Tadgh."

Lianna went to her and took her hand. "I am sorry for bringing ye into a difficult situation. If ye are worried for yer safety, I can send ye home with one of the Lathan guards..."

"Ach, nay, ye canna. Laird Toran would have my hide if I left ye, and left ye with fewer guards than he thought needful."

"Da worries over naught. I grew up with Drummond, Jamie, and Tavish, aye? I can take care of myself." But, could she? After dreaming about David all night, she feared she was falling under his spell, something she vowed before they left the Aerie not to do. And they still didn't know what was wrong with the horses, or if someone in the keep was the cause.

But Jenny's comment about a spy made the hair on the back of Lianna's neck stand up. What if she was right? David had come from France, and Spain before that. What if someone had come with him who meant to do him harm?

DAVID LOOKED up from the ledger he was still trying to make sense of, to see Lianna in the solar's doorway. She leaned against the doorframe, her expression pensive, her brow drawn down and her lips compressed.

"What's amiss, Lianna?" Judging by her posture and expression, something bothered her. "Has someone else said something to ye?"

She shook her head.

Then what? After he tried to kiss her yesterday and she refused him, he feared it was him. That uncertainty sent shivers skittering from his belly to his fingertips. Had he pushed her too far, too fast? He hoped not. Or did she regret turning him away? The thought that she might regret that, and might want to kiss him again, gave him room to breathe.

He was glad to see her. He'd buried himself in numbers, hoping to get the memory of her in his arms out of his mind—and body—but it wasn't working. And now that she was here, he gave up and closed the ledger. She came in and took a seat across the desk from him. "Where were ye married?"

He frowned. What was she asking? "Lucienne, my wife, was French. The daughter of a comte and comtesse." Lucienne had looked somewhat like Lianna, with flowing auburn hair, full lips, and bright eyes. He fell for her because he missed Lianna, but he could not tell her that.

"How long did ye live there?"

"A little more than three years. My daughter was born there. Then Lucienne died of childbed fever."

"I'm sorry."

"Why are ye asking?"

She hesitated, then held up a hand. "I'll tell ye in a moment."

David let her comment pass. "Mirielle's grandparents helped raise her until my father died, and I came back here."

"And did the grandparents agree with ye bringing her here, so far away from them?"

"Hardly."

"Is she the Comte's heir?"

David's gut clenched as it always did when he thought of that possibility. "Not that I have been told. Though her mother was their only living child, there must be a nephew or male cousin who would inherit before a granddaughter. I think even a bastard son, if one exists, would be chosen before Mirielle."

"There's something I think ye should consider." She related what Jenny told her. "She said one thing that makes sense to me. They treat her as if she were a spy. She isna one, of course. But what if there is one here? 'Tis only a theory, but what if the someone harming the horses is from France."

David frowned. He could see where that would lead. "They'd want to force me out, back to France with Mirielle." What if the Comte had no other recourse but to name her his heir? It would explain a lot. David would have to choose between his role as laird and a role as regent for his daughter in France.

Lianna clenched her hands in her lap. "A spy makes a sick sort of sense."

"An agent of the Comte could be behind the illnesses. But who? Clémence? Nay, I dinna believe that. She is with Mirielle nearly all the time. When would she be able to go to the stable unnoticed?"

"Is there anyone else?"

"She is the only one who remained. The guards who travelled here with us returned to France."

"All of them?"

"Aye. I would ken if one or more remained. I would have seen them."

"What if they didna live in the keep, but in the village?"

A chill of a very different kind ran up David's spine. "And came to the keep only rarely, with the other workers? 'Tis possible, I suppose. 'Twould be a risk if I saw and recognized him—or them."

But it was more than possible. Knowing the Comte, it was likely that he'd left more than one person behind to carry reports from Clémence, and to ensure Mirielle was safe. They would have to speak without a French accent, or not at all.

"How can I expose someone like that? Everyone here has been a loyal clan member for all of my life."

"Have they?"

He knew what she meant. Someone, or several someones, were behind the clan's trouble. "Even so, a stranger would be noticed. I would hear if a stranger remained in the area."

Or would he? The Comte could offer many things David could not. Wealth. Privilege. Connections. David had some of those, of course, but the Comte had built his web of alliances over a lifetime. David could only imagine how far his reach extended.

❧

LIANNA WAS GRATIFIED David took her wild idea seriously, but she could be wrong. "I dinna want to be the cause of more trouble."

"Of course. But if ye are right, I should be able to find them." He paused, a frown betraying the direction of his thoughts, his gaze on his folded hands on the desktop. "What if it is not one of the Comte's men, but one of mine who traveled with me? One he corrupted. And that person has recruited others to help."

"How many were there?"

"One died in Spain, two others chose to remain with the lasses they married in France. Only three returned. Two of them chose to live in the village with lasses they married in the last year. They help Tadgh guard the horses when they're in the summer pasture, so they're rarely in the keep. The last one lives in the keep and remains a MacDhai guard. I see him often, of course."

"Is he loyal?"

"Dugall? Kerr talked to him, but nothing came of it. I've never had reason to doubt him. But still..." He flattened his hands on the desk and pushed to his feet.

David painted a disturbing scenario. No wonder he'd been

so solemn when telling her father that the people of his clan no longer knew him.

"I already spoke to the only two I believe could compound a poison—the cook and the old healer," she reminded him. "I couldna swear either one would harm the horses. And why go to the trouble, when they could more easily poison ye?"

"Must I fear every meal? Everything I drink?"

Lianna shook her head. "I doubt it. Not if they havena harmed ye by now. Perhaps whoever is doing this brought something with them."

"That implies a long-term plan—a conspiracy. The French are masterful at that."

"And the Spanish?"

"Perhaps, but to what purpose? I was three years in France before returning here. During that time, I expected Kerr or someone else to succeed my father."

"And yet ye trust him."

"He's given me nay reason to doubt him."

"Ye must be certain. Ye canna accuse anyone without evidence. I have not found anything wrong with the horses' food or water, or with the grounds around the keep. There are no toxic plants in the glen in enough quantity to do what we've been dealing with."

"Have you seen the keep's garden? Cook and the healer grow food and medicinals. Perhaps something from there?"

Lianna jumped up. "Show me."

The walled garden was full of plants, herbs, and flowers, but Lianna could find nothing in enough quantity to harm the horses for as long as David said they'd been getting ill.

Disappointed, she asked David to take her to speak with the healer again. "Where does she grow what she needs, if not in the walled garden?"

"The old woman grows things in a big window. Ye can see

them from outside, through the glass, though 'tis murky," he told her, "but I dinna ken what they are."

Lianna wasn't pleased to be confronting the old healer again, but she had to get answers, and this time, the laird would be at her back.

"I search the nearby glen and woods for anything else I need," the healer said when Lianna asked her the same question.

"Have ye been missing anything?"

The old healer glanced at David. "'Tis hard to tell."

Lianna's hackles went up at that. Her mother kept meticulous notes on each toxic plant she used, measuring its growth, numbers of stalks, estimates of leaf counts if it was very large, and the like. The old healer was either careless or lying or both. Lianna shook her head. "The MacDhai says ye have a window where ye grow some things in pots. Where is that?"

The old woman's gaze darted to the heavy cabinet Lianna had noticed on her first visit, then away again so quickly, if Lianna hadn't been focused on her face, she never would have seen her eyes move. Lianna nodded. So, that *was* an outside wall.

She turned to David. "Will ye ask her to open that cabinet, please?"

His gaze was on the cabinet, a frown creasing his forehead.

Before he could speak, the old woman said, "I lost the key."

Lianna knew it was a lie.

David did, too, apparently. He walked to the cabinet and tugged at the door, then hefted the padlock. "Produce the key or I will break it open," he said, his voice low and calm, but his gaze fierce.

The old healer wasn't intimidated. She crossed her arms and stared him down.

David shrugged, pulled his dirk and struck the padlock with its hilt until the lock popped open. As calmly as before, he pulled the hasp, then opened the doors. Pots lined two shelves, a cloudy, translucent window made up of leaded glass squares behind them, all covered by the bulk of the cabinet. "Lianna?"

Lianna walked to him and studied the contents. This was a more extensive collection than they kept at the Aerie. Why did she have all these dangerous plants? "Poisonous, all of them, some mildly, some deadly. All with medicinal properties—after careful preparation." She turned to the old healer, who watched her with hatred, her eyes glinting with fury. Lianna knew she risked much by challenging her. But she could see the woman had secrets, perhaps dangerous secrets, and not just in this cabinet. She would not tolerate secrets dangerous to David. "This is an unusual way to keep them out of the reach of curious fingers." The south-facing window might also keep dangerous plants alive year-round. Lianna studied the woman with renewed wariness.

David turned to the old healer, whose expression had turned red with fury. "Explain this."

"As she said. To keep the bairns out of things that will harm them."

"And to what use do ye put these?"

David's mild tone didn't fool Lianna for a moment. He was angry.

"I could waste yer time telling ye how I prepare and use each of these to cure everything from headaches to heart problems, but I expect yer lass can do that as well as I."

"I prefer to hear it from ye," David said and settled on one of the two stools in the chamber. He gestured Lianna to the other. "Please, enlighten me."

Lianna reluctantly took the seat next to David. It seemed rude not to offer one to the old woman, but she realized David was determined to get the upper hand with the old healer, one way or the other.

They sat and the old woman talked for the better part of an

hour. Nothing she said, as far as Lianna knew, was untrue, but she minimized the danger of the most toxic plants. Did she think Lianna untrained or unfamiliar with them?

Lianna kept her mouth shut and let the woman talk. None of the plants, as far as Lianna knew, would have caused the set of symptoms she saw in the horses. But there were deadly toxins in each of them that could be used in other harmful ways against people as well as animals. Lianna had the uncomfortable feeling the old woman had extensive experience with all of them.

Finally, the old woman ran down. Lianna touched David's arm. "What we seek isna here."

He stood. "Enough. Close that," he added, gesturing at the cabinet. Then he took Lianna's arm and walked her out of the herbal.

Back in his solar, they settled together in a pair of chairs in front of its small hearth. Lianna related her concern about the healer's casual attitude toward the toxic plants she cultivated. "She downplayed how dangerous those plants can be. Perhaps she's simply old and careless. Forgetful, even. But if there's a conspiracy against you, she could be in on it," she warned.

"She would have to be part of a conspiracy if she has anything to do with what's happened to the horses. I dinna think she could manage it on her own."

"Yet, none of those plants account for what I've observed in the horses. If she used almost any of them, horses would be dead. And this has been going on for sennights. If whoever is doing this grows impatient, she could still prepare something that would kill them outright. Something like a tincture that would not be evident, but could be added to their feed or water."

David blanched.

"But why would the people of this clan do something like this to ye?"

He grimaced and watched the fire. "Perhaps because they were loyal to my father. Or as I told Laird Lathan, because I was gone from here for so long, they dinna ken me." He crossed his arms. "Or perhaps I have a rival I'm unaware of. Kerr and I have discussed the possibility."

Lianna wrapped her arms around her ribs, mirroring his posture, feeling every bit as insecure as the worry about disloyalty within his clan must make him feel. "It may have nothing to do with the Comte and everything to do with someone thinking they're better suited to be laird." She met his gaze. "How do we discover that?"

11

David took comfort from her concern for him, and from her "how do we discover that" question. As though she was his partner. Not in life, as he hoped, but it was a start. Finding the culprit was his responsibility, not hers. Yet she seemed eager to help. He didn't want her to worry, but if it meant she cared about him, he hoped it might lead to more.

"Whom do ye trust?" She leaned forward. "Who will tell ye what you need to know? David, yer life could be in danger. What if horses are just the first step, a warning?"

He shook his head. "Ye may be right, but it makes nay sense for someone in the clan to kill them—they're too valuable. And they have been at this for a very long time. We dinna ken why."

"Some sort of a message?"

"Perhaps, but to what end?"

Lianna shrugged. "Their plan willna work so long as I keep the horses alive. What else might they do? Use some of the old healer's poisons to kill a horse or two? Attack ye? Attack yer daughter?"

"Do ye really think someone is trying to force me back to France?" If even Lianna thought so, the Comte might be behind all of this. "If that's true, the last person in danger would be my daughter. Her grandparents would love to have her back, whether she is the heir or not."

"Honestly, I dinna ken. But ye might consider sending Mirielle to them. Or to Lathan until this is over. She'd be safe there. Unreachable."

"If I send her to France, I might not be able to get her back." He waved a hand, dismissing the idea. "Her grandfather is powerful. At Lathan, aye, she'd be unreachable. But ye wouldna," he told her. "Whoever is behind this could trade ye to yer clan for Mirielle."

"They wouldna give her up."

"At the cost of yer life? Nay, I willna put ye at risk."

"If I'm right, I'm already at risk. I'm delaying them by keeping the horses alive—and healthy."

"So far as anyone here kens, ye are merely someone caring for the horses. But if ye take charge of Mirielle, ye become part of the family. Someone who can be harmed to get to me." She was that already, and more, but no one knew it. Not even Lianna. "I care too much about ye to make ye a target. I always have. Even when I thought ye had forgotten me, and I married another. Ye were always in my heart."

Lianna's mouth dropped open. "Ye never told me." She frowned and looked away. "Ye shoulda told me. Why are ye telling me this now?"

"Because I can. Because I must. And because I hope ye feel the same. There's no one to keep us apart. Not yer brother. Not my father or yers."

David held his breath and got to his feet. Would Lianna admit to feelings for him, too, more than the physical attraction they shared?

"Only us," she replied.

His heart sank, seeing her rejection as the end of his hopes and dreams.

As if she'd made a decision, she took a breath, rose and stepped into his arms. Her touch, her body pressed against his, and the love he saw shining in her gaze were all the answer he needed.

"I'm with you in this. Do ye understand me? I dinna want to see you hurt, or dispossessed. Ye are laird. We willna let anyone change that—unless ye decide to."

He couldn't help himself. He kissed her, and kept kissing her, trying to drink her in, to inhale her essence, to make her a part of his body, so he wouldn't lose her when she stepped out of his embrace. He tasted her mouth, her throat, the graceful curve of her ear, then began again, craving more.

She pulled back first. "David..."

He closed his eyes, summoning the will to calm the need raging in him. "I worry for ye, being here," he said, and brushed a stray lock of hair from her face.

"I never forgot ye," she murmured as she lifted a hand to cup his cheek. Then her lips caressed his, but when she pulled back, instead of hunger, unshed tears shone in her eyes.

He wanted to kiss away her tears, and the anguish behind them, but she clung to them. Still, she'd kissed him, when up to now she'd held him off. He was getting through to her.

"I want ye, lass." Was it too soon to declare his love for her? Or could she see it in his eyes? "I need ye with me." He could tell her that.

"I want to be with ye, too. To help ye, for as long as ye need me."

It wasn't all he wanted. He wanted forever. But as long as she stayed with him, it would be enough for now.

AFTER LIANNA LEFT him to tend to the horses, David stayed in the solar, thinking hard. Lianna cared for him. Her kisses told him she wanted him, too. But did she want more? Or did she mean what she'd said, that she only meant to help him as long as he needed her?

He needed her now and forever. But he didn't think she had forever in mind when she made her offer. Could he make her see how much he wanted her to be his? He dared not scare her away. His clan needed her, too. He had to focus on that until the danger was past. Then there would be time for the two of them.

He got up and started pacing, needing the movement to help him think and to burn off the desire still raging in him for Lianna. They still had problems to solve. He still had time to convince her to stay.

The next step was clear. Talk to the men Kerr had recommended, Griffin and old James. At David's request, Kerr brought them to his solar.

"Good day, laird," Griffin greeted him. Old James, actually the younger of the two, nodded.

David took that for agreement with Griffin's greeting.

"Good day to ye. Please sit." He gestured for them to take seats and nodded to Kerr.

"Kerr tells us ye suspect a conspiracy to weaken ye is the reason for the problem with the horses," Griffin said.

"I do, and I depend on yer insights. Without proof, I willna move against any man, so dinna fear ye will condemn anyone with yer words. But I must ken who ye think could do something like that?"

Only one name came up again and again. Iagan. "He's a hard worker, but he favored Alasdair, even before ye came back," old James told him. "He has influence with the other stonemasons, the blacksmith, some crofters and such."

"It sounds like he would have enough supporters to want to be laird, himself." David exchanged a glance with Kerr, recalling their earlier conversation. David hadn't thought Iagan capable, but this put him in a different light.

Old James laughed. "Nay, he's better working with his hands, and he kens it. He is not yer rival, but he'll support Alastair, or another. Like others in the clan, he's wedded to the old ways. Yer plans to improve the breed of MacDhai horses, management of the crofts, and such, mean change. People dinna like change."

"Even when it makes their lives better? Easier?"

Griffin glanced at his fellow council member. "Even then. After a season or two, once they experience what ye are trying to do, it may go easier. In the meantime, ye must speak with Iagan, find out what he wants, and see if ye can convince him to work with ye, not against ye."

"That's good advice. I'll take it to heart," David told them, and stood. "Thank ye."

Kerr led them out, leaving David to his thoughts. He had a hard time believing Iagan had developed the intelligence or will to cause this kind of trouble. He'd been lazy as a lad, and though he'd sworn fealty to David when he returned to replace his father as laird, Iagan had stayed out of his way ever since.

Old James made sense, but David suspected one of Iagan's reasons was more personal. They had a history. A lass he wanted had set her sights on David. Could he still resent David for that? Enough to cause so much trouble?

David believed the lass was the reason his father sent him to the Continent. When the laird found out about the lass, he'd shouted that he'd not have his only son and heir marry within the clan. David's value in an alliance was too great. He wondered if Iagan knew. And if he'd ever succeeded in capturing that lass's interest.

David hadn't thought about her since he'd left for Spain. He hadn't seen her since he'd been back. Had she married away? He should find out, not because of any interest in her—Lianna would be his if he could convince her—but because she might have been the cause of bad blood that survived to this day. Bad blood that could have serious consequences all these years later. He resolved to send for Iagan just as a messenger entered the solar.

"Beg pardon, Laird, but I have a document for ye." He pulled a missive from inside his jerkin and David fought not to groan. Covered with beribboned seals and addressed in a flourish of French lettering, it could have come from only one person. The Comte.

David stood and took it from him. "Thank ye. Have ye come far?"

"A full day's ride, Laird."

"Then tell the steward to find ye a place to sleep for tonight, and see Cook about yer supper."

The man left with thanks, and David broke open the seals on the latest missive from Mirielle's maternal grandfather.

The Comte inquired after his grandchild. Demanded to see her. For David to bring her to France. He did not mention any intention to allow them to leave the country again, if David was foolish enough to comply.

The missive contained the same demands as every other one the Comte has sent since David returned to Scotland to take over his clan after his father's death. He nearly tossed it into the fire, but as he stood to walk to the hearth and do just that, he noticed something different in this missive. In the bottom corner, a note penned in a tiny, delicate hand caught his eye. The Comtesse appealed to see Mirielle. She was very ill, and could not bear the thought of leaving this earth without another glimpse of the sweet child's face.

David scanned the letter again. There'd been no mention of her illness in any previous missive from the Comte. She'd been in robust health when he left. Disturbed, he crossed to the hearth and tossed the letter into the fire, then poured yet another whisky and sat, musing. Was this a ploy to appeal to his sympathies? If so, it hadn't worked. He'd be a fool to put

Mirielle within reach of her grandfather. Nay, he would not risk losing his daughter.

§

LIANNA'S BODY still thrummed from David's kisses as she headed for the only place she could think of where she felt secure. Useful. Truly needed. To the horses.

Sensations much like the tingles she felt while healing radiated through her body, but they were stronger, and seemed to intensify every time she recalled his lips moving over hers, his tongue teasing her mouth open to his exploration. His breath soft against her ear as his teeth gently tugged at her lobe and lightning flashed along her veins. She hadn't stopped him. Hadn't pulled herself or pushed him away. She hadn't been able to. Her blood had gone hot and thick in her veins. Perhaps she should have tried, but she was glad she didn't. She'd clung to him and feasted on his mouth, his taste, his scent, as if making up for their years apart.

His kiss was everything she remembered and more. He tasted even hungrier for her than he had as a youth, more demanding, but somehow gentler, more attuned to her response. Touching him, lost in his kisses, she could have believed she felt his need for her, the desire burning in him to have her, and how he fought for control. That, though, she must have imagined.

But what if it was real? What if her talent revealed how David felt while kissing her. Not what he thought, what he intended, but his body's response. His body's drive to make her his. If so, his touch, his kiss, had revealed the truth of his desire for her. But not, she reminded herself, his true feelings. A man could lust after a woman, yet not care at all for her. Not love her. And if that was the case, then what good was knowing the strength of David's desire? It didn't help her to know whether he only wanted her now, or wanted forever.

She went to Brigh's stall. There, she could calm herself, get some distance from the storm of sensation David had spun up in her body. In this condition, she was no good to the horses. She couldn't sense anything but her own arousal. She sat in Brigh's stall with her and Conall, whose tail started wagging the moment she opened the stall's half-door. "Settle down, lad," she told him as she bent to pet him. "I'm here to settle down, too." Brigh nudged her and nickered, eager for attention. "Aye, lass, ye are still my favorite. *Dinna fash.*" Lianna wrapped her arms around Brigh's neck and leaned into her shoulder. The contact calmed her. In minutes, she took a deep breath and became aware that Brigh had calmed, too. Once Lianna's heartbeat returned to normal, she checked Conall's injuries, then straightened, satisfied with the progress he had made.

Something about animals had always drawn her to them. Her mother told her when she could barely crawl, she'd taken off after one of the clan's deerhounds, then spotted a cat and rolled to change direction toward it and crawled until she reached it. Aileanna said she knew there was something special going on when the cat, one of the more standoffish of the clan's cats and kittens, the most aggressive when it felt threatened, waited for her to arrive. Before Aileanna could pull her out of harm's way, it permitted her to grab its fur and pull it to her. Instead of hissing or growling and raking her with its claws, it cooperated and curled around her.

She'd been told it was unusual for a talent to manifest in one so young, but all her life, the Aerie's animals had been her friends.

Brigh sighed, letting Lianna know she appreciated their closeness. Lianna patted her and straightened. "I should go clean up. I dinna want to miss supper."

Voices carried down the stable's central hallway. Lianna

recognized Jenny's laugh and Tadgh's deep rumble answering her, then silence returned.

Where were they? "Jenny?" Lianna called for her, recalling that Jenny had said Tadgh was the only one who talked to her. She hoped that was all they were doing.

She heard Jenny giggle, then footsteps approached, lighter and heavier. She gave Brigh a final pat and left the stall. Jenny and Tadgh walked down the stable's central aisle toward her.

"Lianna! Have ye seen the new foal? Of course ye must have. Ye are in the stable all the time. Tadgh just showed it to me."

"Aye, I saw it." One more horse to worry over. Would someone harm a foal so young? Jenny seemed excited and happy, so she didn't mention her concern. Instead, she turned to Tadgh. "Out of a mare I saw in one of the pastures?"

"'Tis the one. She dropped this foal a few days early, but 'tis healthy and strong. Since the nights are still a wee chill, I had them brought in. The laird wouldna be happy if we lost it."

"Has he seen it yet?"

"Nay. One of my men just brought it in today." Tadgh glanced around. "Ah, there he is. Nathair," he called out.

Lianna saw a shape in the shadowed distant end of the stable. But the man slipped out the back doorway and disappeared. "He must not have heard ye."

"Have ye met him?"

"I didna get a good look at him just now, but I dinna believe so."

"Ye will soon enough," Tadgh said and shrugged. The supper bell rang before he said anything else about the man. "'Tis time to head in. Are ye finished here?"

"I am." Lianna brushed her hands on her skirt. "I need to clean up first. We'd best hurry," she added to Jenny.

Tadgh gestured her and Jenny forward. They proceeded across the bailey and into the keep together.

Inside, Tadgh and Jenny exchanged a glance, then she

headed up the stairs with Lianna. He remained in the great hall.

"So," Lianna said as soon as they reached her chamber and closed the door, "he talks to ye, does he?"

Jenny just smiled.

12

The next morning, David sought out Lianna in the great hall, where she usually broke her fast. She had dressed to spend time with the horses, her hair braided down her back as he recalled her mother often did. "Good morrow," he said and sat across from her.

"The same to ye," she replied. "Is there something ye need?"

Yes, he needed her. The table separated them by only an arm's length, but it was too far. He wanted to sit beside her. To touch her. But he needed to see her face for what he intended to ask her. Her tone told him she had backed away from him again. This might not be the best time to make his appeal, but if he didn't speak now, there might never be another chance. She'd melted in his arms yesterday. "I have a request," he told her. "Ye are already doing so much for MacDhai, I hesitate to ask more of ye."

"I came here to help ye." She set aside the bowl of porridge she'd been eating from. "What is it?"

"From what I saw in the bailey the other day, 'tis clear ye have a way with bairns as well as with animals. I wonder if ye could find some time to spend with Mirielle."

Surprised, she cocked her head and frowned. "With yer daughter? Why?"

Because he wanted Lianna to grow to love her as her own. David sighed. "She spends most of her time with Clèmence. I think she'd enjoy being with ye." He could see his request confused her. "And all the cats and dogs ye collect," he added and grinned, hoping to disarm her. "She's a wee bit shy of people and animals. I think being with you might help her get beyond that."

"What about Jenny? Could she help?"

"Certainly." But Lianna was the woman he wanted his daughter to bond with, not her maid. "But she doesna have yer gift with animals and bairns."

Lianna nodded. "I had thought to help keep the lass safe, but wanted to talk to ye first. I didna ken whether ye would want her to get close to me, since eventually, I'll leave MacDhai."

He had already considered the effect on Mirielle. But Lianna would not leave, not if he had anything to say about it. "I still think ye can do the lass some good. I dinna mean for ye to replace Clémence. Only to visit in the nursery now and again, or sit with her in the bailey and let her enjoy the animals ye gather. The other bairns will be drawn to ye, too, so she'll make more friends. I think being with ye will show her she can master what she must when she's ready to leave the nursery."

"I would like to see where she spends most of her time," Lianna told him. "I ken ye have only a few men ye feel ye can trust, but ye can also trust mine. My men can help keep her safe."

He closed his eyes for a moment as relief filled him. She would bond with Mirielle. It would be one more tie to keep her with him.

He appreciated the efforts of her men, but he knew better. "They canna shirk their duty to ye."

"They willna. And David, I ken 'tis not yer favorite idea, but we can even take her with us if anything happens here and we must leave. For that reason, it would make sense for her to become comfortable with me and learn to trust me. But only if ye deem it the wisest course to protect her."

He didn't argue. He couldn't. What she offered made too much sense, as long as Lianna went with her. He studied her for a moment, smiled and nodded. "I'd be grateful for yer care of her."

"Will ye show me the nursery?"

He stood. "Come with me. She should be with her tutor now, but ye can meet him, too."

"What made ye decide to ask this?"

"I thought hard about our discussion yesterday," he told her as they climbed the stairs from the great hall. "I'm fighting shadows. Ye ken that. I appreciate everything ye are doing. Not just the horses, but in trying to ease all of my worries. The top of that list has to be Mirielle. I decided I canna refuse yer help."

He led her to the spiral steps up to the tower. "The nursery is up there."

"I approve," she told him and started up ahead of him. "Though Mirielle is getting old enough not to stay up here. Has she learned to evade her nurse and wander the keep on her own?"

"Not yet." David had to force himself to speak. He was so busy admiring Lianna's shape and the sway of her hips as she climbed each step above him that he could barely breathe. The confined space trapped her scent. It filled his nose, making him hard and hungry for her, and he pushed down the urge to pull her against him and kiss her senseless.

"If not by now, she soon will," she said as they reached the top.

David stayed in the shadows behind Lianna while he fought to get control of his body.

She opened the nursery door he indicated and looked around. The main room served as the play and school area, and a door beyond it led to another chamber containing Mirielle's single bed and chest. On the other side, another door, the one to Clémence's chamber, was closed.

Mirielle looked up as Lianna stepped in, then ducked her head and looked away. Lianna glanced around at him. He nodded approval. The lass was shy, and Lianna had interrupted a lesson. The tutor, the clan's priest, frowned at her. "May I help ye? Are ye lost?"

"Nay. I'm here with Laird MacDhai's permission to visit Mirielle. Dinna let me disturb ye, though. I'll just sit over here and listen." She gestured to a chair that put her out of Mirielle's line of sight.

David stayed out of sight until his body stopped reacting to Lianna's nearness and scent. She did not insert herself into the lesson, but was able to offer a word here and there when the lass didn't understand something in Scots, and the tutor couldn't explain it in French. Even though Mirielle's command of language was that of a small child, her French was still better than the tutor's, probably due to Clémence's influence. The more Lianna assisted, the more Mirielle turned to her when she had difficulty with a word.

David moved to the open doorway as Lianna charmed his daughter. The more help she requested, the more she seemed to warm toward Lianna, which pleased David very much. He didn't know Lianna spoke French, but he shouldn't be surprised. Despite living deep in the mountains of the Highlands, she was her father's daughter—and her mother's. No doubt it never occurred to them to stint her education. Given her father's obsession with making treaties instead of war, no doubt speaking fluent French as it was used in the Scottish court was an excellent skill to have.

Still, David didn't recall hearing her speak another

language while he'd been fostered with the clan. What else did he not know about her?

The tutor hadn't noticed him standing there, and Lianna wouldn't see him unless she turned her head. But Mirielle quickly noticed he was there and gave him a cheeky grin when she thought no one was looking.

By the time the lesson was over, he could see that Lianna had won at least some of the young lass's trust through speaking her first language.

"We have finished yer lesson for today," the tutor announced and stood. "Ye did very well. And bless ye, *mademoiselle*, for yer assistance," he added, turning to Lianna with a tilt of his head.

"I was happy to be of use," she told him and stood.

David stepped into the chamber, which apparently gave Mirielle permission to run to him, crying, "Papa!"

He bent down to wrap her in a hug. "Aye, lass."

"Did ye see?"

"I did. Ye are a very smart lass." He ruffled her curls, straightened, and nodded dismissal to the tutor.

After the man left, Lianna joined him and his daughter near the door. "I'm glad ye are ensuring Mirielle has a good education."

"Trying to, but I fear the tutor lacks some useful language skills."

"I've been teaching him," Mirielle announced. "He talks better than he used to."

David laughed and gave her another hug. "My wise daughter!"

Lianna smiled.

"Can I go riding now?" Mirielle asked.

Lianna's eyebrows arched as she lifted her gaze to his.

"What do ye think, Lianna? Shall she have a riding lesson today?"

"With ye, Papa!" Mirielle insisted.

"Of course, wee one. With me and Lianna, won't we?" His expression pleaded with her to join them.

"That sounds like the perfect way to spend the afternoon," Lianna said to the lass. "But ye must change into something better suited to riding."

"Nurse will help," Mirielle confided with a confident nod. "I ken where she went."

"Very well, my wee lass," David told her and turned her toward the closed door to the inner bed chamber. "Find yer nurse and change yer dress. We'll wait for ye at the stable."

Mirielle ran to the closed door and knocked softly.

David smiled, his heart going with her. She was nothing like her mother, and yet exactly like her, too. He was happy to see her own personality shining through, and wondered what effect Lianna would have if she married him and stayed.

The thought froze his breath. He dared not look aside at her. He feared his thoughts, his hopes, would be all too plainly written on his face for her to see.

"I'd best go get my boots," Lianna said, apparently unaware of his discomfort. She lifted her skirt enough to extend her slippered foot beyond its hem. "I'll meet ye at the stables, aye?"

David cleared his throat. "Aye, we'll see ye down there." He debated waiting for Mirielle in the nursery, but decided his time would be better spent saddling Athdar and alerting the stable hand to bring out her pony. He'd have them wait until she arrived to saddle it. She enjoyed being part of that process, even though she only watched.

He made his way out of the keep to the stable. Athdar greeted him with a low snort, then nickered when David entered his stall and began to ready him for their ride.

Mirielle was ready to go much faster than David expected. He heard her laughter as she crossed the bailey with Clémence and left Athdar to meet her in the doorway. He loved the happy anticipation on her face as he took her hand and walked as fast as her short legs would carry her along the stable's center aisle.

David asked the groom to saddle Mirielle's pony, one of the fortunate ones, so far, that had not succumbed to whatever was making the other horses ill.

David quickly finished with Athdar while the groom, under Mirielle's supervision, was busy with her mount.

As the groom led out the pony, Lianna arrived. She stole David's breath yet again, though she wore an older, rougher fabric cape and boots. She knelt to greet his daughter and David's mind filled with thoughts of her as his bride and Mirielle's mother. And mother to their future bairns, as well.

"I see ye are ready," she told Mirielle. "Can ye wait while I saddle Brigh? And bring Conall?"

Mirielle nodded, then added, "*Oui!*"

"We are going to walk out here in the bailey for a few minutes, so ye have time," David told her. "Athdar is ready. We'll go when ye and Brigh are."

"How is he today?"

"Well, I think."

"While ye two walk the pony, I'll go see."

"Thank ye."

"*Merci,*" Mirielle piped up, apparently wanting to be part of the adults' conversation.

Lianna gave her a smile and a quick curtsy.

While her back was turned, Bhaltair approached and passed by, leading his mount. When Lianna realized who moved behind her, she turned toward him. He said, "If ye are leaving the keep, I'm going with ye."

Lianna didn't argue. Instead, she nodded and entered the stable.

Bhaltair waited outside, his gaze surveying everything around them.

David turned his attention to his daughter, determined not

to let the purpose of Bhaltair's presence affect him and spoil Mirielle's fun. "*Prête, ma fille?*"

"*Oui*, Papa. I am ready." She stood with tiny fists on her slim hips, and nodded.

David grinned at her serious enthusiasm and gestured for her to proceed. He lifted her onto the pony's back and handed her the reins. She flicked them like an expert. The pony responded, moving forward slowly. David always did this with her, walking the pony in the bailey, a safe and confined space, to let his daughter get used to her seat, and to remind her she must control her mount. If the pony bolted, it could not go far, and there were plenty of people about to catch it. He walked alongside, enjoying Mirielle's joy at being on horseback—and with him.

He often regretted the laird's responsibilities kept him away from her. In France, he'd spent as much time with his infant daughter as he wished, though Mirielle was too young to count their minutes together. Since returning to Scotland, she'd grown into a self-aware young lass—nearly four years old— who relished time with him. He spent as much of it with her as he could, and hoped she never had cause to resent the time his position took from her.

Her tutor and her nurse filled in the gaps, but they were not the same as a mother.

Lianna led Athdar and Brigh from the stable, Conall pacing just ahead of her. She smiled at David and stopped, letting him lead the pony and Mirielle to her. He approved of her wisdom. Some might assume horses stabled together would get along, but that was not always the case. Athdar was much larger than this pony, as was Brigh, though she was not as big as Athdar. A smaller steed could be intimidated and frightened into bolting, but Lianna had understood and waited, keeping his daughter safe.

"I believe we are ready to go for a ride," he said to Lianna, then turned to Mirielle. "What do ye think, daughter?"

"I am ready!"

She announced her opinion with great fervor, amusing David. The twinkle in Lianna's eye told him she'd been struck the same way, but followed his lead in dealing with his precocious bairn and held back a laugh.

"Very well." He handed Mirielle her short reins, unwound the long lead from its place on her saddle and mounted Athdar. Lianna mounted Brigh at the same time, settled herself, and nodded approval at the lead in his hand that connected him to Mirielle's pony. It would not get away from them. The larger horses could outrun it, but there was more room to run and rougher ground in the glen. He wouldn't take the chance of his tiny daughter being thrown and injured. Or killed. She would learn to ride under his close supervision.

"Where shall we go today?" Lianna's voice startled him from his thoughts.

"Mirielle?" He always let her choose.

"The glen, Papa." She pointed at Conall. "Whose hound is he?"

"Mine, lass," Lianna told her. "Do ye mind if he comes with us?"

"No. I like dogs."

"I do, too," Lianna told her with a smile.

Mirielle always chose the same place to ride. She loved the nearest part of the glen, especially when the wildflowers were in bloom. And riding its length and back were enough to tire her. When she was older, they'd go farther.

When she was older, he would have to trust in the skills he taught her now. The thought made his belly clench. He could not risk losing her, but he could not deny her such an important skill. His daughter would not be confined to wagons and carts for the rest of her life. She would ride, proudly and expertly, much as did Lianna, who'd been taught to ride before he arrived at the Aerie. Being on a horse looked as natural on her as breathing. He wanted the same for his daughter.

If only Lianna could remain, and teach her.

❧

IT WAS A WARM, sunny morning, perfect for an outing. They rode far enough for Lianna to notice several sycamore trees and point them out to David. None had the skirt of fallen seedlings she'd noticed around the squirrel's tree in the high pasture's woods, where Conall had been hurt. Something had eaten these. Or someone had picked them up.

At the far end of the closest pasture, Conall, who ranged out ahead of them, suddenly stopped, growled and barked. Lianna reined Brigh to a stop. "Bhaltair. David," she called, keeping her voice low and calm. She didn't want to upset Mirielle, who was chattering happily as they rode along. In the fashion of most wee lasses, she had something to say about every different flower she saw, and spoke greetings to passing butterflies and bees.

Bhaltair had been watching their sides and back trail, leaving the front to her and David. Lianna knew him well enough to recognize chagrin in his expression that he hadn't seen trouble ahead of them first. David, whose gaze had been on his daughter, must have heard something in Lianna's voice. He pulled Athdar to a halt, using the long lead to stop Mirielle's pony as well. "Lianna?" He glanced at her, but didn't look up.

She didn't say anything. She nodded toward the low ridge ahead of them. It separated this part of the MacDhai's long glen from the next pasture. She knew the moment he spotted the half a dozen riders on mountain horses watching from their higher vantage point. His shoulders tensed, and he gave her a quick glance before turning to his daughter. "'Tis time to return, Mirielle. Papa doesna wish to speak to those men."

Mirielle surprised Lianna by taking in the solemn expression on her father's face. Instead of arguing or crying as most bairns might do, she nodded and turned her pony back the way they'd come. David handed the lead to Lianna. "Ride. Get her back inside the keep and alert the guard. If need be, I'll delay those men. Bhaltair, go with them."

Lianna didn't argue, either. She called for Conall, then urged Brigh into a trot the pony and her hound could keep up with. If she must, she'd pull Mirielle onto Brigh with her and ride like the wind, but she respected David's impulse not to frighten the child. The men hadn't done anything yet but watch them. Still, she kept watch behind her.

Bhaltair positioned himself between her and the men on the ridge.

David stood sentry, unmoving, his horse, his body, a silent deterrent meant to stop the men from coming any closer. He waited, risking his life, until she and Mirielle were mere yards from the keep's gate before he turned Athdar and raced to join them, riding in the gate immediately behind them.

"Murdoch! Get some men out there and find out who they are. Then close the gates." His shout carried to the guards on the walls. Men scrambled to obey.

Lianna dismounted, touched Conall and told him to return to Brigh's stall, then took charge of Mirielle. She helped her off the pony, then helped her lead it to the side, out of the way of the men and horses charging out of the stable. Mirielle watched wide-eyed, but calm. Once the men rode out of the bailey, Lianna led Mirielle inside the stable and had her give the pony to the stable lads. "Brigh, too, please, while I take this lass inside the keep."

Bhaltair, she noted, had already turned his mount over to

them and left the stable. She saw him mounting the guard tower steps. He'd keep watch with David.

"Come with me," she invited Mirielle. "I'm sure Cook has some lovely treat ready. Ye were so good for yer da," Lianna told her brightly. Mirielle rewarded her with the first tenuous smile the child had ventured since they quit the glen. She'd apparently picked up on the tension, if not before, then certainly after they reached the keep, and she heard her father ordering his men to action.

David would be focused on the possible danger to MacD-hai. Lianna could ensure he would not have to worry about his daughter while his men took care of the threat. Once inside the great hall, she sent one serving girl after cider and sweet cakes for Mirielle, and another after Clémence. Mirielle would be safest in the nursery with her. And then Lianna could assist her father.

She'd seen David's fury as he rode into the gate. In assuming their outing was safe, in riding out into the glen without a larger escort, he'd put Mirielle at risk. Her, too, though she knew she had not been his main concern at that moment. He feared only for his daughter. Before she let the hurt go too deep, she realized he believed she could defend herself, where the lass clearly could not. As he should, he'd put his daughter first.

No doubt, as he'd put himself between them and danger, David had aimed his fury at himself as well as at the interlopers. But now that she and the lass were safe and warm, sipping cider and eating honey cakes, she had leisure to be angry with David for making himself a target.

One well-placed arrow and Mirielle would have seen her father die. The lass would have been an orphan. Because he'd made Lianna responsible for seeing her safe inside the keep, there would have been no time, and no safe way with Mirielle still at risk and strangers on the ridge, for Lianna to return to him and heal his wound. Bhaltair, his duty to her father clear, would have stayed with her, not hurried Mirielle inside the walls. The thought made her shiver.

"Are ye cold?"

Mirielle's tiny, piping voice brought Lianna back from her vision of disaster to the warmth of the great hall. "Aye, lass, perhaps a wee." She caught a hint of movement from the corner of her eye. "Ah, here comes Clémence. Have ye finished yer treat?"

"Aye. Now I am sleepy."

"Very well. I shall see you to your bed," Clémence told her as she walked up close enough to hear Mirielle's reply. She put a hand on Mirielle's shoulder, but her gaze was on Lianna. "Thank you for caring for her. I was told..."

"It was my pleasure," Lianna responded brightly. She saw the concern in Clémence's eyes, and wanted to lighten the mood for Mirielle. "Mirielle rode very well today, and obeyed her da without question. She deserved a treat."

"I see." Clémence forced a smile as she helped Mirielle stand and took her hand. "Ye may sleep for a while, then we will read together, *oui*?"

Mirielle nodded and yawned.

Clémence led her away.

Lianna headed back out into the bailey. David was visible on the wall walk overlooking the area where they'd seen the strangers. He stood between two guards and Bhaltair, each of them tense and focused on whatever they could see in the glen. Suddenly, he turned toward the gate and shouted, "Open it!"

Lianna stayed by the keep's door. Riders would burst through the gate as soon as it opened. She didn't want to be caught in their way crossing the bailey.

David ran down the stairs as soon as the horses stilled. "Murdoch!"

The arms master suddenly slumped over his horse's neck.

Only then did Lianna notice the blood dripping from his shoulder to the ground. She ran to him. "Help me get him down!" David was at her side as quickly as the other men, dismounting, reached her. Together, they got Murdoch off of his horse. Three men carried him into the great hall and laid him on one of the tables there.

"Lianna?"

David's tone was full of questions she feared to answer. Could she help Murdoch? She didn't know. Should she try in front of so many MacDhais? That question was easier to answer.

Nay.

But she had to save the man. He'd already lost a lot of blood. She didn't want to move him again. Not yet. Another delay might mean his life, and he was one of the few men David trusted.

She gestured for David to cut the man's shirt away from the wound, a narrow blade thrust. Probably from a dirk. A sword would have taken off his arm. She was also grateful it wasn't an arrow wound. They often did more damage on removal than when they first entered.

As soon as the wound was clear, she could see blood welling from it. She had to move fast if she was going to save him.

She glanced at David. The apology in his eyes chilled her, but she forced herself to ignore him, and put her hand over the wound. Immediately, searing pain flashed through her shoulder and her knees buckled. Someone shoved a bench behind her. She sank onto it, but left her hand in place to staunch Murdoch's bleeding. Or appear to. She put her other hand on his arm below the wound and *reached* in with her talent. The largest severed blood vessel was easy to find. As quickly as she mended it, the worst of the bleeding stopped. Then she delved deeper, knitted muscle and tendon together as they once were, from the deepest point of the wound upward, grateful she no longer had to press on the wound because she didn't think she could stand the pain in her own shoulder if she did. By the time she was nearly done, she was shivering from pain and cold, and didn't know if those sensations were hers or Murdoch's.

"What do ye think ye are doing to him?"

The old healer's screech startled Lianna out of contact with Murdoch's wound. She pulled her bloody hands into her lap, sagged, and felt David at her back, keeping her upright on the bench.

"She was helping the arms master," David answered quietly.

"Let me see." The old healer shoved Lianna aside.

David gripped her arms to keep her from falling flat across the bench. And, judging by the black look he gave the old woman, to keep from hauling her off her feet and away from the table, Murdoch and Lianna.

Lianna shook herself, surprised at the old healer's strength. As the woman poked and prodded Murdoch's shoulder, Lianna took a breath and felt David's hand squeeze her other shoulder. At least he was aware enough of how her talent worked not to touch the one still torturing her with Murdoch's pain.

"Merely a scratch," the old woman muttered. "But I'll have to bleed him to make sure the wound is clean."

"Bleed him!" Lianna's exclamation surprised even her.

"Dinna do it," David warned. "Do ye see the blood on the hall's floor? If ye like, follow it out into the bailey, through the gate and into the glen. The man's been bled enough."

The old healer looked around, her gaze following the blood trail to the keep's door. "He bled so much from that wound?" Plainly, she thought David was exaggerating.

"Lianna has done what was needful. Leave him be."

"How dare ye refuse yer healer's wisdom over that of a...a

stable hand," the woman persisted, contempt in every wrinkle on her sneering face.

"Wheesht!" David's tone brooked no argument. "Ye willna touch him any further."

Clearly furious at being rebuked, the old healer's eyes blazed. She glared at Lianna, then turned her scowl to David. "Beware, MacDhai," she said, spat and stomped out.

Only then did Lianna lift her gaze beyond Murdoch and the old healer to the people gathered around them. A few serving lasses peered between the men who had ridden in with Murdoch and helped carry him here. In addition, a few older men had pushed their way to the front at the foot of the table. For the most part, they watched the old healer go, but a few gazed at Lianna with uncertainty in their eyes. Could they tell what she had done? Did the men who rode with Murdoch realize how deep his wound had been? The old healer's comments made questions inevitable.

David's solid presence behind her reassured Lianna. His people weren't afraid of her—yet—and his presence made clear his support for her. Bhaltair's presence did, too. He stood off to the side, his gaze on the crowd, watching, assessing, and ready for trouble.

"Move Murdoch to his bed," David ordered calmly, as if the old healer hadn't just threatened him. "And clean up that blood." Then he stepped around to where she could look at him without straining her neck. "What else does he need, lass?"

"A clean covering for the wound. I have a poultice to put on it first. Then he'll need food and rest for a few days."

"Where is it?"

"In my chamber." She put her hands on the bench and pushed to her feet. "I'll get it."

David took her elbow and slid the bench out of her way. "Nay, I'll take ye there. Ye protected Mirielle and helped Murdoch. Ye should rest, too."

"Murdoch..."

"I can slather on the poultice and cover the wound," David told her. "Or Jenny can. Let's get ye upstairs."

"Jenny kens what to do, aye." She reached out to Murdoch, and with a light touch, laid a healing sleep on him, then let David lead her away. Bhaltair followed, blocking anyone from coming up the stairs too closely behind them. Once they were in her chamber and private, she asked, "What will ye face when ye return to the hall without me? There were many eyes watching what I did. They all heard what the old healer said to ye, and they saw the blood." She held up her hands, still coated with red. "She was right. No scratch would leave such a trail."

"*Dinna fash*. We'll go on as always. Those who watched will be glad Murdoch is alive and well. How ye saved him is not their concern. Nor is what that old hag said. She shouldha kept quiet when I told her to. My men will watch her, and she kens it."

"She—and others—could still be trouble."

Jenny entered in time to hear Lianna's concern. She filled a basin with water from a pitcher and wetted a rag. "Bhaltair told me what happened," she said as she handed it to Lianna to use to wash her hands. "I'll take care of Murdoch. I can bring ye something to eat and drink when I'm done with him. He'll remain asleep, aye?"

"Aye," Lianna answered, suddenly weary. "As will I. Where is Bhaltair? Ye shouldna go alone."

"Just outside the door." Jenny accepted the pot and clean cloth Lianna took from her supplies. "Fill the wound, I ken it," she said before Lianna could instruct her. "Then cover it."

"And behave as if Lianna did everything the old healer wouldha done. And naught more," David added.

Jenny left them, and David turned to Lianna. "She'll be back in a few minutes. I must go find out who those men on the ridge were and how the fight started. Will ye be all right if I leave ye alone?"

"Of course." Lianna sank onto the chair by the hearth, grateful for its warmth. As much as she craved being wrapped in his arms, this was not the time to hope for affection from David. He had to go be the laird.

But he'd stood at her back while she treated Murdoch. Lianna could imagine how he looked to the people gathered around them, and for that she was grateful.

13

I n his solar, David met the men who rode out with Murdoch to receive their report. "The interlopers were MacPhersons," one told him. A clan David's had fought for generations.

"What were they doing on MacDhai land, and so close to the keep, before ye chased them off?"

"Trying to steal horses, they claimed."

"Are any of ours missing from the glen?"

"We didna have time to count, laird."

The comment had just an edge of sarcasm. David chose to ignore it. "Nay, of course not. Ye did the right thing, bringing Murdoch back as quickly as ye did."

"We exchanged words. And, as ye saw, blows, but Murdoch was the only one injured before the MacPhersons ran. The cowards."

"That's good." David sat back, musing. Why would the MacPhersons send men to steal horses if they had someone already in place in his keep, poisoning them? The only thing that made sense to him was that they had nothing to do with MacDhai's current troubles.

"One more thing." The man stopped, glanced at the others,

then continued. "Ye may not have noticed in the confusion of bringing Murdoch in, but we captured one of them."

"What?" David stood. "Why did ye not tell me as soon as ye arrived?"

"We bound and gagged him. Edgar, there, tied his mount to his own, so he couldna go anywhere but come with us. We put him in a stall."

"A stall. So he's still alive?"

"Aye, last time one of us looked in on him."

"Come with me." David marched to the stable. Edgar pointed to a stall, where David found the hapless captive sitting on a pile of straw, still bound hand and foot, and tied to a cross-brace in the wall. He pulled down the man's gag. "Yer name?"

The man eyed him as if weighing his response. Truthful or snide? He must have decided on the truth. "I'm a MacPherson. 'Tis all ye care about. What are ye going to do with me?"

David ignored the question. "Ye and yer men came to steal MacDhai horses?"

"Aye. Yers are the best."

"What else were ye after?"

"Naught. Just horses."

MacDhai horses were prized, but there had to be more to bring the MacPhersons so near. "Were ye meeting anyone?"

The man recoiled. "Meeting anyone? Nay. Why would ye think that?"

"Then why come so close to the keep? In another month or two, the horses would be in the high summer pasture."

"But they're not now, are they? And we wanted them now."

"Why?"

"I—I canna say," the man stuttered.

"Ye canna? Or ye willna?"

"I dinna ken."

Of course not. "How many did ye think to steal?"

"As many as we could get away with." David was disgusted,

but ready to let him go when he added, "We ken some are sick. They'd be in the stable, aye? We wanted healthy ones from pasture."

David's blood turned to ice in his veins. MacPhersons knew MacDhai horses were ill? "Who told ye we had sick horses here?"

"I dinna ken."

But someone did know. And a MacDhai had to have told them. "Yer other men ran and left ye behind. Ye dinna owe them yer life. Tell me what ye ken."

The man paled. "Ye canna kill me. I didna harm any of yers."

"Nay? What about my man who came in bleeding."

"'Twas an accident."

"Really?"

"I dinna ken for certain. I was busy with another of yer men." He glared at Edgar. Edgar crossed his arms and widened his stance, smirking.

"Ye'll be busy with me if ye dinna tell me whom ye were here to meet."

"I dinna ken anything about that. We were after horses. Healthy ones."

That had the ring of truth. Whoever led this hapless band might have known whom to expect to meet them, but this man did not. It explained why they didn't immediately attack when he appeared with Lianna, Mirielle, and Bhaltair. Why they didn't attack him while he waited alone for the other three to return to the keep. They expected to meet someone from MacDhai. Seeing them with a bairn surely confused them. Only after Murdoch's men galloped out of the gate would they have been sure the meeting was off.

David turned back to his men, swearing under his breath. "He canna help us. Let him go." Before they untied him, he turned back to their prisoner. "But first, remember this. Tell yer chief if he wants horses, he can pay for them like everyone else. In coin. Else I'll see he pays in blood. Tell him ye have given him my last warning." With that, he stalked out of the stable.

David was still fuming the next morning. He might be willing to accept that the MacPhersons wanted assurances that any horse they took was healthy. In that case, who could tell them? Someone who worked in the stables? Tadgh? Nay, not possible. None of the stable lads, either. The more he thought about it, the more he was certain anyone could have told them. The horses' illnesses were common knowledge in the keep and in the village. Someone benefitted from helping them, but how?

If the MacPhersons weren't the ones using the horses to get to him, or get rid of him, who did that leave? Mirielle's grandfather looked more and more likely. But he needed proof.

When Lianna entered his solar, he had to remind himself that she was here to help because he'd asked her to come, stop his thoughts spiraling into a whirlpool of despair, and give her his full attention. Lianna looked tired, but better than she had the afternoon before.

"Murdoch is doing well," she said by way of greeting. "Jenny did her part with the poultice. There is no sign of fever. I expect him to be up and about later today, but only to eat and walk a wee," she insisted. "He must rest until tomorrow. Oh, and the horses are fine. I was just out there. I didna find any new illness among them."

Relief filled David, but disquiet, too. "Is that good news or bad?"

"What do ye mean?" She sank into a chair on the opposite side of his desk.

"That there are no new illnesses. Has our enemy stopped? Did the commotion yesterday keep him from giving any poison to any more of the horses, at least for a day? Or has he given up using them to discredit me, and his tactics will soon change?"

"I wish I could tell ye, but nay, I canna."

He rested his elbows on the tabletop. "The horses are important, but Murdoch is even more so. As chief, I have too few allies to lose one. Thank ye for saving him. I ken ye would have preferred to do so in private—"

She crossed her arms. "Has anyone said anything to ye today? About that?"

"Nay, but I've been in here since I rose." David sighed. One more problem to deal with, and one that put Lianna in danger if any in the clan recognized and feared what she'd done. Even now, he expected rumors to be running rampant and becoming more exaggerated with each retelling. "Keep at least one of yer men with ye at all times, Lianna, until we see how the clan reacts." He ran a hand through his hair. "I'm sorry, I should have thought of that last night."

"Ye had other things demanding yer attention. Trust me, Bhaltair already took care of me. One of my men is nearby at all times." She took a breath, uncrossed her arms, and leaned back. "Tadgh told me ye asked him to count the horses."

David understood her desire to change the subject. "I did, aye. Our MacPherson guest didna say whether he and his friends had already taken MacDhai horses, only that they intended to." He ran a hand through his hair. "I hope we saw them before they got the chance."

"How long will the count take?"

"It depends on how far the pastured horses have scattered. Later today, I expect." He paused. "I also didna thank ye for getting Mirielle to safety. She likes ye, ye ken."

"I like her, too."

David smiled, grateful for one bright moment in a day that promised to be anything but. "I'm glad."

"Ye said ye have been in here since ye rose. Have ye broken yer fast?"

"Aye, I have. Let me send for Bhaltair to escort ye, then ye go take care of yerself."

"I left him in the great hall. He's not far away. I will be well, *dinna fash*."

"Any threat, Lianna, *anything,* and ye will tell me."

She nodded and left him to his thoughts.

By afternoon, he wished Murdoch could stand with him at his meeting with the council, but Lianna refused to allow it. David would have to manage the clan's council without him.

"MacPherson will go to war over taking their man," Alastair complained after David related all he knew about yesterday's events.

"And we could go to war for their attempt to steal our horses," David replied. "Tadgh reports we didna lose any. We kept the raiders from getting what they came for."

"And they nearly killed Murdoch," Rab complained.

"But he isna dead. He'll be up and about on the morrow."

"The other Chattan clans wouldna stand for another internal clan battle. If ye appealed to the Chattan chief, he'll weigh in with MacPherson to put a stop to any more of this," Rab argued.

The solar filled with grumbles. David let them mutter. The usual few members of the council were being deliberately unhelpful. Their intransigence irritated David, but in this case, he had to sympathize with their anger. A raid so close to the keep offended them and insulted their clan pride. His, as well. If the MacPhersons were getting bolder, he had to wonder why? What made them certain they could approach MacDhai without fear of reprisal? And why risk it? It made more sense for them to wait until the horses were farther from the keep. So why now? Could they be behind poisoning MacDhai horses?

"Send a missive to the Chattan chief complaining about MacPherson incursions," Rab finally continued.

"What do ye recommend I say? Shut them down, or I will?

Ye do ken our horses have been ill. Many still are. And MacPherson wants to steal the healthy ones. We are nay ready to go to war with them."

"Maybe that's why they're being sickened. To make sure we canna fight them off."

A chill ran down David's back at that comment. Griffin was usually one of the more level-headed of his advisors. If he saw that kind of danger from MacPherson, they needed Lianna to work even faster than she had up to now.

Alasdair threw out another disturbing idea. "What if they were a scouting party, not reivers, sent to check on the health and number of MacDhai horses? That would explain their presence, and might tie them to the poisonings."

"Especially if they were meeting someone in the clan who is helping them," old James added.

"What about using the threat of the French? Or the clan ye fostered with? Can we get any help there?"

"We already are," David was happy to remind them. "'Tis the only reason the horses that have sickened are not dead. Or Murdoch, either. As for the French ally, my late wife's father, help from him would be a long time arriving, but," he said, holding up a hand as the room erupted in conversation, "but," he reiterated, louder this time to quiet them, "I can inform him of our issues and ask him to send men." Privately, he'd be happier without the pull and tug from her grandparents about Mirielle. But he also knew if he called for help, he could be certain they would do whatever he needed to protect her. Only once they solved the problem, his risk of losing her would increase. The Comte might insist on carrying his grand-daughter back to France, and claim they could offer her a safer home to grow up in.

Talk turned to the ill horses. "We have no firm answers, and no evidence of who is doing this, but Lianna has treated them.

They are getting better. She will continue to do so as long as needed."

Several of the council spoke up, demanding answers. David nodded. "I want it solved, too. Keep aware. Ye may see or hear something that will point to the culprit."

❧

LIANNA HEARD A RAISED voice as she passed through the great hall near the solar with her Lathan guards. The voice was not David's, but someone she didn't recognize. She paused near the doorway. David might be alone with men bent on doing him harm. Not that it was any of her business, she chided herself. And David was well able to take care of himself.

She contented herself with a glance into the solar as she passed by. David was there, with Kerr and several other men she didn't recognize. They remained in their seats, so perhaps the situation was not as fraught as it first sounded.

None of her business, then. Lianna left the keep and headed for the stable. It was time to check on the horses again. She'd done so every day that she'd been here, and all were improving with plenty of water, dandelion tea, and careful attention to what they ate. She had everyone she could recruit scouring the glen for more fresh dandelions while she continued to put her store of dried herbs sparingly to use.

She waved to the MacDhai guard as she approached. He nodded and let her enter. David had recently doubled the guard on the horses. There would be a man at the back entrance as well.

The improvement in the MacDhai stable should have pleased her, but, like David, it made her uneasy. Why were the horses being allowed to recover? Were the extra guards keeping trouble away? Or was the person behind this still trying to harm them? If so, perhaps her therapy worked faster than the poison. She should be glad of that. But she didn't know! And until a horse began to get ill, her talent didn't tell her which were targets. So she checked on each of them every day, a process that took little time, as long as she didn't have to treat an ill horse, longer if she had to find horses that had wandered far down the glen. She returned from each ride tired, hungry, and no closer to an answer than the day she arrived here.

Still, she enjoyed the time out of the keep. She didn't know if the same was true for her Lathan guards, who kept watch for more interlopers, MacPhersons or otherwise. Brigh and the pup Conall enjoyed the outings, too. He had become accustomed to sleeping in Brigh's stall and being fed by the stable lads, who'd been warned on pain of death not to tease him in any way. She was glad to see him losing his fear.

Once she finished checking out the horses in the stable, she and several men mounted up to check on horses in the pasture. That served both to make sure they were not sick, and to make sure none had been stolen since the MacPherson incursion. Tadgh expected frequent counts. After another foray around the glen, she had nothing to report, except that she had spotted another of the squirrel's trees in the middle pasture without a seedling skirt below it. She couldn't correlate horses let out into pasture with ones that got sick, but she didn't think the horses had cleared the seedlings while they cropped grass below the trees. The wind would scatter them, but in that case, she would expect to find some. Nay, something else was going on. Perhaps they were the preferred food of the glen's squirrels or other animals.

Seeing the tree reminded her she'd given a handful of those seedlings to Bhaltair to hold for her. She must ask him for them. But then what? Feed a few to a healthy horse and use her talent to find out if they made it sick? She hated to do that, but it might be the fastest way to identify the poison. Those trees were telling her something. She just had to figure it out.

David arrived before she finished brushing down Brigh. Her guards had finished with their mounts and had headed for the great hall, except Eduard, whose turn it was to remain nearby. When he saw David arrive, he left the stable. Lianna didn't know whether he'd gone to join the other Lathans or merely stepped outside to give her and David some privacy.

"Have ye found anything?"

"Good day to ye, too," Lianna answered. Judging by his scowl, apparently the rest of David's meeting had gone no better than when she passed by and heard the shouting.

He ignored her sarcasm. "Will we ever be able to solve this mystery? Nothing good is happening fast enough, and problems are mounting up even higher than before I went to the Aerie."

"I'm doing everything I can think of," she replied over Brigh's back. She stopped brushing and regarded him. He was still fuming over the contentious-sounding meeting. But that didn't give him the right to take his frustration out on her.

He was tired. So was she. Tired and frustrated at the lack of answers.

He took a deep breath. "I ken it," he said. "The horses are better under yer care. But what happens when ye leave?"

When she left? Was that bothering him? Lianna's heart skipped a beat. Could that mean he wanted her to stay, and would be hurt by her absence? Or just that he feared without her to keep the horses healthy, MacDhai would be vulnerable to the same insidious attack that had driven him to the Aerie in the first place?

Of course. It was all about the horses. She was here to care for them, not for David. After he kissed her, she'd let herself begin to dream she might have a future with him. With Mirielle, too. But she had to remember, as David had, that she would be leaving at some point. And she had vowed not to let him break her heart again. She should take this opportunity to put some distance between them.

"I ken 'tis frustrating. Ye want so much, and all ye can see is what ye dinna have."

He turned away. "That is truer than ye ken. I felt at home only when I was away from here," he said, and started pacing along the front of the stall. "First at Lathan. Then, when I settled in France as the MacDhai factor, finding and shipping horses. Ye ken that. I truly didna expect to be named Da's successor." He stroked Brigh, then clenched his fist and regarded Lianna over Brigh's back. "I lost so much in the last few years. And what I've gained here, I didna want."

Lianna frowned. Did that include her? "Ye accepted the position, David. Ye are laird. All this," she said and waved an arm wide, "is yer responsibility. Ye need to come to terms with that. Ye will lose the clan if ye dinna make more effort to win over yer people. And to find out who's conspiring against ye."

"What do ye think I've been trying to do?" He turned away from her, his back and shoulders rigid. "I'm fighting shadows, with only a few I can trust—and even some of those may be suspect."

"Kerr? Murdoch? Nay, ye dinna think..."

"Kerr? Nay. The others? I dinna ken what to think, not anymore."

"Then build from them. Find a few more, and more after that. Ye canna keep on pretending the people in this clan dinna exist. They do, and they need ye as much—more—than these horses do."

"Easy to say."

"When is the last time ye spoke to anyone but Kerr or Murdoch, except to give an order to a serving lass or a guard? Do ye ever tell Cook ye appreciate what she does for the clan? Or the blacksmith or the weaver? Do ye say 'good day' to anyone? *Anyone*? Ye werena shy as a lad. Why act that way now?

Ye are the laird. Ye set the tone for the keep. The entire clan. Did ye learn naught from my da?"

Color crawled up David's throat to his face. Was he angry at her set-down, or chagrinned that she described his last year as a failure of leadership?

He nodded. "Ye are right. I did learn better from yer da. I've been so resentful of what life has handed me—most of it—the past few years, I havena been using what he taught me." He nodded. "'Tis time to get over the past and do my job." He leaned over Brigh's back and took her hand. "Thank ye," he added and left.

Lianna stared after him, surprised that he took her censure so well. But if she'd shocked him out of the doldrums he'd inhabited, apparently since returning from France, she may have helped him even more than she thought she was by saving his horses. Unless she was part of the past he intended to get over. Her heart sank. What had she done?

Bhaltair came in soon after, a pouch in his hand. The seeds!

"Ye forgot these," he told her as he handed the pouch to her.

She nodded. "Perhaps on purpose. The only way I can think of to test them is to feed some of them to Brigh. I dinna want to harm her, but I ken Brigh better than any animal here."

"Ye do, lass, and ye willna let her come to harm."

She appreciated Bhaltair's attempt to comfort her and straightened her spine. They had to know if they'd found the poison. "I'll ken the instant a toxin begins to take effect, and treat her for it." Did she hold the source in her hand? It would explain why the nearer trees lacked their skirt of seeds— because someone had harvested the nearer parts of the glen and left the higher-pasture, later-forming seeds for last.

"If I'm going to do this, I may as well start now."

"I'll help ye," Bhaltair said, concern drawing down his brow, his blue eyes communicating concern. For Brigh? Or for her?

With heavy heart, Lianna turned to Brigh. "I'm sorry, lass,

but I canna trust this to any other horse," she told her as she counted out six seeds and laid them in her palm, then held them up to Brigh's muzzle. Brigh sniffed, then blew out a chuff, scattering the seeds. "So ye dinna like them?"

"That did seem deliberate," Bhaltair remarked.

"I'll try again," Lianna said and counted out more seeds, then pushed her palm up against Brigh's mouth, and used her other hand to open it. The seeds went in. Brigh swallowed. Lianna did, too. Tears pricked at her eyes.

"How long will it take?" Bhaltair moved around her to put a comforting hand on Brigh's neck.

"I dinna ken. But I willna give her any more until I've watched her for a while." She let go of Brigh long enough to pat Bhaltair's massive shoulder. "Ye needna stay with me. 'Tis better if I am alone. I can concentrate on her more closely."

Bhaltair nodded, but his pursed lips told her his agreement was reluctantly given. "I'll be right outside if ye need me."

"Thank ye." She turned back to Brigh and laid hands on her, waiting. After an hour, she fed her more seeds, then waited only half an hour to give her more. By now, the first few should have been digested and if they were toxic, she should see the effects soon.

Bhaltair brought bread, cheese, apples, and cider in the middle of the next hour. "The apples are for Brigh," he said. "She might appreciate a treat."

Lianna thanked him. He was right. She used her small knife to cut one of the apples into chunks, then mixed some seeds in with them and fed Brigh those. This time, she ate more eagerly. Was that how the other horses were enticed to eat something harmful to them? Lianna sat nearby to eat and drink what Bhaltair brought her, knowing if Brigh started to sicken, she'd need her strength to care for her.

The next time Lianna reached for Brigh, she felt it. Her heart beat faster and something was wrong in her blood. She wasn't sweating yet, nor had the muscle tremors started, but Lianna recognized the symptoms. She'd found the poison.

If only she hadn't fed Brigh any seeds with the apple. She was going to be sicker than need be, and for longer. Lianna stepped away from Brigh and leaned over the stall door. "Bhaltair!"

He came at a run. "What's wrong?"

"The seeds are the poison. I can feel them working in Brigh. I need buckets of water for her. And the dandelion tea Cook keeps brewed. As strong as she's got. Dinna dilute it. She should have some fresh dandelion greens in the kitchen, too. I want them as well."

"I'll get help to carry it all, and be back as fast as I can."

Hours later, Lianna leaned her forehead against Brigh's neck and breathed a sigh of relief. With the help of Bhaltair, Tadgh and another stable lad whose name she hadn't gotten, Brigh had stayed on her feet, and the poison was out of her system.

"I'm so sorry, lass, to put ye through that."

Brigh nickered.

"I ken ye are well now. I'll leave ye to rest, aye? Tadgh's lads will clean yer stall soon."

She left, exhausted more by worry than by any healing energy she'd had to expend or any residue of Brigh's reaction to the seeds. The effect had been mild and quickly diluted. Damhan remained by the stable entrance to keep an eye on Brigh, and to make sure the lads took good care of her. Lianna didn't want any chance of more seeds being fed to her.

She walked slowly through the bailey, drinking in the afternoon sunshine, headed for the keep to tell David what she'd learned.

DAVID COULDN'T BELIEVE Lianna just walked into his solar and handed him the answer to the question he and his people had struggled with for so long. "Brigh is well?"

"Aye, she is."

Lianna looked exhausted, wrung out, but jubilant, too. "And ye have nay doubt the seeds are the source?"

"Brigh's symptoms came on quickly, mild at first because I gave her only a few seeds, but stronger as she ingested more. We have one piece of the puzzle, David."

"All thanks to ye. Ye noticed the difference around the nearer and the higher elevation trees. Ye gathered enough seeds to prove their effect. Ye found the source of the poison! Now 'tis up to me to find out who was using it to harm the horses and why."

"I am certain ye will," she told him.

He pulled her into his arms and kissed her gently, gratefully, then let her go. "Go get some rest before supper. I'll see ye there."

Her confidence gave him the strength he'd been lacking since before they reunited in the woods below the Aerie. Her censure of him in the stable had been well said and hit close to the bone. She had a better grasp of what a laird was and what a laird should do than he did. Until his self-pity forced her to remind him. Her da would be proud of her.

He had spent the last year resentful of being in a position most would envy; mourning the loss of his wife and the life he'd led with her in France; and focusing on his daughter—at least until the horses began to get sick. He could have turned this down. Kerr could be laird. Or Alastair. But the responsibility belonged to him, not them. It was time he started acting like the laird he claimed to be. Her news took care of one major concern, and gave him a solid foundation to build on—at last.

He still dreaded the confrontations to come. Any sane man would, but he had to know who was trying to undermine his leadership. Three supportive council members had pointed him to the same men Kerr mentioned. Iagan and Alastair, his potential rival on the council.

Iagan served as a mason, one of a dozen men who maintained the strength of the keep's outer walls and repaired the keep's walls, inside and out. It let them move, unquestioned, anywhere within the keep, or without. But only one of them had a history of rivalry with David, even if it had only been due to a lass. Iagan's duties kept him, for the most part, out of David's sight. Today, that would change.

He sent Kerr to bring Iagan to the laird's solar. David stood when Kerr entered, followed by a short, squat man David barely recognized. Kerr made to leave, but David held up a hand, signaling for him to stay. He wanted a witness to the exchange, and Kerr would notice things he might miss.

This was his old rival for a lass's affections? If the situation were not so serious, he might have laughed.

He exchanged a glance with Kerr, disbelieving. The years had not been kind to Iagan. Hard work with heavy stone had made his muscles massive but bowed his back. David quickly realized he would be taller if he stood straighter. David didn't believe he could.

Iagan's gaze roved over the men confronting him. "Why am I here?"

The anger David had been stoking since he'd sent Kerr for this man suddenly deflated. "Have a seat," he directed, pointing to the nearest chair. "Everyone sit down. I will ask questions, and ye will answer them, aye?"

Iagan frowned, but complied, lowering his bulk to the oaken seat.

David sat and dipped his head, his gaze on Kerr, who followed suit, sitting heavily, keeping watch on Iagan. With everyone seated, the tension in the solar eased a bit. At a loss for words, David waited, forcing himself to recall how sick

Athdar had been, how near death the mare Lianna had saved
and others had been. His concern for her safety. His daughter's,
his own. He cleared his throat and spoke. "Ye are aware of the
sickness afflicting our horses?"

"Aye." Iagan's held tilted, questioning in his expression and
his posture. "Everyone is. What has that to do with me?"

"That's what I'd like to find out. Did ye poison them?"

"What? Nay!" He pushed to his feet, grimacing as he
straightened as far as his bent back would allow.

David winced at his obvious discomfort. His work on the
walls had bent his body years too soon into that of an old man.
But David couldn't let sympathy dissuade him. "Do ye ken
anyone who would do such a thing?"

Iagan opened his mouth, shaking his head before he spoke
to deny it, but David held up a hand to halt him. "Or anyone
plotting to remove me as the MacDhai laird?"

Iagan blanched, but continued to shake his head.

"We have a history, ye and I," David reminded him, hating
to ask the next question, but needing to. "Why should I
trust ye?"

Iagan studied him before answering.

David felt weighed and measured, but couldn't guess what
conclusion the man had reached.

"We have a history that involved a lass," he said with a
frown. "Long years ago. And nothing so weighty as a threat to
MacDhai."

"My da would have disagreed with ye," David told him.

He took a step closer to David's desk.

Kerr leaned forward to stand, but David waved him back.
That lass might be ancient history to both of them, but it
appeared Iagan had something to get off his chest. Better he do
it here and now than in some hidden conspiracy.

"A lass who married away from MacDhai while ye were
gone." He paid no attention to Kerr as he verbally challenged

his laird. "She meant little then and naught now." He paused for breath, then spoke more softly. "I have a good wife. I have nay quarrel with ye. And if I did, why would I poison horses and harm the clan?" He stopped and laughed, then waving his arms, shouted, "If I meant to do that, 'twould be easier for me to damage our walls, weaken them, so the next attack brought them down." He paused again, then spoke more softly. "But I would never do such a thing. This is my clan. My home."

David raised a hand, halting him before he continued. "Ye speak sense." He sighed, debating whether Iagan would respect his vulnerability, or if it would be better to feign strength. He decided to be truthful. "Because I was years away, 'tis difficult to judge who might hold a grudge—and for how long. I didna intend to insult yer honor. But ye ken I had to ask."

"I do," Iagan said, softly. "I wouldha, had I been in yer place." He stepped back as if to resume his seat.

David pressed his lips together. After a glance at Kerr, he nodded and raised a hand, stopping Iagan. "Thank ye. Ye may go."

He left and David turned to Kerr. "That leaves us only Alasdair to consider."

Kerr leaned his elbows on his knee and clasped his hands. "At least ye seemed to gain Iagan's respect. He has influence among the working men," he replied,

David agreed. Lianna was right. The more he spoke with clan members, the stronger he would become. "So while this brings us one step closer to finding who's behind this, I dinna think Alasdair will be as accommodating."

14

I nstead of limiting the attendance at his interview with Alasdair to Kerr and himself, David also invited his three supporters on the council. Alasdair might view that as stacking the deck against him, but David wanted witnesses—ones he could count on to accurately relate anything that was said, or that happened, while he questioned his so-called rival. He waited to send for them until after the morning meal the next day, hoping for the calm of full stomachs.

Predictably, Alasdair entered the solar last, making an entrance. "Ye sent for me?" He looked around then, noticing the men in the room, and frowned. "What is this?"

"Take a seat," David directed, after deliberately neglecting to rise from his own. "I have some questions I expect ye to answer."

"Expect? Indeed." After a glance at the other council members, none of whom gave him any indication of what they were thinking or why he was here, he eased himself into the last remaining seat.

"Have ye anything at all to do with poisoning the horses? Planning the campaign, directing it, even feeding poisonous seeds to them?" David increased the intensity of his voice and his expression with those questions, never taking his gaze from Alasdair. Kerr would tell him later how the other council members reacted to his questioning.

"What? Nay. I would never do that. Harming MacDhai horses harms the clan."

"I'm glad to hear ye think so. But harming its laird doesna?"

Alasdair frowned, his gaze sliding around the room. "Have ye been harmed?"

"Not yet. Nor do I plan to be. Ye voted against my approval as laird."

"I did."

They all knew he had done so. There was no point in evading the question, and David hadn't expected him to. He kept his voice matter-of-fact as he asked the next question. "Are ye conspiring to replace me now?" It took Alasdair a moment to get past his easy-going tone of voice to the meat of the question. David could see when he finally understood what he'd been asked. His gaze shot to David, then to Kerr and the other council members, before returning to David. He looked a little less sure of himself.

"Nay. Why would I?"

"Do ye think ye should be laird?"

"Aye." He straightened his shoulders. "And why not? Yer da may have named ye, and the council voted to support ye, but that doesna make ye the best man for the job."

"And ye are?"

"I see where ye are going with this. Nay, I'm not the best, nor am I the only. Nor are ye the best, as we have seen over the last year. The changes ye are making may happen quickly—too quickly for many in the clan—but the improvements ye expect will take years. Do ye ken yer people well enough to be certain they can wait? What if ye are wrong?"

David's gut churned at the condemnation, coming so soon

after Lianna's, and echoing hers. Like her, Alasdair was right about the risk and about how poorly he knew his people, but he was wrong about the answer. "The strength of this clan, how we go forward, depends on all of us. I agree with ye that none of us alone are the best, but together, we can be."

Some of the tension left Alastair's body. "And them?" He nodded toward the other council members.

"They are here to ensure only the truth leaves this chamber."

Alasdair stood. "Ye accuse me of lying—"

"Sit down," David barked. Once Alasdair resumed his seat, he continued. "I accuse ye of naught. I simply recognize how tales fly around the keep and the village, and when tales of this conversation come back to me, I dinna expect them to be altered or exaggerated in any way."

"Ye think I have any control over what people tell each other?"

"The same control as any of us. To tell the truth." David leaned forward and captured Alastair's gaze. "Ye have every right to question the laird's plans. The laird's effectiveness. I dinna fault ye for that." At Alastair's nod, he continued, "But I do expect yer help as a member of this clan. I expect yer advice as long as ye are on the council—and after. I dinna have to like it. I dinna have to take it. But ye can expect that I will listen. I will hear what ye have to say and consider it."

Alastair nodded. "That is fair."

"Then we can work together?"

Alasdair frowned and, after a pause, nodded. "We can."

David stood. He'd already gained more from this meeting than he'd expected. It was time to end it. "Thank ye. Ye may go."

The other council members left with him.

Kerr remained at David's signal. "Ye did a good job with him," Kerr remarked. "He may be the loyal opposition, but I think ye can add emphasis to loyal."

"He's not our poisoner."

"Nay, I dinna think so, either. We need to cast a wider net."

"Aye, but where?"

The question hung in the air long after Kerr left David alone.

A few hours later, Murdoch came to fetch David from the solar, his expression one that David couldn't decipher. He wasn't grinning, exactly. But a corner of his lip quirked up, then smoothed back down as though he thought better of it. Even more strange, he wouldn't meet David's gaze.

"Murdoch! Ye are better?"

"Aye. Lianna approved my release from my chamber." His expression didn't waver.

"Is something wrong? Is everyone all right?"

"Ye willna believe who is at our gate."

"The MacPherson himself has come to apologize for the raid?"

Murdoch held up a hand. "Best ye come see for yerself. If I tell ye, ye will think one of the MacPhersons hit me on the head, or that I've been in the ale all day."

David followed him to the bailey and up the stairs to the wall walk, where the guards studied something on the ground outside the keep. They backed off as David approached, but their gazes followed him as he reached the overlook.

When David saw who waited outside the gate, he glanced at Murdoch and shook his head. "Ye were right. I wouldna have believed ye." He signaled to the men manning the gate. "Open and let them in."

David turned to Murdoch and grimaced. Mirielle's grandparents, the Comte and Comtesse had arrived, and with a full complement of soldiers and servants. This could only mean more trouble to add to the problems already plaguing him.

"Go on," Murdoch said, grinning, and pointed him back toward the stairs.

David pursed his lips. "We really dinna need this added to everything else we're dealing with."

"Aye, but mayhap they do."

He paused and glanced aside at Murdoch. The man's expression had turned solemn. "Mayhap," he said, agreeing, thinking of the Comtesse's tiny request in the corner of the Comte's last missive. "They would not have made the arduous trip from France without a reason—good or bad." He headed down the steps and reached the bailey as the Comte rode in, followed by a covered carriage in which sat the Comtesse, followed by a wagon filled with crates and bundles, and an escort of ten more men.

David was immediately struck by the Comtesse's appearance. Despite the journey, or perhaps in addition to it, the woman did not look well. Was her desperate note on the Comte's last missive written in earnest? Suddenly, his stomach sank. He'd put them off for nearly a year. Their granddaughter had grown from a wee bairn to a lass with a mind of her own. They'd be delighted, he hoped, but they'd missed so much, they could not help but resent her absence from their lives.

Out of the corner of his eye, he saw Lianna step out of the stable, take in what was happening, and duck back inside. Despite the chill he feared she expected to develop between them after scolding him to do his job, he wished he could join her.

"*Bienvenue*," David said as the carriage rolled to a stop. The Comte ignored him and went immediately to his wife, supported her on one side as the driver helped her down, and held her arm while she gained her footing. "*S'il vous plaît, entre,*" he added, gesturing toward the keep's heavy door. She looked as though she needed to be made comfortable before he took care of anything else.

"*La Comtesse* is not well," her husband told David. "Did you receive my missive?"

"I did," David agreed, as he pulled open the heavy door and allowed them inside. "But ye didna say ye were coming."

"There was no time to send another," the Comte said as David signaled for the steward.

"Put my guests in the largest suite," he instructed, "and light fires in all the hearths." He turned to his father-in-law. "Do ye require a bath to be sent up?"

"Not yet, *merci*. My wife must rest."

"Once they are settled, find space for the Comte's escort." The steward hurried to the stairs to make the large suite ready, and David proceeded more slowly with Mirielle's grandparents, showing them the way. It worried him that the Comtesse had yet to speak. If he hadn't already noticed her appearance, her breathing, loud and labored as she climbed the steps, would have told him she was not well. The Comte had said there was not enough time to send another missive? Was her condition so dire? Perhaps Lianna could do something for her. But would she? He wasn't sure he had the right to ask.

He hoped Mirielle was in the nursery with her tutor. He'd prefer she did not meet her grandparents with her *grand-mere* in this state. After they rested, perhaps the Comtesse would feel better.

"Would you like yer belongings brought up right away or would ye prefer to rest?"

"Send them up. My wife will not notice the *agitation*."

"Very well." She must sleep soundly not to notice the commotion of the wagon's contents being carried into their chambers. Fortunately, it had a sitting room and a separate sleeping chamber with a door. With that closed, she might indeed rest peacefully.

Once David saw that they were comfortably settled, he left them to rest and returned to his solar to keep working. It was that or worry over what the Comte might have planned for this visit.

Since he'd been home, David had put off going through several chests his father kept. The ledgers he'd found stacked on this desk, filled with incomprehensible numbers, had been enough of a challenge, for Kerr and for him. Lianna had seen him working on one of them. Since his father had kept them close at hand, and judging by a few dated entries, David knew they were the most current.

He needed to understand every aspect of the clan's finances, but his father's sloppy record-keeping made it a challenge. One ledger described crop yields, but those were haphazardly recorded, making tracking the success or failure of plantings in any season, much less over time, nearly impossible. Another listed where money came from and where it went. Horses played a central role in the clan's wealth or lack of it, but farming and other trades, such as weaving and the blacksmith, also had an impact, earning or spending clan resources as needed.

His father had even kept a ledger recording the clan's efforts at breeding bigger, stronger horses. They, too, were unreliable, though evidence of their success roamed MacDhai pastures even now. Fortunately, Tadgh also kept records. He and David had once spent a frustrating day attempting to reconcile his to the old laird's.

Stymied at every turn, David had made no attempt to open the other three chests. He assumed they contained older ledgers, so he didn't consider them as important as making sense of the last few years, and looking forward to the clan's needs in the future. He lost himself in numbers for the rest of the afternoon.

ϡ

THE OLDER COUPLE surprised David by sending word they would appear at supper and hoped their granddaughter would also be present. Their belongings had gone up hours earlier, so he supposed they'd had time to rest and to unpack a change of garments. He asked Lianna to remain beside him at the high table, put Mirielle on his other side, and left seats for her grandparents beyond her. "Yer grandparents are visiting," he explained to his daughter, wondering if she remembered them at all. She'd been so tiny when they left France.

"I have grandparents?" Mirielle twisted in her seat, trying to see every corner of the hall. "Where are they?"

"They will be here soon, lass. Ye must be on yer best behavior, aye? They are old…"

"Older than ye, Papa?"

"Of course. They are yer mother's parents."

"They must be very, very old."

"Perhaps not so old as that," David equivocated.

Mirielle continued her scan of the great hall, so David turned to Lianna. "Thank ye for sitting with me. I may need an ally."

"I'll help in any way I can," she said, but she looked away.

"Still, I…thank ye."

"I'm pleased—and I must admit, shocked—to see them here," she said softly enough that Mirielle would not hear her, apparently accepting his olive branch, at least for the moment. "We thought they might be behind the poisonings, trying to force ye back to France. Yet if they were able to arrange that from a distance, why would they come?"

"I dinna ken, but soon, perhaps, we will be able to find out." He, too, lowered his voice, though with the rumble of conversation around them, he doubted Mirielle would be able to overhear them. "The Comtesse looked ill to me. I fear this may be Mirielle's only opportunity to spend time with them."

"I'm sorry to hear that," Lianna said.

"Well, it may be a case of keeping enemies within reach. On

their part, and on mine. But for Mirielle's sake, I hope they are not the ones behind our trouble."

When they arrived, the Comtesse leaning heavily on her husband's arm, David rose and guided them to their places at the high table. He seated her next to Mirielle, counting on whatever maternal instinct remained in the old woman to help her regain some of her lost vitality. And tending to her grand-daughter while he and her husband spoke over their heads would keep them both occupied.

"*Merci*," she said as she sat, then turned to Mirielle. "Ah, *ma belle*. I have waited so long to see you."

"Are you my *grand-mere*?"

"*Oui*, I am."

"You are very old."

The Comtesse chuckled. "I suppose I look very old to one as young as you, *ma fille*."

The exchange between women of different generations fascinated David. Trust his daughter to be brutally honest in her assessment.

The woman looked up and met his gaze. "I...*je vais bientôt mourir*," she announced. "And I was desperate to see something left of my daughter before I, too, leave this world, so here we are."

David understood a dying wish. He was here because of his father's. He reached across Mirielle and took the old woman's hand, then lifted his gaze to her husband. His eyes were glazed with tears, but he smiled as he looked at Mirielle, so perhaps they were not all from sadness. His gut told him these people had nothing to do with MacDhai's troubles. Still, David knew from painful experience how crafty the man could be. Could he believe the emotion he saw in his eyes?

❦

LIANNA WATCHED THE EXCHANGE, broken-hearted for the family, yet distant, as though she saw them through cloudy window glass. David should not have asked her to join them at the high table. She looked like she was part of the family. She was not. Doubts she'd held at bay as David tried to woo her arose again.

They'd discussed this. Including her could amplify a threat to his daughter, if any existed. She understood the response to seeing her heal Murdoch had been both good and bad. While some in the clan had begun to greet her with smiles, making her feel more welcome, there were still some who did not.

She searched the room for her men and found them at a closer table than where they usually sat, Jenny with them. Because of the dozen Frenchmen now joining the throng in the great hall? The nearness of her men comforted her, but still, she felt out of place. Left out of the family scene David set.

She doubted he'd invited the Comte, despite his comment about keeping his enemies close. He'd seemed surprised or resigned as they rode through the MacDhai gate. So if he didn't truly welcome them, was he putting on a good face for his daughter's sake? For the grandmother, who was surely very ill? Or just to keep the peace, and as he'd said, to keep his enemies close at hand?

Seeing her daughter's child seemed to have put some strength back into the grandmother's backbone. Lianna thought she sat straighter and her smile was more sure, more serene, as she spoke to the child. Perhaps their visit would be good for them, and for David and Mirielle.

Mirielle, for her part, seemed fascinated by these old people who belonged to her. But she was still so young. If this was to be the last time she saw them, would they haunt her memories as she grew, or would she forget their faces?

David hadn't yet introduced her, but Lianna knew he was too distracted to do the honors, and she did not want to be the one to have to explain her purpose in visiting MacDhai. She didn't belong here. She should go. She tapped David on the shoulder to get his attention.

"Ye dinna need me, and ye dinna want to explain why I'm here, so I will go sit with my men."

He nodded and turned away. She couldn't be sure he'd even heard and understood her.

Well, so much for being an ally during this meal. She stood and made her way to her men's table, regretting that she'd just made herself even more conspicuous by leaving David's side. Perhaps she should have stayed in her seat after all.

The men moved aside and made room for her.

"How's it going up there?" Bhaltair's gaze never stopped sweeping the hall, locating and assessing every warrior, French or MacDhai, in the chamber.

"'Tis heartbreaking, but there was nothing for me to contribute. David barely noticed when I told him I would come sit with ye."

One of her men snorted. "Sorry," he added. "But ye'd be wrong. He watched every step ye took until ye reached us."

So he wasn't entirely consumed with his family. That was interesting. And disturbing. Did he care, or was he simply making sure of her safety until she reached her men? That had to be the reason, she told herself. He had too much else on his mind.

15

"Lianna, come quickly!"

David's urgent shout pulled Lianna out of a deep sleep and a dream in which Cook had covered all the tables in the great hall with either dandelion greens or sycamore tree seeds, and she had to choose a seat. Blinking, she sat up, thinking she'd missed the morning meal, but nay, the sun had not yet risen. Her window was dark.

He pounded on her door, calling for her again. Something was terribly wrong. "Coming." She stepped into her slippers and grabbed a wrap, stumbled to the door, removed the bolt and opened it. "What's amiss?"

"Two horses are down. The stable lad woke and saw them. Tadgh sent him to fetch me. I dinna ken how long they've been sick."

Not Mirielle or her grandmother, thank the saints. "I'm coming. Let me change." Which horses could be that sick so quickly? They'd all seemed well enough this afternoon. How could they have gotten so much worse in the hours since?

"Nay." David handed her a heavy robe. "Here. 'Twill cover ye and keep ye warm. There's nay time."

She let him pull her out into the dark hallway, down the stairs, and across the bailey. The night sky was full of stars, but David never looked up. Lianna fought to stay on her feet as he half dragged—half carried her into the stable past a MacDhai guard. Lanterns had been lit inside several stalls.

"They're here," a lad approached and told them, pointing to two adjacent stalls, "but others dinna look well, either."

"Ach, nay! Brigh!" She dropped to the ground beside her horse and ran frantic hands over her. "God's blood, this is too soon. Ye are so sick because of me. I gave ye those damned seeds. I did this to ye!"

"Lianna, nay. Ye gave her barely any. Someone else has done this." David's grief was palpable, his tone dejected. "Go to yer bed, lad," David told him. "I'll call for Tadgh if we need help."

"I can help."

"I ken ye can, but..."

"Nay," Lianna said, interrupting. "We need him. The horses that ye say dinna look well. Fetch fresh water and make them drink. Have the guard haul up water at the well. He can see the stable doors from there. Keep the horses drinking until they piss, then drink some more. Wait..." she added as the lad turned to run for his buckets. "Get a jar of honey from Cook. Wake her if ye must, or raid her pantry. Several jars. As much as ye can carry, and mix some with each bucket of water."

"Aye, lady," the lad said, and ran to do her bidding.

"I saved Athdar," she muttered, almost to herself. "I will save Brigh, too." Then she raised her voice. "Which is the other horse the lad mentioned?"

"Damn it, one of the Andalusians," David replied from the next stall. "Whoever is sending this message is becoming more direct."

"Fetch more buckets. More water. See if ye can get him up, just like we did with the Percheron mare. I'll deal with Brigh until I get her standing. Should we send the lad to wake Tadgh and the other lads?"

"Not yet. They can take over for us in a few hours if we still need their help." David went to do her bidding and Lianna turned back to her beloved Brigh. She knew David's reluctance to involve more MacDhais was rooted in his determination to protect her. He didn't want the others to have any inkling of her talent, not if she—and he—could handle this on their own. She put that out of her mind as she settled on the straw at Brigh's side. "Ye canna leave me," she crooned as she placed hands on her mare's sweat-soaked side and reached in, feeling the tingle of her healing energy flowing through her fingertips into her parched horse. "Do ye hear me, Brigh? Stand up, damn you!"

Brigh lifted her head, her great eyes rolling to find Lianna. "I'm here, lass. Good, that's good. Come up, lass. Get up." Keeping her hands in place, her link well established, Lianna stood and gave Brigh room to move. She kicked and rocked a little, but looked more like a newborn foal trying to stand than Lianna's well-trained mount. "Come on, lass, ye can do it."

Brigh kicked, rolled, and got her knees under her. David entered then with buckets of water. "Put that where she can reach it," Lianna commanded. He set both buckets below Brigh's nose, then ran for more. "Drink, lass. 'Twill help."

Brigh dropped her nose into one bucket, then the other, acting desperately thirsty. Once she finished, Lianna's talent told her she was stronger. She never took her hands from Brigh's side. "Can ye stand now, lass?"

In answer, Brigh got her front hooves in front of her and pushed up, then settled back down.

David brought more water. Once Brigh drank it, Lianna monitored her while she gave her a few minutes, then had her try again. This time, Brigh pushed to standing.

Tears ran down Lianna's face. She slid her hands up and

wrapped her arms around Brigh's neck. "Ye will make it, lass. I willna let ye die."

She let go and checked the buckets. A little remained in each, so she poured one into the other and bade Brigh drink some more.

David came back with more water and gave it to Brigh, taking the empties with him, running back to the well. Lianna didn't stop to think how tiring hauling up buckets of water must be for the guard, and running them full into the stable and back empty must be for David and the stable lad. But what they were doing would save these horses.

Lianna patted Brigh's side. "I'll be right there," she said, inclining her head toward the stall with the other ill horse.

She left Brigh to do what she could for the Andalusian. He was in worse shape than Brigh had been. Lianna poured herself into him, trying to help. The lad returned with a tray full of honey. "Cook told me she'd have my hide if I dropped and broke any of these. I didna!"

"Very good. Please fill all the buckets ye can find with water. Help him, David. Add some honey to each and stir it. Give one to Brigh, leave two here and give one to each of the other horses that seem ill. I'll stay with this lad." She nodded to David to let him know she would continue to help as only she could.

"Let's go, lad," David said and gathered up as many buckets as he could carry by their rope handles. The lad did the same, then they carried full ones back, one in each hand, as the guard filled them from the well. Once they were all back, they mixed in honey and distributed them as Lianna had ordered.

David rejoined her. She had him try to get some honey water into the Andalusian. He turned the horse's head and dribbled water into his mouth.

"'Tisna working," he groaned. "He doesna swallow it. I've got to get his head up."

"Keep trying," Lianna insisted, her focus within the horse,

trying to slow his fleeting heartbeat. "He's sweating out too much. He must drink."

David waved the lad over. "Get the guard to help me." He got a hand under the horse's shoulder, dug out a shallow trench, and then shoved both arms underneath. Even with the guard's help, he used all his strength to force the shoulder up. They leaned forward, rolling the horse's neck and head upright so it could swallow. "Get some water into him," David ordered the lad, gesturing with his chin toward the bucket. "We'll hold him up as long as we can."

The guard tipped the horse's head enough to get his mouth open, then the lad poured in a cupful of the honey water. The horse finally reacted to that and jerked his head, knocking the men over. But he seemed to swallow some of the water.

"Again," Lianna commanded.

They kept trying, and the horse kept fighting, but they wouldn't quit. Eventually, it rolled far enough upright on its own that David could keep it steady and the guard could go back to hauling up more water from the well.

Lianna could feel the water helping as the horse's heartbeat slowed. "There's something else…"

"The buckets are empty," the stable lad reported.

"Please fill them again and add some honey, just like ye did before. David, help him. There's a good lad, then go to Cook and see if she has any dandelion tea ready. 'Tis safe to leave this handsome lad for as long as it takes ye to do that. He's a little better."

"We'll be back as quickly as we can," David said, putting a hand on the stable lad's shoulder and turning him toward the doorway. "Check on Brigh."

Lianna looked toward the stall where Brigh stood, peering over the wall and watching her. "She's still on her feet. Keep her drinking."

"Aye, we will."

The rest of the night seemed to go on forever, but by the time the sun rose, both Brigh and the Andalusian were on their feet, and the others that had been showing signs of illness all looked better.

The stable, however, had turned into a swamp of horse piss. Lianna laughed to herself. The stable master and the other lads would not be happy to find that mess, but it meant all the horses were better, so it was worth it.

The timing of this attack, for that was surely what it was, bothered her. The next time the lad went for water and she and David were alone, she gave voice to her fears. "Do ye think this has anything to do with Mirielle's grandparents? They're here. Are they responsible?"

David sighed, fatigue from a night of carrying heavy buckets and lifting a heavy horse's head showing on his face. "I canna believe it. 'Twould seem more likely that someone else has taken advantage of them being here, to make them seem guilty. Or to protest their presence."

"Or perhaps they've directed their spy to step up his attack. David, we nearly lost that stallion. I didna want to tell ye at the time, but if ye hadna gotten water down his throat when ye did, nothing I did wouldha helped, and he wouldna be alive."

"I ken it. I saw how ye focused on him, even more than on Brigh."

"I seemed to have a stronger connection when ye were touching him. Did ye notice anything?"

"Nay, but I was distracted. I canna tell ye how much I appreciate what ye did tonight."

"What the hell happened in here?" Tadgh's deep, angry voice rang out from the stable doorway, making both David and Lianna jump.

"Time to face the stable master," David intoned, groaned, and stood.

LIANNA HAD SAVED THEM AGAIN. David's helplessness in the face of her ability tore at him. Before he gave Tadgh a condensed version of what they'd been doing all night, he asked, "Has anyone been in the stable lately who didn't belong? Anyone hanging around, or feeding the horses anything ye didna approve?" David could almost see his mind working, thinking back.

"I havena seen anyone," he reported. "I'll ask the lads."

David nodded. "Do, please. 'Tis important."

"Aye, I can see that."

After filling him in, David helped Tadgh and his lads lead the horses out into the bailey. There, Lianna could keep an eye on them while the stable was thoroughly cleaned. Each time he went in after another horse, the stench of piss choked him after the relatively fresh air of the bailey. Exhausted and yes, angry, nonetheless he felt obligated to help clean up the mess the recovering horses had made. They'd been force-fed buckets full of water through the night, and most of it had been deposited on the straw-covered floors of their stalls a short time later. Any worse and they'd be ankle-deep in stinking mud.

But the horses were improving. Whoever had done this would see his plan had failed. What would he do next?

David stabbed his pitchfork into the ground and leaned on its handle. If this had been his plot gone wrong, what would *he* do next? Use more direct violence? Stab a few horses to death? Nay, he didn't think killing horses was the intent, or they'd be dead already.

He needed Lianna's opinion, but from what she'd told him, he suspected controlling the dose of poison was difficult. Or perhaps the man forgot which horses he'd poisoned and missed dosing a few. And gave double doses to others, like Brigh and David's prize Andalusian stallion. How much would it take to kill a horse? How often would he have to poison them to make them sick? Damn it, he needed to know.

And even more, he needed to find out who was doing this and why. And stop them. He felt certain Lianna was wrong about the grandparents being behind this. Someone else must be. But who? He'd thought he had the culprit in Iagan or Alastair, but he'd been wrong about them. He didn't know whom to trust anymore.

The next time the stable master came by with a wheelbarrow to pick up what David had raked together, the man waited until David finished loading the wheelbarrow, clearing the stall, then added, "Laird, ye were up all night. Go to yer rest and let me and the lads finish this."

Gratitude filled David that someone cared about his efforts for the clan, but he couldn't just walk away and leave this situation to others.

"I am well. *Dinna fash*."

"Ye are dead on yer feet, and so is that lass out there, laying hands on all the beasts. Does she really help them?"

David let his gaze wander through the stable to the open doorways. Outside, he could see horses of all colors and sizes in the bailey, one beautiful lass standing among them, reaching out a hand to each, then directing serving lasses to place water buckets before one here, another one there. He'd had no idea Lianna had continued to use her talent to care for the horses. And that members of the clan helped her. He recognized some of them as women and older lasses who'd been part of her story-telling session in the bailey with the bairns, dogs, and cats. Even better, there were others who had not been present that day. They stood with each horse, keeping them calm, letting Lianna do what she did. The sight nearly brought him to tears.

Even though Lianna had more reason than most to be angry with him for ignoring her at dinner, he thought their shared battle last night had bonded them again. But when he recalled her leaving the table, he wondered. Until then, he thought they were in a good place, but were they? He should not have made her part of the family reunion, not in front of the entire clan. She must have felt out of place. Worse, they'd discussed the risks involved in making her appear involved with Mirielle. He'd taken advantage of her, and he regretted it.

Still, she had worked all night to save MacDhai horses. She continued to do so now, openly, with help from members of the clan, despite her own exhaustion. Once, that would have worried him. After the last year as laird, never feeling like he fit in, seeing the clan pulling together—with him, and with Lianna—made his heart soar and renewed his energy. "Aye, she does," he said in answer to Tadgh's question. "She helps all of us."

❧

AFTER THE STABLE was cleaned and resupplied with hay and straw, the horses were put back in their stalls. Lianna was as close to collapse as she could ever recall being, but as everyone who had been helping dispersed, she decided she wanted to make one last check on Brigh and the stallion before she sought to revive herself with a meal and some time in her bed before supper. She could tell David was furious with himself as well as with the culprit, but he was also exhausted and at his wits' end.

She had no strength left to lend him.

Instead, she watched him head for the keep, then made one more check on the two horses who'd been down when last night started. She checked the stallion first. He greeted her placidly, calmly, not as one desperately ill. She patted his neck, checked that he had water, then crossed to Brigh. "Ach, my lass, she murmured as she stroked Brigh's neck. "Ye had me *scairt*, ye did. How did someone manage to feed ye something bad? For that matter, who dared Athdar's temper before we came here?" Exhausted, she gave up speech and simply leaned into Brigh's shoulder, resting her head against her neck. Standing, she felt herself falling into a doze just as Brigh's head came up, knocking Lianna upright.

Something was wrong. Still in contact with Brigh, she could tell her horse wasn't in trouble. What had she seen? Or sensed?

Lianna moved silently to the stall's half-door and looked up and down the stable's main hall. At first, she didn't see anything unusual, then a man moved from behind a post and began feeding one of the Scottish mountain horses out of a pouch at his waist. She didn't recognize him. He hadn't helped with the day's great cleanup, nor did she recall him from meals in the keep. Had he come with Mirielle's grandparents? He stood close to the stall doorway as if trying to blend in with the posts and walls beyond him, his gaze on the stable entrance, but his hand dipping into the large pouch before rising to the horse's muzzle. The horse liked whatever he offered. It ate with relish, then nosed his hand for more, so he reached into the pouch and lifted his hand again.

Lianna's instincts screamed for her to challenge him and demand to see what he fed the animal. But she was confident she could help the horse, less so that she could help David solve the mystery plaguing his clan, unless she was able to accurately describe the man. He might be a MacDhai, and a rival David was unaware of. So she stayed out of the stranger's view, memorizing what he looked like.

As soon as his pouch emptied, he tucked it into his shirt and left.

Lianna ran to the horse he'd fed. The stable floor outside its stall was clean. He hadn't made her quest easy by dropping anything for her to find. So she forced open the horse's mouth. The remainder of what it had eaten still coated its teeth and tongue. Oats, bits of apple, all designed to please the horse's palate, but the majority of what she saw looked like pieces of seeds she knew, some winged, some chewed into bits. She'd gathered some from under the huge Dule tree in the far pasture. The squirrel's tree. She knew what they could do. If she needed any further confirmation, after feeding them to Brigh, this was it. This horse would soon need water and lots of it.

16

L ianna found Tadgh and asked him to have his lads keep putting fresh water, honey and dandelion tea in front of the horse she'd seen fed. Then she ran to find David. She'd never been to his chamber, but after checking the great hall and his solar, she realized he must have gone up to get a few hours' sleep before having to host the Comte and Comtesse at supper.

"David, open up!" She pounded on his door until he called out, and kept pounding until he opened it. She saw the shock on his face as she shoved past him into the room, but didn't care.

"Close the door," she said. "I have news."

"Sit," he commanded after he did as she requested. "Ye look as knackered as I feel."

"I feel the same," she said as she sank into a stuffed armchair in front of his hearth. She took a quick look around and realized she was in a sitting room, not David's bedchamber. This suite was arranged much as the nursery, except that what she could see of his bedchamber through the open door appeared much larger than the space where his daughter slept.

"What's yer news? We're both tired and need sleep."

So, short-tempered, too. Her news should improve his mood. "I just saw a man feeding one of the horses by hand from a pouch at his waist."

"Ye didna stop him?"

"I thought it more important to be able to describe him to ye. If he's behind the illnesses or part of a conspiracy against ye, he might be a MacDhai. But I fear he came with..."

"The Comte. So, tell me what ye saw."

Lianna spent the next few minutes giving David every detail of the man's appearance, including his posture and his walk as he left the stable, and what he'd fed the horse. "Once that pouch was out of sight, he seemed unconcerned to be found there. If one of the lads had come in, or the stable master, they'd have seen him, too, but they were still out in the bailey, dealing with what we hauled out of the stalls."

David nodded, his expression bleak.

"So, do ye recognize him?"

"I do. He didna come with the Comte's party. He's a MacD-hai. Someone I've kenned all my life, though he's never been a friend. Nathair is his name."

"Why...?"

"That, I dinna ken—yet. But now I think I ken how all this came about. He's the old healer's grandson—and Tadgh's assistant. He's in and out of the stable frequently, unless Tadgh sends him out to the glen." He spread his hands. "No one would think anything of seeing him around the horses. He spends much of his time out of the keep, keeping watch over the pastured horses, but when he's here, he belongs. The guards wouldn't suspect him. They'd barely notice him."

Lianna frowned. "Was he out the day the MacPhersons arrived?"

"Tadgh will ken where he was." David sat forward suddenly. "Damn it, I must make sure he counts the pastured stock again. The man Murdoch captured probably lied. Or they may sneak back." He rubbed a hand over his face, then looked away. "My God. If Nathair's been working with MacPhersons, I'll string him up by his cods from one of those Dule trees."

"What could he hope to gain by helping them and harming MacDhai?"

"It could be many things." David shrugged and turned back to her. "I'll ask him when I have him in chains."

Lianna was still puzzled. "Why have I never seen him before? Not in the stable, and never when I've ridden the glen looking for poisonous plants."

"If he's behind this, perhaps he wanted to stay out of sight. No one would pay any attention to anything he did in the stable because he belongs there." He sighed. "I doubt he came up with this scheme on his own. His grandmother would know what would harm the horses, where to find it, and how to use it."

"I still dinna understand why he—or they—would take out their anger on the horses?"

"When I have him in custody, that's one of the first questions I'll ask." He stood, but Lianna held up a hand.

"Ye are exhausted. Let Murdoch or Kerr take hold of him. Ye can question him in a few hours as easily as now. His grandmother, too. As ye say, she must be involved. Hold them in a locked chamber, if not in the dungeon. MacDhai has one of those, aye?"

David managed a quirk of his lips. "We do."

Lianna got up. "I'm going to my chamber. I'll send Jenny for food, then I plan to sleep before supper. But first, I'll have one of the servants send Murdoch and Kerr to ye."

"Nay, lass, ye go to yer rest. That is my responsibility."

"David..."

"I've no intention of interrogating anyone now. But I ken

where Murdoch is. I'll send him after them, then come straight back here. Will that suit ye?"

She relented. "Aye."

He stepped close to her and smoothed her hair back from the side of her face. "I would like it if ye were here waiting for me. Now that ye are in my chamber, the damage is done."

"The damage?"

"Likely the whole keep heard ye pounding on my door and calling for me. What will they think?"

Lianna stood still. She didn't care what anyone thought. She was near dead on her feet and needed to recover before she dealt with anything else. Especially with David MacDhai. "Ye are exhausted and not thinking clearly," she told him. "Send Murdoch for the healer and her grandson. Ye need sleep. So do I, and ye dinna need me here while ye do it."

"We'd both..."

"Go!" She pushed him toward the door. "Ye are laird. Go order yer men about."

David chuckled and complied, opening the door. Kerr stood on the other side, one of Murdoch's warriors behind him. "Aye?"

"Laird? There was shouting..." He glanced over David's shoulder and colored. His mouth snapped shut.

David stepped back. "Come in. And ye, wait outside, if ye please," David added to the guard at Kerr's back.

Kerr stepped in and David closed the door.

"Lady Lianna, my apologies, I thought there was some trouble."

"There is." David related what Lianna had been so urgently and loudly bent on telling him. "We were up all night with the horses and all morning with the stable master and his lads. I need ye to confine the two we suspect while we get some rest— Lianna in her own chamber—before supper. The Comte may not be amused if I fall asleep in his company."

"Immediately," Kerr said. "I'll alert Murdoch."

"And keep it between ye two and yer trusted men for now."

Kerr nodded and left, taking the guard from the hallway with him.

DAVID TRIED to rest after Lianna left, but tossed and turned in his bed. The man she described was another he'd spent almost no time with since his return as laird. Tadgh's assistant. And the healer's grandson. Why didn't he make that connection sooner? Who better to recognize or devise something to poison the clan's horses, as Lianna had suspected, and to discredit his leadership than that miserable old woman. And her grandson, who had all the access he needed to do her dirty work. Or MacPherson's. But why?

It was time for both of them to face the Laird's Justice.

Later, when Kerr came to wake him before supper, he had bad news to report. The man they sought had disappeared. So had the old healer. Murdoch and his men were searching all of MacDhai, but so far, he'd evaded them. David worried as he dressed. What other mischief could the man cause? Did he know they were on to him?

"Have ye talked to Tadgh? He may have an idea of where the bastard would go. The bothy in the high pasture for one, though he would expect us to look there."

"Aye," Kerr replied. "Tadgh and his lads are helping with the search."

"Who's guarding the horses?"

"Only one man, Laird. The rest are searching, but that includes searching the stable."

David nodded. "Send yer men into the village and the glen in pairs. He could be anywhere, but so could MacPhersons."

David wanted to join the search, but Lianna's words still

rang in his head. He needed to be the laird, not just act the laird. So he dressed and went to the great hall. Many of the men and several women were missing. David assumed they were helping search the keep. There were too many places to hide.

The Comte joined him, without the Comtesse, and requested a word in private, giving David the excuse he needed to move them to his solar.

The Comte observed the niceties while they sampled a fine French wine, much as was done in his home in France. But once they finished, David refilled his glass and settled back for the real conversation the Comte wanted to have.

"I will not mince words any longer," the Comte began.

David tensed, wondering if the Comte was about to admit ordering the healer and her grandson to poison the horses to force him, or more specifically, his daughter, back to France. Sitting alone with the Comte, he was vulnerable to a quick throw of the knife, or an undetectable poison in his wine, but he didn't get the feeling the Comte was prepared to take such direct action. A subtle, long-term erosion of David's ability to control his clan, much as had been underway for weeks, seemed more the Comte's style. Neither Iagan nor Alasdair was the culprit. This man could be.

"The Comtesse is dying," the Comte finally said, breaking the silence. "Her breathing is getting worse and our physician can do nothing for her." The Comte set his glass aside.

David's heart sank for the man, and his wife, all thought of conspiracy fled as the Comte confirmed what the Comtesse's appearance led David to fear. They had treated him well while he lived with their daughter, and put aside any reservations they might have had about him as a husband for their daughter when their granddaughter was born. Lucienne's death shocked and saddened everyone, but hit the Comtesse especially hard. She had taken to her bed for weeks, arising only for the funeral.

"I am so sorry. I ken what the Comtesse means to ye."

"We made the difficult journey here so that she could have time with her beloved daughter's child. This may be the last time either will spend with the other. If my wife is to be gone from me, I will not insist Mirielle return to France. The girl should stay with her father."

"Aye, she should."

"When I, too, am gone, she will inherit an estate with some of my finest horses. She may keep or sell any of it. Her *grand-mere's* jewels, and such other things as a woman would enjoy, will also come to her." He waved a hand as if brushing such inconsequential wealth aside. "As my heir, I have named a nephew with several strong sons, so you will not fear to lose her to such responsibilities. As long as she is safe here, we are content."

David forced his hand to remain steady as he lifted his glass and took another sip. After the Comte's unexpected assurance, he was tempted to empty the bottle in celebration. He needn't worry any longer whether Mirielle would stay with him. But they weren't finished yet. He hated to admit to possible problems with MacPherson, but the Comte deserved to know. Still, MacDhai was no less safe than anywhere else in Scotland, save possibly on the Aerie's tor. Or in France.

He told the Comte the history between MacDhai and MacPherson and the recent confrontation on the ridge. "I dinna ken much about the origin of our difficulty, and my da did not keep good records." He indicated the stack of ledgers on his desk. "He kept a lot of records, but they are so poorly organized as to be nearly useless." He pointed to the chests he'd been ignoring for most of the year. "Those were his. I havena touched them."

"Do you think there may be answers in them? What has kept you from opening them?"

"Reluctance. Memories. Anger. We fought before I left for

Spain. I wanted to go back to the clan where I fostered. But he would not be swayed. He always had a plan for my future. I traveled with MacDhai guards, as ye are aware, so I couldna follow my own...inclinations. After the Andalusians I acquired arrived here, he sent instructions for me to contact ye. And ye ken the rest." He gestured toward the chests with one hand. "Since I've been back, I've struggled to make sense of his most recent records. Opening those has seemed like delving into history I dinna need until I make sense of the most recent events and set the clan firmly on a path to a better future. Delving into historical records feels like putting him in charge of what I do, again. Giving him influence I dinna welcome."

"Even to accept that he is gone, and you are here?"

"I suppose so."

"You are the laird. You cannot afford to indulge in reluctance. If there is knowledge that will assist you to be found in those chests, you must open them."

"I see yer point. I will do so. I must also write a letter to the Chattan chief. He heads a confederation of smaller clans the MacPhersons and we belong to."

The Comte nodded, but remained silent.

David could see him thinking. In France, he was intimately familiar with political battles such as these. David suspected he knew what the man would say, but held his silence, respecting the Comte's careful consideration of MacDhai's situation.

"If I understand your difficulty correctly, a show of strength is called for. Not in battle," he added, holding up a hand after David opened his mouth to object. "But in strategy and diplomacy."

"I agree. I would like your assurance that I can include notice in the letter that MacDhai is fortunate in having a powerful French ally in the family." He smiled, then added, "One I may call upon if needed."

The Comte didn't hesitate. "You may."

The Comte had never offered his support directly. David was glad to have it, though in practical terms, it was worthless unless a situation developed slowly enough for his men to arrive from France.

"I know what you are thinking," the Comte continued. "France is far away. But you are not the only ally I have in Scotland. Many much closer to hand can be sent in your defense."

"I thank ye, and hope they willna be needed."

The Comte raised his glass. "I will drink to that."

After companionable sips, David agreed that including a reference to the French and other Scottish allies in the letter should settle matters, for a while at least. He debated naming Lathan, but decided to keep the Chattan chief guessing.

"I canna express how sorry I am that the Comtesse is ill," he added. Could Lianna help her? Would she?

"She is nearly as old as I. Death comes to all of us." The Comte gave a Gallic shrug.

David knew he was making light of deep feelings. David regretted what he'd suspected about the Comte and Comtesse, his fear that they would take his daughter, his resentment that he'd been forced to take on this position. He dared not voice any of that. Lianna was right. This was the hand he'd been dealt, the hand he'd accepted. But then, Lianna came back into his life. If only he could convince her to stay.

❧

AFTER LIANNA LEFT DAVID, she went to her chamber and cleaned up. She lay down, but realized she was too tired to sleep. The midday meal was over, so she begged food from Cook and took it back to her chamber to eat and drink as much as her belly would hold. Still, sleep eluded her.

The only place she could imagine being able to rest was with Brigh, in her stall. First, she'd check on the horse she'd seen the man feed. She spent a moment wishing she'd interrupted him. If he hadn't been able to feed the horse so many of the seeds, it wouldn't have gotten as sick as it did.

But it was too late for that regret. She'd given David the information he so desperately needed. It was time to stretch out in Brigh's clean straw with a blanket under and over her, and nothing but Brigh's soft chuffing to disturb her rest. If she was lucky, no one would find her until tomorrow. David would be busy with his family, and with his enemy, and would have no time for her. Perhaps that was just as well. If they had indeed found the culprit, and put a stop to poisoning the horses, she would no longer be needed here. She could return to the Aerie.

Somehow, the prospect of returning home didn't excite her. She should be homesick for her parents and her brothers and sister, but she feared once there, she'd be even more homesick for David MacDhai.

How had she allowed that to happen? She'd sworn on the way here that she would not let him break her heart again. Now she was on the verge of giving him the chance to hurt her again. He'd wanted her to stay with him this afternoon. Perhaps he really meant they would only sleep, but she was not foolish enough to believe that. Even if they only finished what they started seven years ago, could she walk away from the feel of him in her arms, or in her body?

She'd been wise to refuse him. Wise not to let him inside her walls again. Not too far, at least. A few kisses hardly counted. She was wise to guard her heart. So then why did her heart feel heavy at the thought of leaving him? Had she fallen in love with David again?

It made her sad and angry all at once. He needed a mother for his daughter. She adored Mirielle, but hadn't been able to spend the time with the child that would truly have allowed them to bond. And with the grandparents here, his family situation was unstable to say the least. Would they insist on taking

Mirielle back to France? Would David let them? The grandmother had seemed desperately ill when she arrived, better in
the company of the granddaughter she'd traveled so far to see.
Was it all a ruse?

Or could Lianna truly make a difference for Mirielle's
grandparents? She had trained with her mother and knew the
basics of care of a person. Aileanna had insisted on that much,
then allowed her to use her talent where she wished, on the
animals and hunting hawks in the Aerie. She'd had little practice caring for people, but it had been enough to save Murdoch.
Was it enough to cure someone near death? Could she help the
grandmother? Perhaps she could at least make her more
comfortable.

This was daft. She was too tired to even consider such a
course. She remembered every time she'd argued with her
mother, insisting she would only care for the animals who
came to her for help. People came to her mother or her brother,
Jamie, and younger sister, Eilidh. The animals had only her to
help them.

Aileanna had tried to convince Lianna that when she
married and moved away, she would want to know how to care
for people, too. If her husband became ill or injured, she would
regret not to be able to help him. Even worse if a child she
loved sickened. She finally understood what her mother had
tried to make her see. If something happened to David or
Mirielle, and she could not help them, it would kill her.

She'd heard her brother Jamie say he regretted the time
he'd wasted fighting against what their mother tried to teach
him. Even he had warned her not to reject any opportunity to
learn. But Lianna was much like him, stubborn and self-confi-
dent, and had done the same as he, determined to go her
own way.

Lianna shook her head as she entered the stable and
headed for Brigh's stall. Her mother was right. She needed to

return home and learn all there was to learn from her before she was faced with something beyond her knowledge and skill.

She stopped outside the stall of the horse she'd seen the man feeding. It came up to her, and she touched its muzzle and neck, reading it. Its heart beat fast, but not desperately fast. Its coat was dry, and its collection of water buckets only half empty. The stable lads had done as she asked, and the horse would survive and thrive. She patted its nose and stepped back.

As she turned toward Brigh's stall, the man stepped out of a nearby stall across the central corridor and approached her.

"Ye saw me feed that beast, aye? And saw what I gave it? Is that why the beast isna ill?"

A rush of fear chilled her. She was alone with the man David believed had sickened MacDhai horses, again and again. She backed away from him.

"I canna let ye tell the MacDhai what ye ken."

The derision in his tone when he named David put her even more on guard. "Why have ye done this?"

"Ye'd like to ken that, would ye? To tell him? Nay, lassie. Ye'll never ken. I'll laugh when yer David finds yer body."

"Nay! Ye willna touch me." She ran for Brigh, but he caught her from behind. She fought, but he was strong, and she was at a disadvantage. The most damage she could do was by kicking at his legs behind her and flailing at his head with her fists. Then she heard voices out in the bailey. The guard! "Let me go! Someone is coming." She raised her voice. "Help!"

He punched her in the temple and everything went black.

17

O nce the Comte left him, David eyed his father's chests. The Comte was right. He'd put off opening them far too long.

They were padlocked, much as the old healer's cabinet of poisonous plants had been. David couldn't help but wonder at the parallel. Would the contents of these be as toxic?

Lacking a key, he knelt and forced the padlocks the same way he'd forced hers, with the hilt of his dirk, removed them and threw them aside. He picked up the top chest and carried it to his desk. Inside, he found several years' worth of journals listing the clan's income and expenses, crop yields, foals and horses traded or sold or deceased. These records were legible and made as much sense to David as the ledgers he'd been trying to understand did not. Many of these would have helped him over the last year as he struggled to learn everything he needed to know about the workings of the clan. Things his father should have taught him, rather than sending him away. Had there been a manager working for his father who left while David was gone? If his father had taken over record keeping after he became ill, that might explain why David could not make any sense of the ledgers he'd been struggling with.

He closed the chest and set it on the floor beside the other two, then carried the next one to the desk. This one contained more clan business. And letters from Toran Lathan and from the Comte to his father about him. Those he would read immediately. The Comte had hinted at other allies in Scotland. David suspected there was much to learn among those pages. He was tempted to start reading, but one more chest remained unopened. He put the second one atop the first, then carried the third chest to the desk.

More letters. He started to close the lid in favor of beginning to read the Comte's letters in the second chest when he recognized the name on the outside of the top missive. *Lianna's*. And the handwriting. *His*.

Dread made him lift the top letter and examine the next and the next and the next, dozens in all. Letters he'd written to her. And even more from her. He spread them out on top of the desk in front of the chest, planted his fists on the desktop, leaned over them and stared, anger at the heartbreak his father had wrought tightening his jaw.

Lianna had written to him. Often. And his father had kept her letters from him. And never allowed his letters to her to leave MacDhai. No wonder she was so angry with him. He had written to her, but she didn't know it. She had never received his letters. She thought he'd forgotten all about her when he left the Aerie. Worse, she thought he'd received her letters and refused to reply.

What a shock Mirielle must have been. Even more than he had feared, Lianna must have felt betrayed. Yet scant minutes later, despite that shock and despite being exhausted from travel, she had thrown herself into saving the Percheron mare. And since then she'd saved nearly every horse in the MacDhai stable, including her own.

Why? The question rang in his head. Why had his father done this? What possible reason could he have had for keeping them from continuing their friendship? Did he fear the feelings they had shared? Unless he found something in his father's correspondence with Toran or with the Comte, he would never know.

He had to tell her. Nay, he had to show her. They could read the letters together. Perhaps then, she would understand his feelings for her, and how abandoned he, too, had felt when he didn't hear from her. How the feelings they'd shared had been genuine. And how he hoped it wasn't too late to find them again.

He gathered up the letters and returned them to the chest, closed it, and returned it to where it had rested. He stacked the other two on top and stood back, heart pounding hard enough to make him light-headed. They'd been there for the year he'd been home, and for years before that, so they'd be safe a few minutes more.

He had to find her. She had to see what he'd found.

He searched for her until Kerr intercepted him to tell him the Comte and Comtesse were already seated for the evening meal. Sharing his news with Lianna would have to wait until afterward. But he would ask her to join him in his solar once the Comte and Comtesse returned to their chamber for the evening.

For David, supper dragged on and on. He wanted Lianna here by his side, but no one had seen her since the afternoon. She wasn't in her chamber, the old healer's herbal, or the library. He'd checked all of those before Kerr found him, and he came down to the great hall, expecting to see her here. But she wasn't here. She wasn't anywhere. Her guards had gathered for the meal and even they watched the stairs as if expecting her to come down them at any moment.

He sent a lad to the stable to see if she was working with the horses, but the lad reported no one was there but the MacDhai guards. Where was she? Why were her Lathan guards not searching for her?

She was helping him save his clan. She'd told him the truth about what he must do to succeed with his clan. She'd told him what he needed to hear when no one else would. She had even been the one to solve the puzzle of how the horses were being poisoned, and by whom. He realized that his future here no longer mattered if it didn't include the lass he had held in his heart and in his memories for the last seven years.

She should be here by now. He needed to go search for her again.

"*Mon fils*," the Comte said and put a hand on his shoulder, "you have not heard a word I have said. Something worries you. What is it?"

David dragged his gaze to the man who had raised his wife, who now missed his daughter. David's lack of sleep made focusing on the Comte difficult enough, without also worrying about Lianna. "I'm sorry. Someone is missing. Someone I care about."

"Then why do you sit here with us? You should go find her."

"How do ye ken 'tis a lass?"

"It is always a woman, is it not?" He chuckled. "Go on. We will be well. La Comtesse has her granddaughter to keep her happy for the evening. I will enjoy the two of them."

David gripped the man's hand in thanks and stood. "I will return as quickly as I can."

"With the woman, *oui*?"

"I hope so." *With her* in every meaning of the word. He'd waited long enough to tell her his truth. He'd hidden how he felt about her. It was time to risk everything, show her the letters, and ask her to become his wife, to be part of his life and his daughter's life, forever.

First he had to find her. Or Murdoch, and get a report from

him. He headed for Bhaltair and the other Lathans' table.
When they noticed him coming, they stood, concern written on
every face. Bhaltair knew he wouldn't seek them out in front of
the entire clan unless something was wrong. Something that
involved Lianna. She would not have disappeared. Not on her
own. She wouldn't leave Brigh, leave her guards behind, or
leave him without a word. The thought of being without her
brought back too many painful memories from years past.
They'd lost each other. Then he'd lost Lucienne. Then his
father. David had lost his way until she found him. He could
not lose Lianna, too. Not again.

LIANNA WOKE up with a pounding headache in a dark, confined
space. Her knees were under her chin. She poked out her
elbows and met the curved surface and edges of wooden staves.
The overwhelming stench of soured ale turned her stomach.
Was she inside a large barrel? Judging by the strength of the
smell, it had been used more than once. She swallowed and
wished she had something to cover her nose. She might never
drink ale again. Dear God, she had to get out of here. How
would anyone find her?

   She couldn't think for the pain in her head. She slowed her
breathing to control her panic, then used one of the methods
her mother taught to tamp down on the pain. Once she calmed,
she focused on how to get out. She could barely lift her arms to
touch the lid's inner surface with her fingertips. She had no
leverage to push it up and open. Under the gagging stink of ale,
she smelled old, rotted wood, but had no room to swing her
foot and kick out any of the staves. She was upright, so she tried
rocking from side to side, hoping the barrel would break open
if it fell over, but it didn't budge. When nothing worked, she
resorted to crying out.

"Help! David! Can anyone hear me? Help me! Somebody, get me out of here!"

She thought she heard low laughter and feared it was her captor, come back to make good on his promise to kill her. She remembered hearing voices before everything went black. That must be why she was still alive. He'd been interrupted, hit her, then dumped her in the nearest empty barrel. Was she still in the stable? There should be guards nearby. Unless they were in on it. The voices stopped and she heard nothing at all, so she called out again. And again.

"Lass?"

Someone finally heard her! "Help!"

"I hear ye. Where are ye?"

"Here!" She pounded on the only surface in reach. "I'm here." In moments, she heard tapping at the lid and swearing. He made the barrel shake a little, but not enough to help.

"I canna get it open. I need a tool. I'll be right back," the voice said.

"Get David!" She didn't want to sound like she was begging, but her eyes filled with tears. "Get David," she said more softly. "Please." An image of him filled her mind, reaching for her, love and longing in his deep-set gaze. Did he love her? At times, she thought he did.

She needed him. She couldn't let whoever had done this hurt him by harming her. David would blame himself and never get over it. And his horses would still be vulnerable. She swore when she got out of this barrel, she would not let that happen. She loved David enough to stay, and to be a mother to Mirielle. She would tell him. And she would help him win over the people of his clan, even though it meant risking her life with people who might fear her talent.

It seemed like hours, but she knew only minutes had passed when she heard clinking and swearing as someone pried off the barrel's top. Hands reached in to grab under her arms and lift her out. "Lianna, love, who did this to ye? Nathair? How long have ye been in there?"

It was David. She turned, crying out as cramped muscles and joints protested suddenly straightening. He wrapped her in his arms and lifted her off her feet, but she groaned, so he put her down again.

"It was him," she said, pacing in a short arc to stretch her cramping legs. "The healer's grandson."

David swore and lifted his head to address the men gathered around them. MacDhais and Lathans, both. "That grandson of a bitch is still around here somewhere," David growled. "Find him."

As soon as the men left him alone with Lianna, David swore he'd kill the bastard with his bare hands, He'd hit her and stuffed her into an old barrel outside the buttery. "Did he do anything else to hurt ye?" He dreaded the answer, but he had to know.

"He hit me on the head when we heard someone approaching the stable door. But before that, he threatened to kill me."

"He'll never touch anyone else once I get done with him," David promised.

"Is that so?" Nathair appeared from the darkness behind barrels stacked between the buttery and the wash house. Before David could react, he grabbed Lianna's hair and pulled her back against him, a blade to her throat. "How would ye like to watch her bleed, *Laird* MacDhai?"

She didn't scream, but David wished she'd had time to do just that. Their men could not have spread out too far yet. He could see dismay and anger in her eyes. "If ye so much as scratch her, ye willna live to see moonrise."

"If ye take one step closer, neither will she," the man threatened.

David took a chance and slid his gaze from his enemy to Lianna. She quirked her lips, a gesture the man behind her could not see. That quick change of expression told David she was ready, and what to expect. She'd done this with her brothers countless times, and countless times they'd fallen for it. Or rather, she'd fallen, leaving her brother holding empty air, vulnerable to attack. David blinked his agreement and readied himself to move. He dared not appear to tense up or Nathair would notice. Instead, David slid his gaze back to the man, and shifted his stance at the same time, unlocking his knees and flexing them ever so slightly. "What do ye want?"

"I want ye gone. Her, too. Ye bring nothing but strangers and foreigners to MacDhai. The clan isna the same. The keep isna the same. Pah!" He turned his head aside and spat, then looked back at David. "Ye and yer Continental horses and yer new ideas."

His movements shifted the blade a fraction away from Lianna's throat, the opening she needed. She tossed her head back, catching her captor on the nose with a satisfying crack. Then she went limp and dropped while he howled with the pain she'd caused. She ducked out of David's way as he tackled the man around the chest and fought to control the blade in his hand as they fell.

David felt her roll clear from under his legs. Then he was too busy holding Nathair's arm over his head and pounding the hand holding the blade against a rock to be aware of her.

The bastard had a grip of iron. He wouldn't release the blade. He writhed and fought, trying to force David off.

But if David let go for an instant, before he could roll clear, the blade would be buried in his back. He hung on grimly and used his knees and feet to do as much damage to the man's lower body as he could. Nathair groaned as they rolled to their sides. He must be tiring. David could see desperation in his narrow gaze.

Just then, Lianna delivered a punishing kick to Nathair's kidneys. He cried out and his grip on the knife loosened slightly. If he survived, he'd piss blood for days.

But David meant to end this now. Lianna was putting herself in danger to defend him and fight her attacker. He kept a strong grip on the man's wrist with one hand, hauled back with the other and slugged the point of his chin. Nathair's head snapped back with a resounding crack. He went limp.

David wasn't fooled. He kept control of the hand holding the blade until Lianna pulled it from Nathair's grip. Only then did David accept that he was really knocked out. He rolled aside, then shoved Nathair onto his belly.

Lianna used the man's own blade to cut a length of rope from a loop by the wash house.

David tied his hands behind his back, then shoved to his feet, tempted by pure frustration to follow Lianna's example and kick the man in the kidneys. Instead, he bent forward, hands on knees, and got his breathing under control. Lianna stood aside and watched him until he straightened and raised a hand. "I'm well. Ye needna use yer strength to care for me."

"Took ye long enough," she observed, wiping blood from a shallow cut on her neck. "Do ye ken why he did this?"

David gave her a look. Long enough? "Not yet. If we havena killed him, I will have answers. If not from him, then from his grandmother." He touched her throat gently. "And he hurt ye again. He'll pay for that."

"I'm fine." She crossed her arms and backed up a step, then took a deep breath, bent and put a hand on the man's neck, ignoring her own injury. "He's alive, for now. Ye shouldna hit him so hard. Do ye want me to wake him?"

"Nay. I'll not have ye risk yerself for the likes of him."

"Ye want answers, aye?"

David ran his hands through his hair, his gaze lifted to the clouds above them. What was he to do with this woman? First she fought with him, then she insisted on taking his enemy's pain into herself to make sure David got the information he needed.

"He's going to be out that long?"

"Aye. Hours. Or he may not wake up. His head hit a rock when he fell."

He shook his head and capitulated. "Then do what ye must."

Lianna dropped to her knees, winced, and took a breath, then put her hands on her attacker, one on his neck, one on skin exposed by a tear in the back of his shirt. "God, I hate this part," she muttered.

David managed not to laugh, but it was a near thing. Lianna glanced up at him, suspicion in every nuance of her expression.

"He had a knife to my throat. And now I have to touch his skin." She gave an unladylike shudder.

David pursed his lips. His sympathy was for her, not Nathair. "Let him die."

"Nay, he's going to answer yer questions first." She closed her eyes, shutting David out.

He settled on the ground nearby with a soft groan, ready to wait as long as it took. In moments, Bhaltair and Murdoch arrived. David glanced at Lianna, then waved them off. Bhaltair nodded and pulled Murdoch away, headed into the keep. David was certain the next person out that door would carry a tray of food and drink for Lianna.

He wasn't wrong. Bhaltair himself did the honors. Good thing. It took a man his size to handle the weight of what he'd loaded on the tray he carried at chest-height. The pile of food nearly reached his chin, flanked by pitchers.

"Ye are planning to feed how many people?" He spoke

softly, so as not to disturb the work Lianna was doing on his behalf.

"I never ken how much effort goes into...that," he said as he set down the tray and settled on the ground beside David.

David marveled that the ground didn't shake.

Bhaltair nodded toward Lianna, still bent over their attacker. "She's going to be stiff as hell."

"Aye, first from the barrel he stuffed her into, then this. At least she got a few of her own licks in."

"Good lass. I trained her well."

"Ye and her brothers, ye mean."

Bhaltair shrugged massive shoulders.

Lianna chose that moment to straighten and open her eyes. She nodded appreciation to Bhaltair when she saw the tray he'd brought, then winced and rubbed her head. "Bind him well and lock him up somewhere," she said and gestured to the man beside her. "He'll sleep till morning. Then he's all yers."

"Thank ye," David said and pushed to his feet. What a warrior this woman was. "Ye handled yerself well, Lianna. Ye kept him from killing me."

Her eyebrows raised, but she nodded. "Ye saved me, too, remember?"

"Aye." He didn't want to think about how close he'd come to losing her. "I'll be back in a few minutes. While I'm gone, get started on that." He pointed at the tray and gave her a meaningful stare.

"I'll help carry him," Bhaltair said and stood, then split the night with a whistle so loud, even Lianna jumped.

"Warn me, will ye?"

Her complaint didn't faze him. He watched for a moment, then nodded as another of the Lathan guards approached. "Stand guard over Lianna," he instructed. "We'll be back shortly."

He pulled the attacker off the ground by his arms with a

wrench that should have dislocated his shoulders. Then he tossed the man over his shoulder like he weighed nothing, and gestured for David to lead the way.

David heard Lianna's tired snicker and studiously avoided meeting her gaze. Instead, he headed for the keep, forcing himself to look forward to the morning, not back at Lianna, resting on the ground against the wall of the buttery with her Lathan guard. At least now she could eat and rest. Tomorrow, he'd get answers.

18

Clémence met them at the keep's door. "Laird, I cannot find Mirielle. She is not with her *grand-mere*. Not in her bed. No one has seen her."

David ran back to Lianna. "Ye must wake him up." He reached for her hand to help her up.

"What?" She set aside the morsel she'd been about to eat and glanced at her guard, then let David assist her.

"Wake him up. My daughter is missing."

Murdoch hurried up then and David told him, "'Tis Mirielle. Clémence canna find her."

"I heard," Murdoch told him.

"Check the herbal. Find the old healer. She may ken where he put my daughter."

"Are ye sure he has her?"

"Are ye sure he doesna? Search the keep. Wake everyone if ye must, but find her."

Murdoch turned away and called for his men. David turned back to Lianna and took her hand. Together with Bhaltair and his burden, they went to the solar. Bhaltair dumped the man on David's hastily-cleared worktable, then left to join the search.

Lianna didn't make him ask a second time. She touched the man's head, closed her eyes for a moment, grimaced, then stepped back and nodded. "In a moment..."

Nathair groaned. His head rocked side to side, then his eyes opened, unfocused at first. When he saw David, they narrowed and he spat. He missed.

"The length of yer life," David told him, "depends on how quickly ye tell me where my daughter is. And yer grandmother."

Nathair turned his head away, which put his gaze on Lianna. He grinned.

David grabbed his chin and twisted his head back. "Look at me. She isna here to help ye. She's only here to make sure I dinna kill ye too fast." David took a step closer and let his gaze travel the man's body, then returned to regard his face. "Ye must be uncomfortable, with yer hands bound underneath ye like that."

The man frowned, then nodded.

Thinking about how Bhaltair had jerked Nathair off the ground, he added, "It must put a terrible strain on yer shoulders. I can help ye. But first, ye must tell me something. Where is my daughter?"

"Ye'd like to ken, aye?"

"I asked nicely. I willna for much longer. Where is she?"

"With my gran."

"And where is yer gran?" David kept his tone light, fighting back the fear and fury filling him every time he met this man's gaze.

"Where ye'll never find her."

"With the MacPhersons?"

"They promised to take care of us."

"Take care of ye? More likely, they'd take over the clan and expose ye as the traitors ye are. How long do ye think ye'd last, then?"

They couldn't have left MacDhai, could they? The gate closed at sunset. This time of year, that was well after the evening meal. How long had Mirielle been missing?

David clenched his fists, but after one glance in Lianna's direction, kept them at his sides. She was exhausted. He could beat this man nearly to death, but if he didn't give up his secrets, she'd pay the price to bring him back every time David went too far. He couldn't do that to her. He wouldn't. He fought to control his fear and fury.

"Nay," David said as Nathair's expression failed to reflect any dismay. "They're still here. Oh, I'll find her. Ye will tell me. The discomfort ye feel now is naught to what my men are getting ready for ye in the dungeon. Have ye ever been down there? Nay? Not even as a lad, going where ye were forbidden to go? Well, ye have much to experience, then."

Lianna's face had gone pale. David paced to the end of the table beyond his captive's head. Out of his sight, David rolled his eyes and shook his head. She took a breath, telling David she understood.

He moved back into Nathair's line of sight, but kept pacing. "Our ancestors kenned how to extract secrets while keeping their prisoners alive and screaming. Ye'll be screaming what I want to ken before I'm done with ye." David kept talking as he moved, watching the man's complexion fade, the more he embellished. It was all a lie, meant to intimidate Nathair into telling David what he desperately needed to know. MacDhai's dungeon had no torture chamber the likes of which David described. His men weren't down there preparing anything. They were searching the keep, and if they failed to find Mirielle, they'd search the village, the glens and the mountains in all directions until they brought her home. Or until David terrified this man into speaking.

Lianna caught his attention when he stopped for breath, held up a hand and tipped her head toward their captive's legs. Then she moved to the man's bound feet. His boots were gone, maybe kicked off in the fight. David hadn't noticed until she pointed to Nathair's feet. She pulled down his hose, touched a finger to one ankle, and shuddered. But she didn't stop. She untied the knot and without removing the coil of rope holding the man's legs bound together at the ankle, loosened it.

He shrieked and drummed his heels on the table.

David frowned. What had she done?

"'Tis only blood returning to yer feet," she said.

David was sure the information was as much for his benefit as his prisoner's.

"It doesna harm ye at all. In fact, ye need that blood to keep the flesh of yer feet alive, ye ken? Before the MacDhai's men cut them off, they'll want to be sure ye can feel them. But for now, 'tis damn painful for a few minutes. Imagine how yer hands, arms, and shoulders are going to feel." The look she gave the man was positively feral, then she gripped the ends of the rope and yanked them apart, tightening the looped bindings yet again, and secured the knot.

"I thought ye a healer, but ye ken how to harm, too, aye? Like my gran." The man turned wild eyes to David. "She'll be in the dungeon?"

David didn't bother to meet her gaze. He just nodded. Then smiled, imagining all the things he'd like to do to this man, but wouldn't.

"Dinna let her near me. She's a devil! I'll tell ye everything. Just keep her away!"

"Then talk. Where are they?"

"In the back, inside the buttery. Not outside in the empties where I stowed *her*. Behind the full barrels. Gran has a taste for ale, ye ken. The wee lass is tied up." He choked off at the look that crossed David's face at that admission. "She isna harmed, I swear it. 'Tis just to keep her quiet with Gran."

"Watch him," he growled to Lianna. "If he moves, hurt him."

She bared her teeth at Nathair, and David ran for the bailey. When he found Lianna, he'd been close to his daughter, but he'd never known.

The buttery was behind the kitchen, but could only be entered from outside. He saw Murdoch and waved to him as he ran. Murdoch and a few of his men angled to meet him. "Buttery," David said before he asked.

David entered first and made his way to the back, past rows of butts and kegs of ale and mead stored for years. He couldn't think when he'd last been in here. Murdoch followed him, a torch held aloft. This was no place for flame, but it would be pitch black in here until the moon rose and some light leaked in the door and the high-set windows on either side of it.

Then he saw her. Mirielle, curled into a ball as far from Nathair's old gran as the rope connecting her to the old healer would allow. With an oath, he gestured for Murdoch to take the old woman, pulled his dirk, cut the rope and gathered his daughter into his arms. She blinked awake as he pulled aside the rag tied over her mouth. "Papa?"

"Aye, love. I've got ye. All is well."

"Nay, that mean man and that old gran want to hurt ye. My gran is not like her," she added with clear contempt in her voice.

That old gran was sputtering awake, screeching as Murdoch and another of his men pulled her to her feet. They were not gentle about it.

"I ken it," David told Mirielle as he walked out of the buttery, leaving the grandmother to Murdoch and his men. "But they canna hurt us, and they never will. We are safe, ye and I, and everyone else here." He no longer cared about the old healer. Mirielle was safe. But he turned back as Murdoch approached, leading his men and the old woman out of the building. "Lock her up, but not with her grandson. I'll get Mirielle settled, then I have a few more questions for both of them."

LIANNA TURNED her grin on their captive. "Alone at last. Just not how ye pictured it, aye?" She paced in a wide circle around the table. Though he was still tied up, she kept carefully out of what would be his reach if he got an arm loose. She wanted him to think she was confident and in charge of him, but that didn't mean she wasn't careful. Good thing her knees were below his line of sight. They were shaking hard enough that if she stopped moving, surely he would notice how they made the rest of her vibrate.

Her fury from the attack had abated, and all she wanted to do was throw herself into David's arms and stay there forever. Why had he left her alone with this man? "Ye could save yerself a lot of trouble—and pain—if ye tell me why ye did all this. Why poison the horses? Why take me and the lass? What do ye have against the MacDhai?"

Her captive did his best to follow her movements as she walked around him, twisting his head from side to side, leaning his torso to improve his angle. She was completely out of his view only when she stood behind his head. He couldn't crane his neck back far enough to see her unless she stood too close for comfort.

That she would not do.

Those few seconds out of his sight gave her a chance to take a deep breath, clench her fists, or do anything else that helped her fight her fear of being left alone with him.

Then she'd move into his view again, her guise of calm confidence firmly in place. She had to force herself to look at him. "Ye may as well tell me. The MacDhai's men will get it out of ye soon enough."

Nathair had the nerve to laugh. "Keep telling yerself that. Ye will be disappointed."

Something in his tone made her pause by his side. His grin went daft, lips pulled back over his teeth, and his eyes narrowed. Shaken, she took a step back.

He struck, rolling toward her, then reached for her. She tried to dance back but he was too fast. Before she knew it, he'd dragged her atop him, his hands a slowly tightening vise around her throat.

"I've got ye now, witch, and I'll finish what I started. Ye want to ken why we did all this? Money. Revenge. Ye'll have to ask Gran about that. Ye'll see her in Hell soon enough. When I'm done with ye, before I disappear, I'll finish her, too."

He was mad. She fought to break his hold, fought to breathe, to scream, but nothing worked. He kept increasing the pressure on her throat until she saw stars.

She was dimly aware of the solar door opening, David framed in the doorway, then with a roar, he leapt for her and pulled the man's hands from her throat. Lianna fell back, gasping for air, pulling David with her. He twisted as they fell, so she landed on her side on top of him, rather than crushed under his greater weight.

As she rolled off him and David sat up, Nathair also sat up and sawed at the rope around his ankles. He had a *sgian dubh*! As she pushed to her feet, David stood and shoved her toward the solar door.

"Call the guards." The rope binding Nathair's feet parted. David pulled his dirk and got between her and their captive. "Ye canna get away, so drop that."

"I'll finish ye before they get here," the man taunted and charged at David, his short blade held over his head for a downward slashing blow.

David ducked aside, but that cleared the path toward Lianna.

Nathair took advantage. His blade made a bright arc as it came rushing toward her.

Instinctively, she reached up to block his arm. Blood sprayed across her torso, shocking a shriek from her. Then David yanked Nathair back and dropped him face-first on the floor. He pulled his dirk from the man's neck as he fell.

Lianna stood, frozen, her gaze jumping first to the blood on her shirt, then down to the dead man, then up to David's bloody arm and hand, then back around again.

David bent to make sure he was dead, then wiped his dripping dirk on the man's back and tucked his blade away. Only then did he move to Lianna and wrap her in his arms.

"Lass, I'm sorry. I never shouldha left ye alone with him."

"I kept walking around the table. He kept moving. I thought he was trying to watch me. He must have been fighting his bonds. Loosening them. He grabbed me." She fisted her hands on David's chest. "He must have had the blade tucked in the back of his trews." He'd loosened the rope enough to get a hand out of it, then both hands. He'd attacked her, then gone for his blade when David pulled her away.

"Ye are safe now. I think we all are."

"The horses, too?"

David laughed. "Aye, them, too."

"He said they did this for money and revenge. To ask the old healer."

"I will, never fear. Once I talk to her, we'll ken what all of this meant."

"Then what are ye waiting for?"

"Now that I have ye in my arms, I'll nay hurry. The old woman isna going anywhere. But ye must let go of me, so we can go somewhere else to talk."

Lianna realized she had a death grip on his shoulders. She

released him, then stepped out of his arms, shaking her cramping hands. David's expression told her he hadn't finished with whatever he wanted to say.

Kerr arrived then. "What happened?"

"He got loose and tried to kill Lianna—again. He's dead. Get him out of here. And have someone bring a basin of hot water for Lianna."

Kerr nodded and went to get help.

David took her arm and led her out into the great hall, to a seat by the large hearth. There they washed away the worst of the night's violence and the maid took the basin away. Another brought food and cider.

She took one look at the trencher and turned away. She didn't have the stomach for food right now. Instead the cider was sweet and cold and helped wash away the night's violence.

David didn't touch the food or the cider. He watched her until she slowed down, then he took a breath. "I ken this isna the right time..."

"Right time for what?" Lianna looked up from pouring another cup of cider. She set down the pitcher when she saw his expression, solemn, yet hopeful.

"When I saw ye with that blade to yer throat, and again with his hands around yer neck, I couldna breathe. Lianna, I canna lose ye. Yet twice tonight, I thought I might."

"Ye didna lose me. We fought, and we won." She tipped her cup in a mock toast, then set it aside. "But we're not done finding out all ye need to ken. We have more to do. So, what are ye trying to say to me?"

"I found yer letters to me. And mine to ye. My father kept them from us, but he saved them."

"Ye wrote to me? Where are they?"

"Aye. I ken that ye believed I left the Aerie and never thought about ye again, but I didna. The letters are in a chest in the solar. We can read them together, later, after all this is settled. Lianna, we didna forget each other. He stood in our way. He kept us apart."

"Ye wrote to me? I could kill yer da for what he did."

"Not if I killed him first. But he's out of our reach, and despite what he did, we're here, together."

"Seven years, David. He cost us seven years." She looked away. "What am I saying? If he hadna done what he did, ye wouldna have Mirielle."

"And ye..."

"I am not as important as yer daughter."

"Ye are important to me. Canna ye see that? I've been trying to tell ye. To show ye." He reached out and took her hands in his. "I think of ye all the time. I want ye, ye ken that, aye? But more than that, I love ye. Marry me, Lianna. Stay with me forever. Or none of this will have been worthwhile."

It had been an awful day, but suddenly she could put it all behind her. She no longer cared that because of his father's schemes, she'd thought David had forgotten her, and broken her heart. Or that he was once married to and loved another woman, who gave him a daughter. All that was in the past.

They'd forged a new bond—even more fully than she'd dared hope. David loved her.

"I love ye, too, David MacDhai. I always have. I never stopped loving ye, even when I thought I'd never see ye again. When I thought ye still had a wife. Being yers, being with ye the rest of our lives, aye, that makes me very happy. Of course, I will marry ye."

He stood and pulled her up into his embrace, then kissed her, gently, reverently. She kissed him back, gladly, hungrily, not caring who might see them.

David leaned back, and his lips parted for a moment before he spoke. "Yer da..."

Lianna gave him a reassuring smile. "He'll be thrilled. My brothers, less so. But I dinna care what they think. Ye have always been the lad I longed for. Ye are the man I want to spend my life with."

"Ye didna mention yer mother."

"She practically told me to marry ye as we were leaving the Aerie." She grinned. "Though she was very subtle about it."

David laughed. "Then we'd best send word for her to prepare for a wedding."

"Aye. Da will want to invite all his allies. Ma will want the entire clan and all my siblings, which means Jamie will have to travel here, too."

"So, a big wedding?"

"Aye, probably more people than ye have ever seen in one place at one time. Ach, nay, likely ye saw more in France."

"That doesna matter. I will wed ye in front of three people or three thousand."

Kerr approached then and cleared his throat, his presence a jarring reminder of their unfinished business. For David's sake, Lianna fought not to glare at him. So much for enjoying a few minutes of uninterrupted happiness.

"That matter is taken care of," Kerr said as David frowned up at him. "The maids are...removing the last traces. And the grandmother is guarded, upstairs."

"Come with us, Kerr." David took Lianna's hand. "Are ye willing to join me? Ye'll understand better if she admits to her part in all this. To the poison."

She didn't want to talk to the grandmother, but neither did she want to leave David's side. "I'll go with ye, but we already ken what she used. The Dule tree seeds."

"Too bad we canna hang the grandson from one of those trees," Kerr remarked. "'Twould be fitting."

David's expression was grim, but Lianna appreciated the irony.

He led her upstairs to a chamber guarded by one of Murdoch's men.

The old woman sitting inside looked up when the door opened and they walked in, then gasped at the blood on Lianna's shirt, now smeared on David's too. "My grandson?" Tears leaked from the corners of her eyes.

"Dead," David confirmed. "It didna have to end this way. So make his death worth something. Tell me why."

She dropped her head into her hands. "Lachlan Mackintosh."

"The Mackintosh chief's murder?" David frowned and turned to Lianna. "Da's foster-brother was blamed for killing the Mackintosh chief a dozen years ago, while I was fostered with ye. In fact, I mentioned it to yer da that first meeting at the Aerie." He turned back to the old healer. "What has that to do with harming MacDhai's horses?"

"'Twas the reason yer da sent ye away again." She crossed her arms and bent forward over them, as if her belly hurt. "Mackintosh kept the men who killed their chief in chains for years. One of them was my poor son. But that wasna enough. Then they tortured them and finally, hanged them." She straightened on a groan and narrowed her eyes at David. "They put my son's head on a pike! When that news came, yer da feared more reprisals and sent ye to the Continent for safekeeping, not because of some lass. I'd lost my son. Yers protected ye, something I couldna do for my lad. So I took it upon myself to avenge him. To ruin the MacDhai line—or destroy it. I couldna kill yer da's foster-brother, so I took yer da's life instead."

"Ye killed him?" David shook his head. "Nay. I was told he was ill."

She cackled, and the hairs rose on the back of Lianna's neck.

"There are many ways to kill," the old woman taunted. "Never anger a healer."

David looked to Lianna. She nodded. She could think of many ways to use those plants in the locked cabinet downstairs.

"Were ye planning to kill me?" David's tone was flat, emotionless.

"Ye have only a daughter. Since yer line ends with ye, I planned to force ye back to France. 'Tis why yer horses are sick. So ye would suffer the disgrace of being removed as laird. So the council would name another in yer place. I thought I'd made sure of that. Dule tree seeds will kill horses. Eventually. If the council didna act, some woulda died. But then ye brought *her* to MacDhai." She glared at Lianna. "Ye let her question me. And ye chose to stand with her over me. So I told my Nathair I didna care if both of ye died tonight. Yet here ye stand. And my grandson..."

David's gaze locked with Kerr's, then he turned back to the old woman. "Who else is helping ye?"

"No one."

"Ye lie," Kerr barked.

"What about MacPherson?" David's tone was calmer, but no less sharp.

"How did ye ken about that?"

"MacPhersons kenned the horses were sick. And yer grandson admitted helping them. He said ye would explain. How long have ye been planning this?"

"I had to wait for the trees. The seeds. MacPhersons cornered Nathair out in the glen two months ago. Rather than kill him, they used him. They wanted to ruin MacDhai's reputation and take our horses while they did it. Since it fell in line with what I'd planned, I let Nathair do it."

"Why should I believe ye?"

"Because my grandson is dead." She gestured at the blood on David's sleeve. "Killed by his laird. His father died because of yer foster-uncle. In trying to ruin yer family, I destroyed mine, too."

They left her then, and David sent a guard to call the council to his solar. "Stay with me," he said, when Lianna made to leave him. "Ye had a role in ruining the plot against the horses, so ye should have a say in this. The council may have questions ye can answer." After they gathered, he related what the old healer confessed. Kerr confirmed it, then David asked the council for recommendations.

"Hang her. 'Tis the just reward for what she put in motion," the youngest of the council demanded. Others agreed.

"Clan law demands it," another added, his expression grim. "Despite her long service to the clan, she murdered yer da and tried to harm ye and the clan. Ye have nay choice, Laird."

David's expression mirrored his. "There's nay alternative in the law?"

"None."

"But is there nay room for mercy in her case?"

Lianna didn't know these men, but she was glad to see one of them trying to calm the angry council.

"What do ye suggest?" David's hands were tied, but Lianna could see that despite everything, he was reluctant.

"Banishment. Let the MacPhersons have her. They'll ken we discovered their plot and will keep their distance."

"Nay! She kens too much about the clan and the keep," one objected who'd been silent up to now. "She must hang from one of those trees she used to poison our horses."

Ayes rang around the solar at that suggestion. Lianna shivered at the memory of Kerr suggesting a similar fate for her grandson.

"Very well," David finally agreed. "She is condemned by her own words. She'll hang at noon tomorrow."

Kerr, who'd stayed by the door to keep the meeting private, spoke up. "I'll tell her." At David's nod, he left the room.

Lianna stood to follow him and David held up a hand. "Thank ye, Lianna, from the clan, for all ye have done to save MacDhai—not just the horses, but our good name and our future."

The council echoed David's words with *ayes* and clapping.

Lianna accepted their approbation, her gaze on David. "I'm glad I could help." Then she let her gaze sweep the chamber. "Good night to ye all," she said, wondering if any on the council would deem it so. With his decision weighing on him, would David spend this night dreading tomorrow? With nothing more she could do, she left to find her bed at last.

❧

LIANNA WOKE the next morning from a nightmare in which Nathair still had his hands around her throat, his foul breath in her face, and her life slipping into blackness. Shuddering, she sat up, then threw aside the covers, left the bed and opened the shutters to let light and air into her chamber. She stood in the open window, breathing great lungfuls of cool air, letting the morning sun warm her face. The light dazzling her eyes helped her shake off the unsettling effects of the dream. By the angle, she judged she'd slept late into the morning. Then she recalled what was destined to occur at midday.

A soft knock at the door preceded a serving lass with a tray filled with bread, butter, honey and a pitcher of cider. "The MacDhai asked that I bring this to ye," she said and put it on the small table by the hearth. "He thought ye might wish to rest today, and I'm to bring ye anything else ye would like. He said to tell ye they found the old healer cold dead in her bed this morning, so there is nay need for ye to bestir yerself."

"Thank ye," Lianna murmured, though her heart was pounding. Dead? "That is sad but welcome news." As angry as David had every right to be, she knew he had dreaded hanging the old woman. Perhaps her heart had given out during the night. Or she'd had some poison hidden on her person. Either way, she'd found an easier death than she would have met at noon.

"I heard they found her with an empty vial beside her," the maid confirmed, as if reading her thoughts.

Lianna nodded. She could see the old woman choosing poison over the indignity of a noose. Poison was her chosen method to kill David's father and sicken the horses. She'd prefer it.

Lianna recalled the lass was waiting for her to tell her what else she might want. She gestured at the tray as her stomach rumbled. "This is plenty for now."

The girl stirred the fire in the hearth and added more fuel before leaving Lianna her privacy.

Lianna fell to, suddenly ravenous, ate her fill, then yawned. Perhaps David's idea was a good one. Unless someone called for her help with an animal, she would stay in. She eyed the bed. Its plush covers and promises of peace and quiet she'd yet to experience since she'd arrived here lured her back.

Yet one thought kept intruding. How was Mirielle? The lass had been traumatized last night. How was she today? Lianna couldn't rest until she knew, so she dressed and headed for the nursery.

The Comtesse greeted her as she entered. "Mirielle, she is sleeping. I read to her a happy story."

"I'm glad," Lianna told her. "Do ye ken if she slept well last night? She was so upset."

The Comtesse shook her head. "*Non*, Clémence says she fretted and awoke several times through the night. Her father stayed with her for hours, but he must sleep, too, *oui*?"

Yet he was up before her and sending a servant to see to her needs. Jenny must still be asleep. She had been awakened by the commotion and had stayed up to see Lianna safely to bed.

"*Oui*. It was an upsetting day. I'm so sorry they frightened Mirielle. But the man is dead and the old woman, too. She'll never harm anyone again."

"That is good." The Comtesse took a deep breath. "There is

something I wish to say to you." She patted the seat beside her. "Please."

Lianna joined her, wondering what was on her mind.

"I think you will be a good mother to my granddaughter."

Lianna didn't know what to say to that. David had only offered for her last night. "How do ye ken that?" News must travel as fast here as it did in the Aerie.

"I have lived long enough to know when a man is in love. David looks at you that way. I hope you will be happy together."

So the Comtesse hadn't yet heard they were betrothed. Lianna supposed David would make an announcement at supper. She was tempted to share her news now, but decided to wait for David.

And now that they knew who and what had harmed the horses and had put a stop to it, she could return to the Aerie until the wedding. But the thought of leaving David and Mirielle made her heart heavy. Best she think about something else, like what she might uniquely be able to do for Mirielle's grandmother, and thereby, for Mirielle.

Lianna took her hands. "I hope so, too" she said to distract the Comtesse as she used her talent to put the woman into a light sleep. She closed her eyes and sought what made the woman so ill. Parts of her lungs were hardened and filled with fluid. She helped where she could, quickly, so that the Comtesse wouldn't notice anything odd about her touch when she awoke. Instead, with her help, the Comtesse would go back to France in better health and in better spirits, knowing her granddaughter would be well loved.

19

The Lathans arrived at MacDhai a hundred strong, bringing carts laden with Lianna's belongings, tents, flour, apples, eggs, and other food that would travel several days, Cook and her top helpers, guards, and more. David turned a bit pale, but welcomed them through MacDhai's gates with more aplomb than Lianna thought he'd be able to muster. He told her then that this wedding would be the biggest event in MacDhai memory, and he hoped he didn't embarrass her by forgetting anyone—like her father.

Lianna had laughed at his discomfort, but today, the memory of that laughter resurfaced to plague her. Standing before the small kirk in the keep, waiting for the priest to open the doors and let people in, David looked masterful, eager, and happy. She was the one now pale and nervous, sitting on Brigh's back, across and farther down the bailey, wondering what she had agreed to. While she loved David and Mirielle to distraction, doubts about the radical change she was making in her life had crept in.

Then she recalled sitting with David, reading their letters to each other in turn, and her doubts evaporated. They'd laughed and cried, hearts full, over the hope and longing, the dismay and distress in each letter. And finally, the grief and hope for the future contained in the very last letters they'd written to each other all those years ago. Her memories of writing those letters filled her with poignant emotions.

David's expression as he read his words to her made her believe that he'd felt much the same. Sad, frustrated, even angry, yet always with the hope that she would respond to him. It broke her heart that for years, he thought she never did.

She loved David. Marrying him today meant they'd never lose each other again.

Lianna sat sidesaddle atop Brigh, who was bedecked with garlands of spring flowers matching the ones pinned in Lianna's hair. She waited by the stable to make the short but symbolic ride to the kirk. Horses were MacDhai's lifeblood. Lianna had been riding Brigh when she found David. She rode to MacDhai on her, and had worked tirelessly to save MacDhai horses. Athdar stood near the kirk, ready for David when the time came to leave the kirk as a married man. She could no more imagine marrying David without Brigh and Athdar as part of the ceremony than David could imagine doing it without Mirielle in attendance.

The lass was in the custody of her grandparents, though while they waited, she ran back and forth between them and her father. Her nurse Clémence tried to keep up, looking harried. But the Comtesse! Everyone remarked on how much better she seemed. Lianna had told her mother what she'd done, and Aileanna suggested more ways to help her, if Lianna had the chance before the pair returned to France. Today, the woman stood tall and steady next to her Comte, then bent to cuddle her granddaughter, all without difficulty and with good color in her cheeks.

This wedding was truly a combined event, Lathan and MacDhai. Lathan guards were paired with MacDhai guards around the keep. Bhaltair took point on the outer walls. Conall remained in the care of one of the stable lads he'd bonded with and Damhan, one of her guards, near the kirk.

The MacDhai cook had complained at first about the Lathan cook and kitchen staff's invasion in her kitchen, but eventually, the two women came to some accommodation. For the past week, they had worked as smoothly together as could be hoped for. And accompanied by sufficient guards to frighten any quarry over the next mountain, the Lathan and the MacDhai had hunted together, surprisingly successfully, to feed the enormous crowd.

Aileanna and Lianna's younger sister Eilidh had brought all manner of garments, but even more importantly, they'd brought Moina, the Lathan's head seamstress and dressmaker. Lianna had not envied her task, to alter one of the many dresses they'd brought into one suitable for her wedding. Or to create one from scratch out of the fabrics, all with the nervous bride, her mother and sister looking over her shoulder. But the end result pleased them all.

Lianna, now that she could see the adoration on David's face, was certain he approved as well.

In the end, she had not worn her mother's wedding dress, green for the healer, though Moina had changed it here and there to suit Lianna's shape and preferences. Instead, Lianna had fallen in love with fabric the color of bright summer berries that Moina brought with her. The dress she created suited this warm early summer day, leaving Lianna's shoulders almost bare save for straps of the same fabric. Translucent fabric in the same color served as a wrap around her shoulders. More of the same floated over the skirt and fell in a layer so light and sheer, it mimicked the glow of a beautiful dawn. As Lianna moved, the skirt swirled around her. She pronounced it magical.

Her mother had been moved to tears, and unable to say

anything. Her sister Eilidh merely told Moina she hoped she'd create something as wonderful for her when she married, though she hoped that would not happen for many more years.

Most of Lianna's brothers remained at the Aerie. Drummond, as heir, was required to hold the keep against his father's return, or to take over as laird if the worst happened. Tavish remained behind to help Drummond. And more than likely, out of embarrassment for how the brothers had treated David when he came to Lathan injured and in desperate need of help.

But Jamie had come with his bride, Aftyn. Lianna had enjoyed seeing her again. At their wedding, Eilidh had told her new sister-in-law that with her wed to Jamie, the number of girls finally equaled the boys. Lianna was about to bring a new brother into the family. She hoped Eilidh would not be too disappointed to once again be outnumbered.

Among the other surprise guests were her father's best friend Jamie, for whom her brother had been named. Married to the Fletcher, he'd left his wife at home, seeing to her clan. And Donal MacNabb, arms master to her grandfather and her father until he married the MacKyrie laird and seer, Ellie. She, too, remained with her clan. Lianna would have liked to speak to her about Tavish, Eilidh's twin. Given his burgeoning talent, Lianna expected their mother had already written to Ellie, making Lianna's concern redundant.

Lianna took a breath and looked around her. She would soon be a married woman. Wedded and bedded, and lady of MacDhai, married to its laird. She knew Da approved—he'd worried for years about finding a match for her who would love her and keep her safe, somewhere her talent would be accepted. Here, after she saved MacDhai's horses and Murdoch, her talent was accepted by most, if not truly understood. Over time, everyone would learn its value.

The kirk's doors opened, and the conversation in the bailey swiftly fell silent. The priest motioned for the families to enter, so the grandparents went first, with Mirielle. Aileanna reached up and grasped Lianna's hand, then took Eilidh's arm and joined Toran, both Jamies and Donal. They entered together. Kerr, Murdoch, and the rest of David's council went in next, followed by Lathan clan members and friends, leaving the bailey lined with MacDhais, staff and servants, none of whom would fit in the small kirk. They would watch the ceremony through the open doors.

It was time. Lianna leaned forward and patted Brigh's neck. Ever attuned to her mistress, Brigh waited a beat for Lianna to straighten, then walked slowly forward. Lianna's gaze never left David, but she was peripherally aware of the people lining both sides of her path, clapping, cheering and shouting well-wishes as she passed. Lianna smiled and waved. Before she knew it, Brigh stopped in front of the kirk. David walked up to her and raised his arms. Lianna leaned forward and let him grasp her around her waist and lower her to the ground, her arms around his shoulders. She relished the comfort of his touch, his scent, and the smile he gave her as he set her on her feet and gazed into her eyes.

"Ready, my love?"

"For years, aye. For ye, always."

He took her hand and kissed the back of it, then walked with her into the kirk, down the center aisle past their family and friends, until they reached the priest, Mirielle's tutor, and knelt before him.

The prayers, the ceremony, all passed in a blur until the priest asked David if he took her to wife, to love and honor, to protect and cherish all their lives. The sound of David's enthusiastic, "Aye," made her heart beat fast, and she drew a breath, knowing her turn to make the same vow came next.

But David held up a hand and stopped the priest before he could ask her the same questions. She turned to David, confused by the pause.

He smiled, reassuring her, then pulled her to her feet and kept her hands in his. "I ken 'tis not the usual way a wedding 'tis done, but I have more to say to ye, Lianna, before our families and friends. I love ye. I fell in love with ye many years ago, and though our lives diverged, ye were always locked away in my heart. I came back to ye in great need, for myself, my clan, and my daughter. Ye protected them, worked hard to save them, and showed me that no other lass could ever again be a better partner for me, or to become Lady MacDhai. Ye unlocked the memories I'd kept hidden all these years, and proved the love I held in those memories was real and true and worth all the pain to find it again. I'm proud to call ye my lady, prouder still to give ye to my clan as my lady, and my love. And, in a few moments, my wife, mother to my daughter, and to all the bairns I hope we will have. I will spend my life making ye glad that ye came to me—to all of us—and chose to stay."

Lianna's throat closed as she fought not to sob, happy tears streaming down her face as David turned her back to face the priest and resume kneeling.

The priest cleared his throat, making Lianna stifle a giggle. Then he asked her the same question he'd posed to David. She said, "Aye," but softly, then turned to David, found her voice and repeated it. "Aye!" Then she stood and faced the audience and said it even louder, "Aye." Then she turned back to David, who'd gained his feet. "Aye, forever and always, my love. I waited for ye for seven long years. I'll never let ye go for seven times seven times seven years again. I'm proud to take ye as my husband, and Mirielle as my sweet daughter. And I hope for more bairns as well. After all, a lass needs some brothers to boss around." She grinned at Jamie as the audience chuckled. David smiled, then cupped her face. He leaned in to kiss her, paused and glanced at the priest. "Father?"

The priest rolled his eyes. "Very well, I pronounce ye man and wife. Kiss yer bride, MacDhai."

Everyone laughed at that. David swooped in and gave Lianna a long, slow, simmering kiss that promised a lifetime of love.

§.

DAVID WANTED to spend the entire wedding dinner and celebration with his new bride. He'd sent Mirielle off to bed hours ago, in the care of her nurse and her grandparents. He had no responsibilities except to enjoy the celebration and ensure Lianna did, too. But the men kept pulling him aside for another drink or a story of their wedding and wedding night. He was beginning to think the men were deliberately keeping him from her.

Suddenly something went missing from the chamber, and he noticed the lack immediately. He looked around to the high table where Lianna had stayed with her family between dances. Toran, Jamie, and Donal were still there, but the women had disappeared.

It was time, or nearly so, for him to make his way to his chamber and claim his bride. He had waited for this day for seven long years. It wasn't his first wedding night, but he fervently hoped it would be his last.

After another toast, he mentioned his need to go relieve himself, which started the other men cackling like overexcited hens. He didn't care. He escaped by way of the bailey, where he accomplished what he'd told the men he was going to do. Then he made his way through the kitchen, up the back stairs, anticipation tightening his muscles and heating his blood.

Aileanna waited outside the door. "Are ye drunk?"

"Nay. I spilled more than I drank, and set aside full cups after a sip."

"Good lad. Take care of my Lianna."

"All my life, foster-mother, with all my heart."

Seeming satisfied, she nodded and left him to begin his marriage with her eldest daughter. He was acutely aware she had not touched him, but had granted him the privacy that her talent would not allow her to bestow if she so much as brushed his hand.

Anticipating the coming night with her daughter, he was in no condition to be probed by her mother's talent. Grateful for her forbearance, he put a hand on the door, then paused and thought better of simply opening it and barging in. Instead, he took a deep breath and knocked. "Lianna, 'tis David."

"Come in, then." Her voice, laced with amusement, penetrated the thick oaken door.

He opened it, stepped inside, then closed and barred it. Unless the keep was on fire, he would brook no interruptions.

Before he turned to face her, Lianna asked, "Mother met ye in the hallway?"

"Aye. Drummond is not the only Lathan protective of ye. Yet she very carefully didna touch me." He did turn then.

Lianna sat beside the bed in a padded chair. Her hair was down and hung loose around her shoulders and upper arms, covering part of the exquisite lace bodice over her breasts. She held out a hand.

He moved to her and took it, then pulled her up and into his arms. "I kenned the moment ye left the hall. Something was different. Lacking. I missed *ye*. I came as soon as I could get away."

"Ye did well to escape so quickly, Husband." She brushed her hands up the outside of his arms to his shoulders, then tunneled her fingers into his hair.

He dipped his head and tasted her lips. So sweet.

"I missed ye." He repeated and kissed her again. "Husband. I like the sound of that word on yer lips, Wife."

"And I like the sound of 'wife' on yers."

The smile she gave him spoke of love and longing. He was

glad to see that she longed for him. They had lost years that could have been spent together. Love, trust, shared memories, and sacrifice bound them together fully, though not in the same way as Mirielle once bound him to Lucienne. "I could almost thank the old woman and her grandson for how they chose to try to get rid of me. The damage they did forced me to the Aerie. To ye. Without that, I might never have returned. Or returned too late, after Toran married ye off to some other man."

"He wouldna. I waited for ye. I kenned with ye, I'd be safe."

"And if I never came?"

"When ye found the letters, ye wouldha come. But if not, I wouldna wed. I wouldha remained in my father's care, and when the time came, my brother's. Or I wouldha come looking for ye."

"I'm glad ye didna have to."

"As am I, though I regret what ye and yer clan and yer horses suffered."

"Ye suffered, too."

She shrugged it off, as if her efforts had not cost her exhaustion and pain, again and again.

"Then let's not think about regrets tonight. This is our time." He had wanted her for so long, he could barely contain himself. But he would take his time with Lianna. He was no frantic youth. He had been married, and knew how to protect her and to please her. She, so far as he knew, was untouched. He vowed he would give her joy, and more, before the sun rose again.

"I've waited a long time for ye, Husband."

"Then wait nay more, Wife." He stepped back and brushed her hair behind her shoulders. "So beautiful," he whispered, meaning every syllable.

"The gown? Aye, Moina does exquisite work."

"She does, but I was referring to my bride."

Lianna's cheeks pinked, and she dropped her gaze to his chest. "I dinna ken why I'm nervous. I ken what we'll do."

"There's a difference between kenning and having done, love."

She lifted her gaze to his. "Then show me."

※

LIANNA'S HEART beat like a bird's, faster and fiercer than she'd ever felt before. David stood before her. Her husband, gazing at her with love and hunger and the weight of all their years apart. All the memories they shared—and those they did not.

Candlelight brought out the gold in his hair and lit the darkness in his deep-set eyes. As she pushed his shirt from his shoulders, firelight burnished his muscles, endowing every strong curve with light and shadow that shifted and rippled as he lifted his hands to her head and tangled his fingers in her hair.

When his lips found hers yet again, she melted into his kiss, relishing his taste, the sensation of his tongue teasing her lips apart, his teeth nipping gently at her lower lip. She answered in kind, determined to explore him as he explored her, to know her husband better than he knew himself. She might be a virgin, but she was not ignorant. She was, after all, a healer's daughter.

Each kiss brought a pleasurable tingle that spread from everywhere David touched. Only when he released her and stepped back to remove his boots and hose did she recognize what she'd suspected when he kissed her. Her talent shared what he felt with her, and amplified her own desires for him.

"David."

"Aye, love?" He touched her cheek, a question in his gaze and his lifted brow.

"I think I feel some of what ye feel. My talent, my senses... like when I touch an animal to help them."

"I'm not injured."

"Nay, but I can tell a difference in what I feel when ye touch me, and when ye dinna." She could see lots of potential for enjoyment in the future. "This will give us many reasons to try..." she trailed off, at a loss for words.

"I see," David said and grinned. "Ye will enjoy being together even more than most, is that what ye are trying to tell me?"

"I canna judge. So I must experience it. Make me yers, David. Forever. Bloody sheets and all."

"That's my brave lass." He gave her another heart-stealing grin and reached for the ribbons holding her gown closed. "Ye dinna fear anything, do ye?"

"I fear many things, as any wise person would. But I dinna fear ye, nay."

"Good." His fingers brushed her upper chest as he untied the first ribbon, then slipped lower, to her breasts, for the next three. He paused there and slid a strap off one shoulder, baring one breast. As if he didn't believe what he was seeing, he murmured, "Breathtakingly beautiful," then bent to kiss the upper slope of her breast and traced down with his tongue until he took her nipple between his lips and teased it with his tongue.

Lianna's body burst into flame, her own, and a wildfire of need echoing from David.

David pushed her bodice aside and turned his attention to her other breast. Lianna wrapped her arms around his waist and held on, certain if she let go, she'd fall to the floor in a puddle of need.

He took her mouth in another blazing kiss, then ran a hand down her back to her bottom. "I need to see all of ye, love."

"And I, ye."

"Then unless ye wish for this lovely gown to be ruined..." He tugged at the bodice as if he was about to tear it from her body.

She squeaked in protest, unable to get a word out past her horror of him ruining Moina's hours of dedicated, heartfelt effort for her.

Laughing, he slid both straps down her arms and watched as the fabric slipped down her body to the floor.

She knew then that he'd never wanted to tear it. His threat had been intended merely to get a rise of out her and perhaps ease some of the tension that was growing between them. She would happily punch him, but his chest expanded on a deep breath as he gazed at her, no longer teasing, but drinking her in. She unbuckled his belt and let his great kilt join her gown on the floor, then reached for the hem of his shirt and pulled it up.

David stripped it over his head, then stood before her, naked and aroused. She took a deep breath of her own, not caring that it made her chest rise and her breasts lift toward his hungry gaze. She admired David, from his dark-golden hair to the muscles defining every plane and curve of his body, to his manhood, which stood proudly and massively between them, to his strong thighs and elegant feet. Unbidden, her hand lifted to her chest. Her husband was even more magnificent unclothed than dressed and fighting to protect her. Lianna leaned toward him instinctively.

As if sensing her weakness, David picked her up and laid her on the bed, then stretched out beside her. She reached for him, needing his weight and the solid strength of him close to her, filling the emptiness that had bloomed inside her.

"I remember ye as a slender lad," she said, running curious hands over his chest, down the muscles of his arm, across to his hip. "Ye have changed."

"And ye were a barely budded lass, dealing with her first

moon blood and not liking it one bit. 'Tis how I wound up trying to show ye there would be much to enjoy when ye were ready."

"And how my brothers found us, fortunately clothed after ye taught me what ye were willing to, then." She glanced down. "I see ye have much more to show me now."

David chuckled and caressed her breast. "Aye, as do ye, Wife."

"I've often wondered what wouldha happened if they had found us earlier."

"I'd be dead, or they would, or if not, then we would have been betrothed that day and married soon after."

"Too young. And we wouldna have Mirielle." She lifted her hand to his face, then turned to align her body with his, touching him everywhere she could and feeling his manhood hot and hard against her belly. "Nay, it all happened as it should, and brought us back together at the right time."

"I think so, too." He rolled her to her back and leaned over her, supporting his weight on his arms. "As much as I missed ye, and held ye in my heart, it wasna our time. *This* is our time."

Lianna kissed him, putting all the love and longing in her heart into her kiss.

David responded, stroking her body while he made love to her with his lips and teeth and tongue. When he reached the juncture of her thighs, she opened for his questing fingers. Heat raced from the place he touched throughout her body, multiplied by what she sensed in him. He built a need in her that threatened to burn her down and take him with her. She arched against him, wanting more, needing more. He gave it to her, increasing the pressure of his fingers as his mouth left hers. He kissed his way down her body, giving her chills to race alongside the fire he'd set, then replaced his fingers with his tongue, stroking and sucking gently until the fire in Lianna exploded, sending sparks shooting skyward behind her eyelids, making her body tremble and buck with a fierce pleasure she'd never known it capable of achieving. David had given her that, as he'd given her a gentler pleasure when they were younger.

She lost the ability to speak, but told him with her embrace, pulling him up over her, what she needed.

David met her gaze, his expression solemn. "This may hurt the first time."

"I ken it. Take me, Husband. Make me yers forever."

He kissed her softly, gently, and she became aware of him at her entrance, stretching her ever so slightly. He moved slowly, giving her time to adjust to his size before pushing deeper. It made her oddly uncomfortable, but that was overlaid with David's fierce pleasure at being inside her, and his concern for her. She felt when he reached her barrier, both within herself and by David's awareness. "'Tis time," he whispered.

"'Tis *our* time," she answered and nodded.

He pushed through. Something tore with a sharp, bright pain that lasted only seconds as David waited, giving her a chance to catch her breath, to let the pain subside. It did, more quickly than she expected, and she nodded again for him to continue.

He pushed until he could go no farther, then slowly withdrew and entered her again, keeping his strokes slow and sure. As his arousal built, so did hers. "'Tis like feeling everything doubled," she gasped, and her blood burst into sparks again. David's strokes quickened and in moments, she felt his climax burst through his body. He slowed then finally stopped, still joined with her. His head dropped to her shoulder, then he lifted it to kiss her again and again and again.

"I dinna think I would survive if I felt that doubled," he told her. "But I feel something...more. More than I've ever felt before."

Lianna laughed, suddenly giddy. "I'm glad. Now I understand what ye tried to show me all those years ago. Thank ye."

David lifted up to one elbow and regarded her. "Are ye thanking me for now or for then?"

"Ach, then, of course. Ye are not done with me yet. Or are ye?"

His manhood hardened and expanded, filling her fully again. "What do ye think?"

"I think I'm glad ye barred the door."

EPILOGUE
THREE YEARS LATER

L ianna watched her twins' reactions as David introduced them to Athdar, Brigh, and a few other horses. This was their first visit to the stable, the first of many to come, she was certain. She only hoped David managed to impress upon them how dangerous the horses could be for small creatures such as wee bairns. They would learn to ride soon enough, but in the meantime, David insisted he wanted them comfortable around the great beasts, not afraid. Mirielle, now nearly seven-years-old, stood beside her father and patted the nose of any horse that dipped its head low enough for her to reach. Her blonde curls bobbed with her laughter, and hearing her, the twins laughed, too.

Good. Exposure like this would keep them from being afraid. And David had done a good job teaching Mirielle when she was younger to respect the horses, so Lianna had every confidence he could do the same with the twins.

Soon enough, David turned their small brood and led them to where she sat on a bench outside Brigh's stall. Mirielle stayed by her father, but the twins climbed up on the bench and leaned into her, gently patting her rounded belly.

The baby she carried kicked as if it knew its siblings were eager to meet it. Lianna looked forward to that happening as well. As easy as her pregnancy with the twins had been, this one was difficult. She'd been tired and sick long past the normal first few months. Though her due date was still two weeks away, David was concerned enough to send for her mother. If all went well on their journey, Aileanna and an escort were due to arrive later today, and would spend the remaining fortnight before the due date—or as long as it took for the bairn to arrive—watching over her, here.

Lianna would be grateful to have her mother to monitor the bairn's progress during delivery. If there was trouble, Aileanna would take care of it. Lianna expected to be too busy with the birthing to be able to call on her own talent.

The first thing Lianna wanted her mother to do was ease this damnable back ache that had started earlier this morning. She must have slept in an awkward position.

David helped her to her feet, and they all headed back into the keep for a midday meal. While they ate, Kerr brought David a stack of correspondence.

"Nothing urgent," he reported, "but there is one personal missive there on top."

Lianna glanced at the stack and recognized the Comtesse's handwriting. She hoped all was well with Mirielle's grandparents in France. Perhaps they were planning another visit. Mirielle barely remembered the last one. It would be good if she could spend time with them, now that she was old enough to keep memories of them with her as she matured. Lianna envied her that. Her own grandparents were gone before she was born. But she had both her parents and her clan, as well as an extended family that included so-called aunts and uncles, such as the Fletchers and the MacKyries. Thinking about them, she could not complain. She was lucky to have so many good people in her life.

David broke the seals on the missive and read, then frowned, glanced aside at Mirielle and turned to Lianna. Her heart skipped a beat. Did the letter bring bad news?

"The Comte is ill, his heart, she thinks. But she still hopes they will be able to make the trip here in another month. She writes that Clémence is doing well in her new marriage and her husband treats her very well, but there is no sign of a new bairn on the way yet."

"I'm happy for Clémence, but wish we were closer, to be able to help the Comte."

"I am, too. I hope he is well enough for them to make the trip. If not, and if ye are able, perhaps we'll go there."

"To France?" Lianna had never been. But the thought of such a long trip in the company of three young children and a newborn? "I canna think such a trip so soon would be good for this bairn," she said, patting her belly. "'Twould be best if only ye and Mirielle go. She doesna remember where she was born. It would be good for her, and for the Comte and Comtesse." If only the Comte could live long enough.

"I want ye to go with us," Mirielle piped up. "And the twins. And the new bairn." She gave her father her best wide-eyed, pleading look.

Lianna fought not to laugh. Their eldest had not lost her self-confidence. Indeed, it had grown with her. She had no fear of expressing her opinion, certainly not to her father, who doted on her.

"I understand, lass. Perhaps if we waited until this bairn is older?"

"Perhaps," Lianna answered, giving Mirielle a look that forestalled any further objections. She didn't need the twins to take up the campaign. She had other things to do first, like deliver this bairn.

David grinned at her, knowing full well the direction of her thoughts. He doted on the twins as well. He had his heir, and his minutes-younger brother, as well, to guarantee the future of the clan. At two years old, they were already insatiably curious, hence the visit to the stable, supervised by their father. It would take several more with David to convince the lads this was no place to wander into and no place to play. Tadgh, the stable master, would be on guard against them, as well. When they were a little older, David and Tadgh would begin their riding lessons, much as David had done with his oldest daughter.

In the meantime, everyone in the clan stayed busy keeping them out of trouble. Lianna was grateful Jenny remained with her and had taken over the nursery when Clémence returned to France with the Comte and Comtesse three years ago. Jenny and Tadgh had settled into a comfortable courtship that neither seemed in a hurry to consummate, though Lianna worried they never would. Perhaps their friendship was enough, but Lianna hoped for more—for both of them.

A disturbance at the keep's door turned out to be Aileanna's arrival. Lianna tried to stand, but her mother waved her down as she hurried toward her, then bent and gave her a hug.

"Oh!" Aileanna's soft exclamation startled Lianna.

"Oh?"

"Oh?" David echoed Lianna's question.

"Oh, 'tis naught to *fash* over. The bairn is coming."

"Now?" Lianna suddenly understood the reason for her backache.

"Aye, soon now. As usual, I've arrived just in time."

DAVID HAD Jenny take the children up to the nursery. That left him the leisure to pace around the great hall while nature took its course upstairs. He wasn't worried. The best healer in Scotland was with Lianna. Not that Lianna couldn't take care of herself, but in this circumstance, that could prove to be too much of a challenge. He thanked the saints for his impulse to send for Aileanna, and was grateful she'd arrived as quickly as she did.

Hours passed. Kerr, Murdoch, and members of the council came in and out, checking, sitting with him over a dram for as long as he could bear to sit before he felt the need to be up and pacing again.

Finally, Aileanna came downstairs, moving gingerly and looking tired, but jubilant. "She's well, and ye have another daughter," she announced.

David raced upstairs and into their chamber, where Lianna rested with the bairn cuddled close in the crook of her arm. He paused in the doorway, taking in the scene. "Lianna?"

"I'm well. And look! Yer new daughter is beautiful."

"Our daughter. Let me see." He sank onto the side of the bed, leaned down and kissed Lianna's temple. Then he looked at the bundle she held. A sweet face with rosebud lips and deep blue eyes gazed up at him as if she already knew him. "She's..." He stopped, at a loss for words.

"Hard to look away from, I think ye mean."

"Will she have a talent like yers?"

"I dinna ken. But with those eyes, I'd be surprised if she didna. Mother thinks 'tis likely. She seems to have an old soul behind those eyes. I wonder who she was before she came to us."

David knew exactly how to respond to that. He turned his gaze to his wife. "We canna ken. But I will make her the same promise I made to ye on our wedding day. I will spend my life making her glad that she came—to all of us—and chose to stay."

AUTHOR'S NOTE

Clan Davidson, or MacDhai, as it has been known through the centuries, has a long and bloody history with both Clan MacPherson and Clan Mackintosh, fellow members of the Clan Chattan confederation.

The incident I use as the motive for the attack on the clan's horses is historically real, though details vary. Some accounts say a John Malcolmson and two Davidsons were involved, possibly with others, in killing Lachlan Mackintosh, the 14th Mackintosh chief, in 1525, while he was hunting at Ravoch. Malcolmson was the Davidson chief's foster brother and believed the Mackintosh chief destroyed his prospects for marrying a rich widow.

The killers were captured and kept in chains in the dungeon on Loch-an-Eilan for seven years. After a trial, Malcolmson was beheaded and quartered, and the two David-sons were supposedly tortured, hanged, and their heads mounted on pikes at the spot where they committed the crime. Other accounts claim they were cut to pieces as soon as they were caught. I chose the former fate for the Davidsons, since it gave the old healer years to worry for her son and nurse her grudge against those responsible—as she saw it—for his death.

As for the horses' illness, after finding an abstract in the Veterinary Record of the British Veterinary Association, I queried veterinary schools for more information about sycamore poisoning in horses. I'm grateful to Dr. Murl Bailey, DVM, Diplomate, American Board of Veterinary Toxicology, for helping me make some sense of what I read and providing more detail on the poison's effects. In short, the sycamore toxin attacks the liver, and cascades into kidney and causes other problems. Its effects are characterized by rapid heartbeat, sweating, muscle tremors, dark urine, difficulty standing, and more. The toxin is water-soluble. Even today, affected horses are treated with intravenous fluids and close veterinary care. Sadly, the mortality rate is high.

I used literary license concerning how many of the seeds a horse would have to eat, how often, and for how long before symptoms would present. To come up with a 16th Century treatment, I looked to herbal medicine. Dandelion is thought to cleanse the liver, so I chose dandelion greens and tea, along with copious amounts of water combined with honey and a little salt (medieval sports drink, anyone?), as the therapy used to save the MacDhai horses. Lianna uses her talent to quickly identify afflicted horses so they can be treated successfully, to slow too-rapid heartbeats, and to support the horses as only she can, but even she says water and dandelion therapy did most of the work.

I love second-chance romances and hope you enjoyed David and Lianna's. Look for Book 3 in my Highland Talents Heritage series, *Highland Reckoning*, Drummond Lathan's story, in June 2022.

Drummond Lathan has never wished for any form of the strange talents that curse his mother's bloodline. Serving as his father's advi-

sor, negotiator, and second-in-command, his position as Lathan heir and his highly honed skill as a warrior garner him more than enough attention, without the added burden of the hushed whispers his talented siblings have to bear.

Morven MacComas knows the destructive power of whispers. A year and a day after handfasting, her husband denied her and disappeared, leaving her disgraced and brokenhearted. When she discovered he also left her pregnant, she vowed that there would be but one love in her life—her child. Five years later, even as she struggles to deny her attraction to the Lathan heir, Morven fears his recent arrival is somehow linked to a daring daylight raid on her clan. Along with cattle, reivers have taken her young son.

Drummond has always had a knack for finding lost things, but believes his success is simple good fortune. As the attraction between Drummond and Morven grows, his heartfelt attachment to her becomes a bond that could lead to the boy—if Drummond can accept that his talent is real and valuable. And if Morven can allow herself to trust in love again before her son is lost forever.

ALSO BY WILLA BLAIR

His Highland Heart

His Highland Rose

His Highland Heart

His Highland Love

His Highland Bride

Highland Talents

Heart of Stone

Highland Healer

Highland Seer

Highland Troth

The Healer's Gift

When Highland Lightning Strikes

Highland Talents Heritage

Highland Prodigy

Highland Memories

Highland Reckoning

Sweetie Pie (A Candy Hearts Novella)

Waiting for the Laird

When You Find Love

ABOUT THE AUTHOR

Willa Blair is an award-wining Amazon and Barnes & Noble #1 bestselling author of Scottish historical, light paranormal and contemporary romance filled with men in kilts, psi talents, and plenty of spice. Her books have won numerous accolades, including the Marlene, the Merritt, National Readers' Choice Award Finalist, Reader's Crown finalist, InD'Tale Magazine's RONE Award Honorable Mention, and NightOwl Reviews Top Picks. She loves scouting new settings for books, and thinks being an author is the best job she's ever had.

Willa loves hearing from readers!
Contact her:
www.willablair.com
authorwillablair@gmail.com

Sign up for my Newsletter
Find links to the rest of my books